REA

AC...

DISCARDED

Don't miss the previous books in this series

Love Underground
Persephone's Tale

SUPER ROMANCE

OCT 0 5 2005

THE GODDESSES

FATAL ATTRACTION

Aphrodite's Tale

Alicia Fields

A SIGNET ECLIPSE BOOK

SIGNET ECLIPSE
Published by New American Library, a division of
Penguin Group (USA) Inc., 375 Hudson Street,
New York, New York 10014, USA
Penguin Group (Canada), 90 Eglinton Avenue East, Suite 700, Toronto,
Ontario M4P 2Y3, Canada (a division of Pearson Penguin Canada Inc.)
Penguin Books Ltd., 80 Strand, London WC2R 0RL, England
Penguin Ireland, 25 St. Stephen's Green, Dublin 2,
Ireland (a division of Penguin Books Ltd.)
Penguin Group (Australia), 250 Camberwell Road, Camberwell, Victoria 3124,
Australia (a division of Pearson Australia Group Pty. Ltd.)
Penguin Books India Pvt. Ltd., 11 Community Centre, Panchsheel Park,
New Delhi - 110 017, India
Penguin Group (NZ), cnr Airborne and Rosedale Roads, Albany,
Auckland 1310, New Zealand (a division of Pearson New Zealand Ltd.)
Penguin Books (South Africa) (Pty.) Ltd., 24 Sturdee Avenue,
Rosebank, Johannesburg 2196, South Africa

Penguin Books Ltd., Registered Offices:
80 Strand, London WC2R 0RL, England

First published by Signet Eclipse, an imprint of New American Library,
a division of Penguin Group (USA) Inc.

First Printing, October 2005
10 9 8 7 6 5 4 3 2 1

PUBLISHER'S NOTE
This is a work of fiction. Names, characters, places, and incidents either are
the product of the author's imagination or are used fictitiously, and any
resemblance to actual persons, living or dead, business establishments,
events, or locales is entirely coincidental.

The publisher does not have any control over and does not assume any
responsibility for author or third-party Web sites or their content.

AUTHOR'S NOTE

An old man is telling a story, weaving his characters out of the smoky firelight. The prince of a fortified hill fort and his sons and male guests are listening. Behind a screen the women of the house may be listening, too (as long as they do not appear immodestly among the men) to this tale of a time when women were not so confined. Listening wistfully, perhaps, to the story of a ten-year war and the queen it was fought over, and the goddess who started it all. It was a golden time, when their great-grandfathers were lords of golden cities. Looking back on it, they decide they must all have been gods, those heroes of that golden age.

This is how myth is born.

Very little is known of the ancient civilization of the Mycenaeans who fought that war, beyond the paintings they left on their walls. The Olympian gods, and the religion that we think of as that of the ancient Greeks, developed long after the terrible battle between Mycenae and Troy, in the Greek Dark Age, when invaders from the north devastated the land and rebuilt it as their own. It is in times like that that stories of memorable heroes—and heroines—grow in the telling, to remind a scattered people that once they were great. And slowly these stories encompass the invaders, too, incorporating the gods they have brought with them and knitting them all into the fabric of the conquered land.

We know that the ancient Mycenaeans brought much of their culture from the island of Crete, where evidence of that older religion is found in statues of bare-breasted priestesses in flounced dresses, dancing with snakes; and pictures of young men and women leaping over the horns of bulls. A similar fresco of bull leapers was painted in the palace at Tiryns, near Mycenae, and so I have based my speculations about the religion of Mycenae on the rituals of Crete. And because the start of it all was the promise of the most beautiful woman in the world to the prince of Troy by Aphrodite, I have put her story at the heart of that dreadful war.

I

Wave Born

Everyone knew she was trouble from the start. Even Zeus knew it the minute he saw her. For one thing, she didn't have that look that newborn babies always had—slightly squashed and slit-eyed, as if they weren't quite awake yet. This one's eyes were wide open, and she looked like someone who had arrived to take charge. *I am here*, that look said. *Watch out*. And she was beautiful, which newborn babies also rarely are. Her eyes were the color of lapis lazuli, not the slate blue of normal newborns, and her hair was a cloud of rose-gold curls just as long as the first joint of his finger. Like everyone else, he fell in love.

The farm he brought her home to was in Argolis, on the fertile plain that lay below the hill-fort village of Tiryns. There his family raised cattle, goats, and olives and were a power in the world. The rest of the household took one look at her and knew trouble when they saw it, too. To begin with, Zeus claimed he had found her on a fishing trip off Cythera. He said, casually, that she had been lying in the surf, an exposed baby left to die, as surplus girl children often were.

"And why exactly do we need another one?" Hera inquired. She fixed the baby with a steely gray eye, looking from the child to Zeus and back again, perhaps measuring their features against each other. "We have a daughter."

"A playmate for Hebe," Zeus said jovially.

Hebe looked up from her dolls and smiled at Mama and Papa. Hebe was a biddable child.

"This house doesn't need another mouth to feed," old Rhea said, stumping into the nursery on her two canes.

"Let me worry about that, Mother," Zeus said. His mouth compressed slightly and a tic started under his left eye, the tic that his mother always produced in him.

"Always bringing home your bastard brats." Rhea mouthed the remaining stumps of her teeth. "You'll be putting your poor mother out into the snow next, to make room for them."

"It hardly ever snows, Mother."

"It might as well," old Cronos said, joining her. "Death song for this farm. Going to go under soon, the way you and your brothers run it. I might as well die now."

Zeus looked at his father with exasperation. Cronos was nearly as bent as Rhea; they were like two malevolent bears, half crouched over their canes. Hera stood with her arms crossed, tapping her long fingers on the folds of her gown. This was between her and Zeus. Stubornly, she refused to take advantage of his parents' opinions on the child. Shortly after her marriage, Hera had found herself drawn into the ongoing war in which Zeus, his siblings, and his parents continually engaged, and from which no one ever escaped.

"If you'd married a woman with some fire to her you wouldn't be out rutting with serving maids in a hay barn every night," Cronos said, reminding her why.

"I told you, Father. I found the child," Zeus said between his teeth. "In the surf. She was wet and cold."

"No need for another girl," Cronos said. "Waste of resources."

"Should have exposed the last one," Rhea said.

Hebe, playing with her dolls on the nursery floor beside her brothers, pretended she hadn't heard that. Hebe was seven, quite old enough to understand things. That particular thing she had been hearing all her life, so that she hardly took notice anymore.

"That other one, too," Rhea said. "The deformed one. Ill luck to keep that one. I said so." She pointed a wavering finger at Hephaestus, who sat with his brother and Hebe, pounding a wooden block with his wooden hammer.

"That will do!" Hera turned on her mother-in-law with fire in her eye. "Get out!" She flapped her mantle at Rhea as if she were shooing chickens. "Out! Get out or I *will* put you outside. I'll put your bed in the barn!"

"Zeus! Are you going to let her talk to me that way? She's wicked! She'll freeze me to death! Save your poor old mother!" Rhea sucked her teeth at Hera with a malign glare, tottering on her canes. She shifted both of them to one hand and crossed her fingers against the evil eye with the other, nearly toppling herself over.

"This isn't your business, Mother."

"Ungrateful children come to a bad end, always,"

Cronos grumbled. He had been tall in his youth, but was bent so nearly double with age that he had to cock his head to look up at Zeus with a mad eye.

"Or yours." Zeus put a hand on each. "Now go and sit down and rest, or I'll call a servant and have you carried."

"It's come to this," Cronos said, stumping along on his cane, closer to his son. "All my children betray me."

"Heracles!" Zeus shouted, and a muscular servant appeared. "Take my parents to their sitting room, please."

"Yes, Lord." Heracles scooped up Cronos in his arms and carried him off while Cronos beat at him with his cane. In a few moments he came back, slightly battered, for Rhea.

Zeus let out a deep breath. "Patricide begins to look a more acceptable option daily."

"You won't, though," Hera said. "You're still afraid of him."

"True, alas." Zeus ran a hand through his coppery hair, as if combing his father out of it. "Now . . ." He peered into the rush basket where he had laid the baby, and tickled her. She cooed at him. "About the child . . . I thought, a playmate for Hebe."

"Hebe has her brothers," Hera said. She and Zeus were united in their opposition to his parents, but only in that. The two boys on the nursery floor eyed them watchfully, with considerably more attention than they had given their grandparents. When Mama used that tone, someone was often sorry quite soon. Hephaestus went on pounding his hammer on his blocks, his odd twisted feet stuck straight out in front of him, but Ares got up from his toy soldiers and trotted over to peer into the rush basket at the baby.

"Pretty," he said. "Can we keep her?" The shrieks of two more little boys outside the window claimed his attention, and he darted out the door, abandoning the baby for them. In a moment they heard louder shrieking.

"We need another girl," Zeus said cajolingly. "With all these boys."

Hera's mouth flattened out. The two boys outside, Dionysus and Hermes, were Zeus's, but they weren't hers. Their mothers were servants on the farm, among the many who had received his attentions.

"Always room for one more. That's my sweet." Zeus slid an arm around her.

"That's generally been your theory," Hera said. She eyed the baby again. "You've been overpopulating the farm for years." She had milky skin and shimmering hair the color of chestnuts. She was the most beautiful woman in the village, maybe even in the city of Tiryns, but the simmering anger she directed at her husband made it a fearsome loveliness, like the statue of some dangerous goddess that only Zeus had the nerve to approach.

Hebe and Hephaestus watched in silence. When their parents struck sparks, things caught on fire, and it was better not to be in the direct path of the flames.

"What would you like?" Zeus asked. "Some splendid present for being such a good wife? For putting up with troublesome old Zeus?"

"I'll think of something," Hera said between her teeth, because she knew he was going to keep this baby no matter what she said. "I put up with a lot, so it had better be extremely splendid." She swept from the nursery, leaving Zeus with the baby, who began to howl. He shouted for the nursemaid.

*　　*　　*

So she stayed. Zeus claimed she wasn't his, but he never had a good answer for why he had brought her home. He had never been the best of fathers to the children he had already, male or female, calling them to him to pet them like puppies and dismissing them carelessly when they bored him, and sometimes seeming to forget their names. But he named this one himself. He called her Aphrodite, meaning "Wave Born."

The farm he brought her to was on land that had first been worked by the ancestors of his clan, and handed down over the years to Cronos and Rhea. The rocky hillside supported olive groves, and the lower land pastured cattle and goats or was tilled for grain. A terraced vineyard climbed the slope in between. Of Cronos it was rumored that he had killed his father for control of the land. The old couple were now too feeble to run the farm themselves, but still able to tell their children when they were doing it wrong. They terrified Aphrodite as she grew, sitting in their armchairs at the center of the great hall like spiders. They appeared to unnerve her aunts and uncles as well. There were four of them besides Zeus—Poseidon and Hades, and the sisters Demeter and Hestia, plus Poseidon's wife, Amphitrite—and they all avoided the grandparents' scolding tongues when they could manage it, sending the unfortunate farm servants to care for them, and gritting their teeth through dinner as Cronos expounded on the numerous errors Poseidon made in his training of the young horses, and Rhea complained of Hera's supervision of the kitchen and Amphitrite's lack of children.

Zeus and Hera's children, who ate in the nursery with Zeus's other sons, got most of their information on family matters from eavesdropping on these conversations.

"When I am grown," Ares said, "I will lock them up in a tower, if Father hasn't done it already by then."

"He would have," Hephaestus said, "but Grandfather threatened to curse him, and Father thinks he can."

"Always another mouth to feed," Rhea's voice came querulously through the wall. "And in these hard times. Likely your poor old parents will starve for you feeding your bastards all our food."

"What hard times?" Hermes asked. He had never noticed any. His mother was a maid here, but he was petted and spoiled by Zeus.

"Grandmother says it's hard times," Hebe said. She was the oldest, at nine. "She caught me in the garden yesterday and told me I'd never have a dowry, and I'd have to go on the streets."

"Spiteful old witch," Dionysus said.

"She's always saying I should have been exposed. She thinks poor little Aphrodite should, too."

"She's afraid because she's old," Hephaestus said. He was well aware of what his grandmother had always said about him. He was eight and Ares seven. Hermes and Dionysus were five and six.

"Lots of people are old," Hebe said, "and they don't tear at each other like jackals."

"Our family does."

Hermes pointed at the baby, now two, banging her spoon on the table. "Maybe Father brought us that one to give them something new to complain about. Keep them off his back."

"Didn't work," Ares said.

"Baby, don't do that." Hebe took the spoon away

from Aphrodite before she could smack her cup with it. "Before this one they complained about you," she said to Hermes.

"Do you think she's Father's?" Dionysus asked.

"No!" Ares said. "He found her. He said so."

Hephaestus snorted. "There are enough of Father's children to go around the village twice."

"This one is different," Ares said stubbornly.

Hebe sighed. The only time Ares ever stopped fighting with his brothers or the village boys, or lining up armies of bugs and trying to make them fight one another, was when Aphrodite toddled into the yard to find him. Hebe knew that even at two, Aphrodite was dangerously beautiful. Her beauty wasn't just to the eyes; it was a presence, a force like an overpowering scent. There might be other girl children as beautiful, or maybe even more so, if you painted her picture and showed it to people and asked them to vote on the prettiest. But no one who saw her in person ever saw anyone else to match her. She was going to be more beautiful than Mother, Hebe thought, and that was going to make more trouble yet.

Aphrodite wasn't sure when she had figured out for herself that she was beautiful. She had simply always known it. Wherever she went people looked at her, and they would do things for her without being asked. If she asked, they would do nearly everything. Or the men would. Hera told her not to get above herself, and Hebe told her to be careful. The shepherd boys made her wreaths of daisies when she came out to play with the new lambs, and Heracles carved her a little wooden horse on wheels. Ares pulled her around in his goat cart, and Uncle Poseidon gave her rides on his shoulders. Animals liked her, too. The goats and Hera's chickens followed her everywhere she went.

When Aphrodite was five years old, a woman who ran a very high-class house of hetairae in Mycenae tried to buy her. (Hera would have sold her if Zeus hadn't been there.) Aphrodite wasn't sure what the woman had wanted, but she had promised her beautiful dresses and to teach her to play the lyre, and Aphrodite had wanted to go with her.

"You wouldn't have liked it," Hephaestus said solemnly. But he thought she might have.

When she was seven, two twelve-year-old boys in the village outside Tiryns fought over her, and one pushed the other off a wall and broke both his legs. Aphrodite watched them with interest, twining one rose-gold curl around her finger. She yearned for those boys, for both of them. They were so wonderful and strong, and she liked the way they moved inside their skin, like young horses. They gave her an explosive sense of power, rolling in the dirt like that, pummeling each other for her sake.

"You come home!" Ares said, grabbing her by the arm. "You belong to us!"

"Ow! You're hurting me!"

Ares loosened his grip. "Sorry. But you stay away from those louts."

"Why?" Aphrodite demanded. "They gave me a sweet. One of them did."

"You can't take sweets from strange boys," Hephaestus said, hobbling beside her.

Aphrodite looked at him thoughtfully. He always seemed to know things. The boys in the village teased him because of his feet and threw rocks at him because they knew he couldn't catch them. When Ares was with him, Ares caught them instead and beat their heads together. Aphrodite knew Hephaestus didn't like that when it happened, but she didn't understand why. Who would want rocks thrown at them? "Why can't I have the sweet?" she asked.

"Because they will want something for it," Hephaestus said.

"Because you're ours," Ares said.

When she was ten, a group of mothers from Tiryns came to the farm to complain to Hera that Aphrodite had been in a cattle shed kissing boys, each in turn, in exchange for a silver bead or a bronze bracelet, or whatever he could offer her. She was wearing the offending bracelets when Hera turned her over her knee.

"Disgraceful!" Hera's hand came down wielding an ivory hairbrush.

"Ow!" Aphrodite thrashed on her lap as Hera got a good grip on her hair with her other hand.

The brush came down again. "No child of my household will behave like a trollop! In a shed! With seven boys!"

"Ow! Stop!" Aphrodite wailed, kicking her feet, her face slick with tears.

"Stay! Away! From boys!" The brush came down with each word.

Hebe stood to one side with her lips pursed. Hebe was seventeen, and she would not have thought of kissing a boy until her parents presented her with a suitable husband, and then she would kiss him *after* the wedding.

"There!" Hera grabbed Aphrodite by the shoulders and stood her on her feet again. "You are not to go into the village alone again! Do you understand me?"

Aphrodite sniffled, rubbing her backside. Hera's anger sparked out of her gray eyes like lightning, but

Aphrodite still didn't comprehend why. "Yes, Mother," she said, because it was easier to say that than to argue. But it had been fun kissing those boys. It had felt very nice in places that Aphrodite hadn't noticed before. She looked sorrowfully at her bare wrists. Hera had taken the bracelets.

"You need work to do," her Aunt Hestia said, taking her by the ear and leading her to the kitchen, where she washed dishes for a ten-day until her hands were raw, snuffling at her misfortune to the household snake, who came out of his basket and wrapped a sympathetic coil about her ankle, his flat head resting on her foot. After that her Aunt Demeter took her into the kitchen garden, where she set out bean seedlings until all the nails on her red hands were broken to the quick. The Aunts frightened Aphrodite almost as much as the grandparents did, and she obeyed them implicitly, but dishwater and beans didn't make her stop liking boys.

Hephaestus was sixteen then, old enough to know danger when he saw it, but he couldn't help feeling sorry for her as she mourned her confiscated bracelets. He had begun to take over the forge on the farm by then, sitting on a stool he had built, his lame feet dangling as he hammered out bridle bits and sheaths for wagon wheels, spear points for hunting, and cauldrons for the kitchen. Sometimes Aphrodite would sit and watch him, her tame hen in her lap, or one of the other farm animals who always came to her hand. Today it was a goat, its knobby head resting on her knees. She looked so sad that, on impulse, he said, "If I made you something, Mother would let you keep it."

Aphrodite's face brightened. "Would you? What would you make me?"

"I have a little gold. I could make you a girdle to wear with your good gown. Not all gold, bronze mostly, but I could put gold ornaments on it. What do you like?"

Aphrodite's eyes shone. "I like doves. They make such a sweet sound. There's one that sits on my windowsill every morning. Could I have doves on it?"

"Doves it shall be," Hephaestus said.

Aphrodite beamed at him. A ten-day later, when it was finished, she fastened it around her slim hips to admire herself. The girdle was forged of delicate, spiraling links of bronze, with gold rosettes between the links, and the buckle, as promised, was a pair of gold doves, facing each other.

"I made it so you can move the buckle when you get bigger, and you won't outgrow it," he said.

Aphrodite sighed with delight and danced across the yard. "I'm going to go look at myself in the pool!" she called to him. Hera possessed a silver mirror, but just now Aphrodite felt it might be unwise to borrow it. She ran along the wagon road that sloped down from the farmyard into a grove of trees. From the road, the path to the sacred spring branched off, and she darted along it.

It was cool and mysterious in the woods by the spring where the Goddess lived. The Goddess was old, older than anything else except maybe the sacred serpent who slept at the heart of the Earth. She was the mother of them all, the mother of everything: of the rabbit, and the wolf that ate the rabbit, and the man that hunted the wolf. She was the giver of new babies, and the dark doorway that people went through when they died. Aphrodite could feel her when she went to the spring, an old power deep in the water and the rocks, in the heart of the woods where an olive tree stood guard over a spring-fed pool and a stone altar, all three so old they had been there in the time of Erebus, the first of Cronos's clan, so Mother had said. Beside the altar sat the omphalos, a round stone shaped by an ancient hand, and nearly as tall as Aphrodite. The omphalos was the navel of the world, older even than the altar and the tree. Aphrodite thought that the Goddess talked to her here sometimes, but she had never said so to anyone. She suspected she would have been spanked for impertinence, as it was common knowledge that the Goddess spoke only to her priestesses in her temple. But Aphrodite had heard her.

This morning she knelt beside the pool and looked into its black water. Her pale face shimmered back at her, and around her waist shone the magical, marvelous girdle that Hephaestus had made for her. Aphrodite held her breath, staring at her reflection. The girdle glowed, it sang, it felt warm against her hips and waist.

On impulse she unbuckled it and dipped it in the water. "Make everyone love me," she asked the Goddess. Its bronze spirals flashed like golden fish in the depths. Ares had begun to run after older girls and leave her behind. "Make him love *me*," she told the water and the golden belt.

Be careful what you wish for, the water whispered back.

"Why?"

No other sound came back to her except the liquid *plop!* of a frog at the far end of he pool. Aphrodite put her marvelous girdle back on, feeling its still-warm links imprint themselves on her waist.

II

✦

The Festival of the Goddess

When she was twelve, her Uncle Poseidon asked
Zeus for her.

"You're already married," Zeus said. "And aren't
you afraid she's mine?"

"I don't care."

Zeus chuckled. "Neither do my boys. Ares has
asked me for her already."

"Ares is only seventeen," Poseidon said. "A man
should be at least thirty. Stable. Ready to provide
a household."

"Father says we're both still too young," Ares said,
glowering. "But you're mine, you understand that?"

"Of course." Aphrodite snuggled her face against
his chest. The hay tickled her ears, and she pulled
her mantle up to cover it and lay back down. She
had always known she belonged to Ares. All those
other boys were just practice, but practice was fun.
She didn't say that to Ares. He was too jealous.

"Have you done this before?" Ares asked her suspiciously.

"No." Aphrodite widened her eyes at him. She loved Ares. Loved the way his chestnut hair curled over his left eyebrow, and the way his eyes went from pale blue to gray when he was angry. Hermes and Dionysus didn't count; they were just so she would know how to do it. And she hadn't actually done it with Zeus, not strictly speaking. She ran a finger down his bare chest. "What about you?"

"It's different for men," Ares said.

"Why?" That didn't seem fair.

"Because girls have the babies," Ares said. "And you have to know whose baby it is."

"It's the girl's," Aphrodite said.

"No, it's not. A baby belongs to the father. He's the one who decides if they're going to keep it or expose it."

Aphrodite sat up. There was hay in her hair. "Well, that isn't fair!"

Ares shrugged. "It's the way it is." That was always the way it was. You couldn't have women in charge of things.

"What, forever?" Could Zeus still decide to expose her? That would be silly; she wouldn't die if he did it now.

"No, he has four days," Ares said. "After that, he has to keep it."

"What if he's at war or something?"

"I don't know," Ares said. "I hadn't thought of that. I don't pay attention to babies anyway. That's for the women."

"Then I shall have all my babies while you're at war," Aphrodite said decisively.

Ares gripped her arm. "You had better not. Then how will I know they're mine?"

"I'll start them before you leave, silly." Aphrodite bit his earlobe.

"Well, there isn't a war right now," Ares said. He looked grumpy about that.

"Good. I don't really want you to go to war."

"Well, I do. That's how a man proves himself."

"You promised to take me to the festival on the Goddess's day. That's more fun than going to a stupid war," Aphrodite said.

Ares shook his head, but he kissed her on the nose. "You don't have to worry about war. You're a girl."

What girls worried about was staying respectable, according to the Aunts, and to Mother, who said, "Now you stay with Ares and Hebe, mind you. No running off by yourself."

Aphrodite promised, bouncing with excitement. Festivals were always thrilling, but the Goddess's were the best, when everyone danced in the streets and the priestesses paraded in their flounced red and blue and yellow gowns, bodices framing bare breasts the way they had worn them at Knossos in the old days. "Immodest," said Hebe, who would have died before she let anybody see her her without her top, but priestesses could do things other people couldn't. Aphrodite, studying her own breasts in a bronze mirror, thought she would look very nice in one of those dresses. She put on her own best gown, which Dionysus's mother, Semele, had stiffened with flour starch for her, so that the flounces on the skirt rustled nicely, and pinned it at the bodice with the bronze pins set with amber that Uncle Hades had given her last Solstice night, and fastened the girdle Hephaes-

tus had made for her around her middle. She dressed
her hair in a knot with stray curls falling fetchingly
about her face and down the nape of her neck, and
buckled her good blue leather sandals that Uncle Poseidon had brought her back from the horse fair at
Mycenae.

When she was satisfied with the results, she
danced down the corridor to the kitchen and gave
an extra saucer of milk to the household snake,
where he lay coiled in his basket behind the cook-
stove. "Make something exciting happen," she whispered to him.

"Are you changing your clothes again?" Ares
shouted outside her chamber door. "Come *on*. We'll
miss it all!"

"I'm coming!" She ran back down the corridor,
spinning in a circle as she caught up with him. "How
do I look?"

His eyes ran over her with the hungry look that
she recognized on men now. "You stay close by me,"
he told her.

Outside, the grandparents were being loaded, complaining, into a wagon. Hephaestus perched beside
Uncle Poseidon on the driver's seat, and in the back
Cronos and Rhea had been propped in cushioned
chairs. Beside them, Amphitrite was nursing the baby
she had finally had. Zeus held the reins of a chariot
crowded with Hera and the Aunts, and Uncle Hades
was in another with Hermes and Dionysus. Ares was
to take Aphrodite and Hebe. Behind them the household servants trailed on foot, laughing and passing
a wineskin back and forth, their heads crowned with
flower garlands. The family wore wreaths of spring
flowers, too, braided by Hebe and Aunt Demeter that

morning. Aphrodite patted hers into place and giggled at Uncle Poseidon, who had a daisy hanging over one eye.

"Drive carefully," Uncle Poseidon shouted at Ares. "If you play the fool with my horses you'll be sorry."

"Yes, Uncle." Ares shook out the reins and the team began to trot. When they had passed down a dip in the road and into the trees that ringed the farm, out of sight of Uncle Poseidon, he urged them into a gallop. Aphrodite clung to the chariot's side with one hand and held her wreath on her head with the other as they careened out of the trees and past the fields knee-deep in new wheat. The spring air flew in her face and went to her head like wine.

"Slow down!" Hebe shouted at Ares. "You'll have us in the ditch!"

"Don't be a stick-in-the-mud," Ares said. "Or go ride with the Aunts."

"Mother says I am to ride with you," Hebe said, lurching as the chariot bounced. *To keep an eye on you*, was implied but not spoken.

Hebe was turning into one of the Aunts, Aphrodite thought. Neither of them had married, and Hebe didn't seem to want to, either. Zeus was in no hurry to send her off. There was plenty of work to be done on the farm, and a dowry was always troublesome to provide. "He won't turn *me* into an old maid," Aphrodite had said to Hermes, and Hermes had laughed until he couldn't breathe.

"No danger of that, my dear," he had gasped.

She had smacked him for being impertinent, but he had just laughed some more. It still seemed a shame to Aphrodite. Maybe she could find Hebe a husband. She would ask the Goddess about it.

The Festival of the Goddess marked the midpoint

between the spring equinox and the long, hot sunlight of the summer Solstice. It was the springtime hinge of the year, when the world turned from winter into summer, and everything was reborn. The road into Tiryns was crowded with holidaygoers, and just past the border of the family's fields, Ares had to slow down whether he wanted to or not, as a procession of the neighbor's farmhands and a flock of sheep appeared suddenly in the road. Ares threaded the chariot between oxcarts and wagons and a herder driving a dozen pigs. The air was a clear crystalline blue, the dusty sunlight bouncing off the limestone walls of the city that crowned the hilltop, so that Aphrodite had to squeeze her eyes half-shut not to be blinded by it. The crowd grew thicker as they climbed toward Tiryns through the warren of mud-and-thatch huts that clung to the lower slopes of the hillside, and she caught the smell of roasting meat from the first sacrifices to the Goddess. White gulls circled above them, looking for scraps, the detritus that humans left behind. Aphrodite leaned over the side of the chariot as it jounced up the rutted road, staring at the city cut into the sky above them, magical and beckoning. At the top, they rattled up the cobbled street, past an old woman carrying two live chickens by the feet, and a man prodding a dancing bear along on its hind legs.

"Oh, stop! I want to see the bear! Ares, stop!"

"Can't stop here," Ares said, swerving the horses and chariot expertly between an oxcart and a lamp seller with a crate of bronze lamps on his back.

"Put me down then!"

"You stay here!" Hebe said, her hand on Aphrodite's arm.

Aphrodite pouted, but the sight of the priestesses

distracted her. Their procession was moving through
the outer gates just ahead of the crowd, and from
her vantage point in the chariot, Aphrodite could see
the priestesses' pale faces and bright eyes as they
came down the steps from the temple, their breasts
bared and tinted with rouge. Their hair hung in wild
dark ringlets from beneath crowns of gold and lapis
lazuli, and the first three carried live snakes twining
about their arms. The trio behind them bore the
double-bladed ax that was the Goddess's symbol,
and the final three carried small bronze braziers. Two
small boys in white tunics followed, playing the
pipes, and behind them came two men leading a
spotted bull and a black ewe. The bull's eyes rolled
wildly, and he snorted and danced sideways on his
lead as the crowd dodged his hooves and wide, curving horns. The crowd hushed as the servants of the
Goddess went by, mothers clutching children by the
hand, reaching out to touch the priestesses' skirts
for luck.

Ares edged the chariot through the gates, monstrous jaws of cut stone that loomed above them so
that Aphrodite felt as if the city were swallowing
them. Inside was a courtyard and a second pair of
gates at right angles to the first. Through them she
could see a stone bench soaked in fresh blood. The
smell hit her nostrils abruptly, and she nearly
gagged.

"All right, you two, get down here." Ares drew
rein. "I'll take the horses to the inn stable and come
back to meet you."

Aphrodite tumbled down from the chariot with
Hebe behind her. She stood on tiptoe, trying to see
what the priestesses and their attendants were doing,

but a huge man in a farmer's broad hat was just in front of her. The bull bellowed somewhere beyond the press of people. She could hear the high, thin voices of the priestesses over the murmur of the crowd, and the blood smell intensified. The black ewe bleated and then was silent. Aphrodite wrinkled her nose.

There was the man with the bear. It stood on its hind legs, muzzled by a leather strap with a tinkling bell. Aphrodite followed it, forgetting Hebe, who was making her obeisance to the Goddess. It wasn't a very big bear, and it looked sullenly out past its muzzle, so that Aphrodite felt sorry for it. But beyond it in the courtyard was a man with dogs jumping through hoops. One of the hoops was on fire. Aphrodite abandoned the bear and stood watching the dogs fly through their fiery rings. A man was selling sticky sweets on a tray, and Aphrodite reached into the purse that hung from her girdle and gave him a coin. He beamed at her and gave her two sweets instead of one. She stood sucking on them and watching the dogs, her eyes bright. It was all so wonderful—dancing bears and dogs and the priestesses with their beautiful dresses. She didn't care for the sacrifices, but you had to give the Goddess her due.

"Where are you from? I haven't seen you here before."

A boy was standing next to her. He looked as if he might be about fifteen. He had no beard yet, not even the trace that Ares had managed to grow, and his tunic was edged with the Tyrian purple that came from sea snails and was so expensive that the younger members of her own family weren't allowed to wear it yet. He wore a gold torque around his neck and a cap on his dark curls. His accent was odd, but she could understand him.

"I haven't seen you, either," she said, licking her fingers.

"I am from Cyprus. My father has a merchant fleet and he takes me with him sometimes to learn the business. We have been here a ten-day this trip."

Aphrodite had no idea where Cyprus was. "We have a farm here, outside the city. That way." Aphrodite waved a hand vaguely in the direction of home. She smiled at him. He was really a very beautiful boy. "What did your father's fleet bring to Tiryns?"

"Ivory and sandalwood on this voyage. And copper. We're taking on jars of olive oil here, and then we'll go inland to Mycenae with the rest of the cargo."

"Mycenae is even grander than Tiryns," Aphrodite said. "I've never been there."

"This city is all very well," the boy said, "but there are many grander. I am Adonis. What's your name?"

"Aphrodite. Will you show me your ships?"

He smiled at her. "Gladly. Er, isn't someone with you?"

Aphrodite smiled back. "My sister, Hebe. But I think she's lost herself somehow."

"Well, then!" Adonis gave her his arm with alacrity, and they went past the bear and through a crowd watching a man juggle plates and apples, and out the gates again, dodging a pastry seller's cart.

"Oh, I want one of those." Aphrodite stopped, drawn by the pastries. They were made of layers and layers of fine dough, with nutmeats and honey in between, arranged in little cups of fresh leaves. Adonis bought her one, and by the time they reached the harbor on the far side of the city, he had also bought her a cup of fresh milk and a blue bead to wear around her neck and keep off the evil eye.

His father's ship was docked and being loaded, its white sails furled and oars drawn in through the locks. A sailor bobbed his head at Adonis and eyed Aphrodite askance, but he didn't say anything. Aphrodite hopped along the gangway that had been dropped onto the dock, craning her neck to see everything. She threw the last bite of her pastry at two gulls and laughed as they squabbled over it. The winner perched on top of the mast with his prize. "Oh, it's wonderful! Do you like living on a ship? What if it storms?"

"We hug the coastline, and sleep ashore most nights," Adonis said. When her expression made it plain that that sounded awfully tame, he added, "But sometimes we have to ride out a gale. It's very thrilling. Exhilarating, just us against the sea." A sailor behind him snorted, but Aphrodite didn't hear.

"Oh, I want to sail in a ship!" Aphrodite sighed as the deck rose on the gentle swell under her feet.

"You would get bored with nothing to do. I miss hunting and racing my horses when we're at sea."

"You could come and hunt with my brothers!" Aphrodite said. "Ares and Hermes are always going out with their bows and a spear. Will you be here long? I know they'd take you."

Adonis looked as if he were less certain of that. "Where are they now?" he asked, mildly wary of the fact that she had brothers at all.

"At the festival. Somewhere. We got separated."

Aphrodite explored the deck and peered into the little cabin that sat in the stern. "Is this where you sleep? Show me!"

Adonis followed her in. "Father and I share this when we must sleep at sea. It's really quite comfortable."

"I can see that." Aphrodite looked around her admiringly at the red and blue cushions on the floor and the little lamp that hung on a chain from the roof. "It's just like in a story." She sat down on the cushions. She had asked the snake to make something exciting happen, and he had done it. She would give him a whole new bowl of milk when she got home.

Adonis sat down beside her. She took off her wreath of flowers, snatched the cap from his head, and, laughing, put the wreath in his hair. "There. I will trade you."

He grinned at her, rakish under the drooping wreath of anemones. She tried on the cap, fitting it to her head. It was blue, embroidered with scarlet thread. "How do I look?" She posed for him.

"Lovely. Like a painting on a vase." He put his hand on her knee, and when she didn't push it away, he slid it up her thigh. "You can keep it if you like."

"I will. I'll wear it every day after you sail and think about you," she said.

"You don't mind that I have to go away?" he asked her, puzzled.

"Oh, no. Ares wouldn't like it if you stayed. But I'll go to the sacred spring and ask the Goddess to keep you safe." She swayed toward him dreamily, waiting for him to kiss her.

"Where is she?"

The commotion outside made Aphrodite sit up

abruptly, smacking Adonis's nose with her forehead. She heard Hebe's voice and heavier feet on the deck. "Oh, dear."

Adonis, holding his injured nose, looked frightened. "It's just Hebe," she said soothingly. She stood and pulled down the flounces of her skirt, shook out her mantle, and wrapped it about her in a dignified fashion. When she poked her head outside the cabin, Ares was standing on the deck, his face red with fury.

He grabbed her by the wrist, jerking her out of the cabin. She could see Hebe and Hera and Zeus behind him. "Let me go!" she said indignantly.

"What have you been doing?" He narrowed his eyes and stuck his face in hers.

"I went to see the bear," Aphrodite said, affronted. She didn't like being shouted at.

"That's not a bear!" Ares glared over her shoulder. He turned his attention to Adonis. "I'll break your neck, you little son of a pig!"

The sailors on the deck moved forward threateningly, and Adonis took note of them. "My men are here," he said. "Watch yourself, peasant."

Ares shoved Aphrodite aside at that, flinging her into the grip of Hera. He lunged at Adonis, catching him around the throat, and knocked him down. Adonis fell backward through the door into the pile of cushions, feet thrashing, with Ares on top of him. They flailed among the cushions, cursing, while Adonis's father's seamen tried to push past Zeus. Zeus stood in the doorway like a plug in a bottle. His sword had somehow appeared in his hand.

Hera's fingers dug into Aphrodite's arm, "You have disgraced us all!"

"I only wanted to see the bear," Aphrodite said

sullenly. "And Ares is awful. I hope Adonis kills him!"

"And you were supposed to watch her!" Hera snapped at Hebe.

Hebe opened her mouth to defend herself and closed it again. She *had* been supposed to watch her, but watching Aphrodite was like watching a grass-hopper that zoomed about the room until you were dizzy and took your eye off it.

Zeus drove the seamen back with his sword and gripped Ares by the hair with his other hand before they could come at him again. He yanked Ares back-ward off Adonis, and Adonis scrambled into a crouch, fists up.

"That's enough!" Zeus bellowed. The seamen stopped in their tracks and looked at each other, per-plexed, as if they weren't quite sure why.

Adonis wiped his nose, which was bleeding now. "When my father hears of this, you will all be sorry," he spat.

"When your father hears that you tried to seduce a respectable young woman whose own father owns forty hectares here and pays his taxes, he will more than likely turn you over his own knee!" Zeus roared.

"Seduce her?" Adonis looked scornfully at Aphrodite now. "She thrust herself at me like a com-mon tart."

"I wanted to see your ship, you stuck-up little toad!" Aphrodite said, overcome with indignation. "I wouldn't be seduced by you if you were the last boy in Tiryns! And I hope Ares broke your nose. So there!"

Zeus towered over Adonis. "You would be wise

to keep your tongue between your teeth about my daughter," he said. "Any loose talk in this town or elsewhere will get back to me, you may be sure. And your father, whoever he is, doesn't have enough ships to get you out of my way."

Ares tried to push past Zeus. "You should have let me kill him." His cheek was scraped raw where it had come in contact with the signet ring Adonis wore on his right hand. His eye was going to be black in another hour.

Zeus shot out a hand and shoved him back the other way. "And you be still!"

Ares looked at Aphrodite, and she turned her back on him.

Zeus gave Adonis one long, last threatening look, and announced, "We are leaving now." He pivoted, his cloak swirling majestically behind him, and they all trotted dutifully along the gangplank before him. Adonis watched them go, holding his bleeding nose. His face wore a look of angry, puzzled yearning.

Zeus stalked along the wharf, herding them along. A certain amount of attention followed them. Hebe pattered beside Hera and Aphrodite. "I'm sorry, Mother. I did try to . . . but there were so many people . . . and the Goddess . . . I . . ."

Hera sighed deeply to indicate her displeasure with everyone in general. She pinched Aphrodite one last time and let her go.

Aphrodite marched ahead, chin up, displaying her injured dignity and sniffling. Her arm hurt where Hera had held it. When Ares came up abreast of her, she turned her face the other way.

"I would have killed him if Father hadn't come along," he said. "I'll kill anyone who touches you."

"You didn't have a knife," Aphrodite said scornfully. "Father doesn't let you wear one because you try to kill people."

"I would have strangled him. I could have. You're mine."

"I'm not going to be yours if you behave that way. I just wanted to see the bear."

"You were in bed with him! Like a slut!"

"I wasn't! I let him kiss me is all."

"Who said you could let some boy kiss you?"

"Who said I couldn't?"

"You smirched the honor of this family!"

"Oh, pooh. Father kisses girls all the time."

"That's Father. It's different for men."

"Well, I've heard the rumors." She lowered her voice to a hiss. "You needn't think I haven't. Hephaestus isn't Father's. Everyone on the farm says so. So there!"

He grabbed her arm, and she flung herself angrily away from him. "Be quiet about that!" he said.

"Fine!" She stumped in sullen silence up the road from the harbor. In the courtyard of the Goddess they found the Aunts waiting for them.

"Brother says we are to take you home," Aunt Hestia said.

"Noooo!" Aphrodite wailed.

"Right now," Aunt Demeter said.

"But I haven't seen the jugglers yet. There is one who does it with fire. And I wanted to buy some ribbons! And I'll miss the Bull Dance!"

"You should have thought of that earlier," Aunt Hestia said. "Mother and Father are tired and want to leave now, so you can just come right along." She pushed Aphrodite toward the gates. "Hephaestus is waiting with the wagon."

Aphrodite wondered if Hephaestus wanted to leave yet, either, but you couldn't ever tell with him. His face was expressionless, his feet planted at their strange angle on the footboard. He probably hadn't wanted to come in the first place, she suspected. Who would, if they had to drive Grandfather? And anyway, Hephaestus had a way of talking about things like festivals and market fairs, with their attendant amusements, that wasn't quite a sneer but was close. He didn't say anything when the Aunts prodded her toward the wagon. Grandfather and Grandmother were settled in the back in their chairs, glaring around them, and Aphrodite protested when Aunt Hestia climbed up in the wagon bed beside them and beckoned to her.

"I want to ride in front!"

"Well, that's a shame," Aunt Demeter said, settling into the seat beside Hephaestus.

Grandfather Cronos prodded Aphrodite with his cane as she climbed in, and she scooted as far away from him as she could get. "Come to a bad end," he said, glaring at her from under wild eyebrows.

"Ought to have been exposed," Grandmother Rhea said.

"Hush, Mother," Hestia said.

"So ought you," Cronos said, scowling at both the Aunts. "Worthless. Couldn't get a man between you."

Hestia flinched, but Demeter swung around from the wagon seat. "That will do. *Be quiet*," she said.

Cronos went on muttering, and Aphrodite slipped an arm around Aunt Hestia, even if she was mad at her. Aunt Hestia hated even to leave home; she went into Tiryns only to honor the Goddess. Aphrodite knew Aunt Hestia didn't *want* to get married and that Zeus had made Cronos leave her single, but he couldn't make him be quiet about it. Cronos was an evil old man. Aphrodite was glad he wasn't really her grandfather. She fingered the blue bead around her neck. Maybe it would take care of Grandfather.

At least she still had her blue bead. She rubbed its wide-open eye with her thumb, and brightened somewhat. And she had had an adventure. When you asked the snake for something, you had to take what he gave you. He was part of the Goddess, and her ways were mysterious.

When they got home she was banished to her chamber to be ashamed of herself until dinner. Aphrodite sat on her bed, kicking her heels against its frame and dutifully attempting shame. She had put the blue bead in her clothes chest, an oak box with a row of poppies carved on its hinged lid, that sat against the wall. Above it, midway up, a scroll of blue waves ran all the way around the white walls, and beneath it green and yellow fish and a pinky-brown octopus floated. Aphrodite liked her chamber; it was like lying on top of the waves. If Ares hadn't found them, Adonis might have taken her out in his boat. She decided she would make Ares suffer for a while before she allowed him to apologize.

Zeus, once out of earshot of his children, was inclined to be amused. The girl had spunk. "She hasn't done any harm," he said. "Just a little adventure. Scared that boy to death, I expect."

"She needs to be married," Hera said. "As soon as it can be managed." Zeus was impossible, Hera thought. The girl was like a female version of him, ready to lie down with anything that passed by her.

"She's only twelve," Zeus said. "Give her a few years yet. Hebe isn't married."

"That is irrelevant." Hera sighed, vexed. Hebe was sweet, but she wasn't beautiful. And she wouldn't exert herself. She would end up with an unsuitable match if they weren't careful. "In a few more years Aphrodite will be a scandal clear to the court at Mycenae," she said, returning to the annoyance at hand. "Marry her off now, mark my words, or you'll be sorry."

"She'll be a scandal if she is married," Zeus said cheerfully. "And where will we find a match who'll put up with that?"

III

❧

Training a Cat

So naturally, Hera's eye fell on Hephaestus.

She had always considered Hephaestus her private property. Cronos and Rhea had demanded that she expose him the day he was born, when they saw the twisted feet, but for some reason Hera, who demanded perfection in everything else, found that those ill-made feet stabbed at her heart. Secretly she wondered if they were her punishment for having, in her anger, gotten herself with child independently of Zeus. She wasn't entirely sure that Hephaestus wasn't his, but it was certainly likely. Zeus had been chasing that slut Metis, and Hera, just that once, had not been able to stand it. The urge to serve him his own sauce had taken hold of her, and she had done it under his nose, with a grain merchant who had business dealings on the farm. While Zeus, who thought he was the only one who could behave like a goat with no consequences, had been sleeping off the night's wine, she had slipped silently from their chamber into the guest quarters. And then the baby had been born with deformed feet, so that they dragged at every step, and he could never go any-where unheard. Hera saw the justice in that, and knew it was her fault.

When Cronos told her to expose the baby she spat in his eye, and Zeus hadn't had the nerve to go up against her. And so Hephaestus lived, and while the other boys were learning to hunt and fight, Hephaes-tus spent his time with old Demodocus at the forge. Now he had a reputation as the best smith in or around Tiryns, and even the king in Mycenae sent him work to do. Hephaestus had made the king a breastplate with the sacred serpent coiled across the front that had earned him a purse of silver and a steady stream of customers who wished to emulate the king. Hephaestus's hand with metal was magical, Hera thought, some gift from the gods to make up for his lameness. Everything in the world was bal-anced; she had learned to see that. And if Aphrodite was upsetting the balance of the farm, then who bet-ter to settle her down than a man who could call fire to his command? And, the thought crossed her mind, if Aphrodite really was Zeus's, there was always the useful fact that Hephaestus probably wasn't.

Hera broached the idea to him once he had had a few months for the memory of her escapade in Tir-yns to dim. He was making a bridle bit for of one of Poseidon's restive horses, leaning his dark head against its black flank, talking some indistinguishable language to it, as he fitted the cooled bit between its great teeth. Hera fanned herself in the heat from the forge. It was a boiling day outside, and the forge was like sticking your face in a volcano.

"It isn't good for you always to be here, and never to have any company," she said.

"I have plenty, of company," Hephaestus said. "Grandfather was here just now telling me how to handle this horse."

She thought he grinned at her under his dark beard, but with Hephaestus you were never sure. "Lovely for you," she said. "I meant . . . well, I meant a wife, and a family . . . what all men want."

"Do I want that?"

"Well, you must. Mustn't you?"

"Must I?" He tethered the horse outside the forge and inspected the bit. "Women don't exactly flock to my side." He gripped the bit with tongs and stuck it in the forge until it glowed.

"You are not ineligible, all the same," Hera said indignantly. "You have a reputation, and wealth. And a man with a steady disposition is what a young girl needs."

"What young girl?" Hephaestus inquired, hammering the bit on his anvil.

"Well . . . darling, do stop for a moment. That makes such a dreadful noise. Young Aphrodite, for instance. She needs a steadying hand."

Hephaestus went on hammering. "I would rather stick it in my forge."

Hera looked exasperated. Hephaestus had always been an unwieldy child. He was never persuaded by the arguments that swayed other people. Hera couldn't quite put her finger on why. He saw the world from some odd angle, she thought. "She's very beautiful," she suggested.

"So is fire." He held the red-hot bit out to inspect it, and nodded his satisfaction.

"You've always been kind to her. She respects you. And you wouldn't have to marry her right away. She *is* young, as your father has pointed out. She could be trained properly first."

Hephaestus eyed the ginger-colored barn cat slinking after a sparrow in the yard. "When you have trained a cat, I will believe you can train Aphrodite."

Hera sighed. Hephaestus laid the bit aside and picked up another length of bronze bar. When he didn't say anything else, she left him there. As she crossed the yard, the cat exploded into a flash of gold, rolling across the dust with the sparrow in its jaws.

Hephaestus watched his mother stalking, thwarted, back toward the house. He had few illusions about Hera. He knew, for instance, that she loved him but that she also considered her children much as she considered her household: Order was important, and her urge to straighten things out was fierce. He had been quite young when he had first heard the rumors about his parentage, thrown at him by neighbor boys along with the rocks. He held neither against her. That was the way of the world.

But marry Aphrodite? No. As he thought, she flitted past the forge doorway toward the chicken house, a basket in her hand. Persuading Aphrodite to do any chore about the farm was difficult, especially since she did most of them so badly, but for some reason, the hens liked her. They never pecked her hands when she came to rob their nests, the way they did the maids, and the crossest of them actually came when Aphrodite called her. He watched her now through the gold shadows of the henhouse door, standing on tiptoe to reach the topmost nests, her hair a windblown tangle down her back. She was beautiful enough to stop any man's heart, but it wasn't just beauty that lured the hapless into her net. She exuded a kind of eldritch glamour, a force with its origins somewhere in the heart of the Earth, a promise, like the plant sleeping in the seed, of wonders to come.

Aphrodite liked him, he thought—she liked everyone—but she would not love him, not even the way she loved the boys her passing fancy lit on, much less the way she loved Ares. There was very little good, he considered as he worked the bronze, to come of forging a dagger to stab yourself with. He stood thinking, scratching Poseidon's stallion between the ears. And there was Ares. As if summoned by his brother's thought, Ares came down the dusty road that wound past the laurel trees where the Goddess had her sacred spring, and up the cart track to the farmyard, a trio of rabbits slung over his back and his dog at his heels. When he saw Aphrodite in the henhouse he made a detour, dropping the rabbits at the door, and caught her by the waist. Aphrodite spun around, spilling her eggs, and kissed him while Hephaestus rolled his eyes. If Mother saw that, she would try to marry Hephaestus to her tomorrow. Aphrodite and Ares were as unreliable and dangerous as a basilisk's egg among the hens, apt to hatch fire and uproar at any moment. Their amours were marked by grand passion and shouting matches, and they fell out and made up like two bonfires. He knew that Ares wanted to marry her and had already talked to Father about it over a year ago, but no one but Aphrodite and Ares thought that would be a good idea. They were unfaithful, vengeful, and jealous of each other now. If they married, Hephaestus

considered it very likely that one would murder
the other.

Aphrodite saw Hephaestus watching them, and
she winked at him over Ares's shoulder. Hephaestus
would never tell on them, unlike Hebe, who considered it her duty to save Aphrodite by preventing
her from so much as looking at a boy. And that was
all very well for Hebe, who, Aphrodite happened to
have figured out, was languishing for love of Heracles, who was her father's servant and thus completely ineligible. Hebe wouldn't sneak off with
Heracles, she just followed him with her eyes and
sighed, and he probably didn't even know it.
Aphrodite saw Hebe coming from the olive grove
and pushed Ares out of the henhouse. She picked
up the eggs, which had fortunately fallen in the
straw. No one seemed to care what the men did,
but everyone watched *her*. It wasn't fair. Aunt Hestia had lectured her about virtue and chastity and
dedicating your body to the Goddess, but Aphrodite
wasn't sure. After all, the Goddess's business was
seeing that everything made more of itself—crops
and people and animals. And anyway, how could
something that was so much fun be something you
weren't supposed to do? That didn't make sense. If
you weren't supposed to do it, you would think the
Goddess would have arranged it so that it wasn't
fun.

Aphrodite thought about that over the next few
months, while Hera tried to instruct her in wifely
duties. All women were the Goddess in some small
part, Hera said, because the moon belonged to the
Goddess. Men, on the other hand, had the Bull,

whose dance was still an offering to the Goddess. The Bull and the sacred snake were one in some way; they were both male, but the Goddess ruled them both. Therefore, Aphrodite knew, it was wise to give your best attention to the Goddess.

According to Hera and Aunt Hestia, the Goddess also valued the ability to clean squid.

The squid lay on the kitchen table, glistening and opalescent, bulging eyes staring at her reproachfully from their tentacled heads.

"Ewww." Aphrodite scrunched up her nose and drew her hands back.

Hera took a small cleaver and sliced neatly through a head behind the eyes.

"This is how you do it," Hera said briskly, turning the milky body inside out. She pulled the translucent entrails out and laid the empty tube flat on the chopping block again. "You cut it in rings, not too thin, mind. And don't forget the tentacles."

Aphrodite watched with revulsion as Hera sliced the tentacles from the severed head. When they were cooked, she knew, they would curl up like a flower. Hera handed her the knife and she backed away. "Why do I have to do that? Cook can do that!"

"And when you are married, how will you know that your cook has done it properly?" Hera inquired.

"I don't care if he hasn't," Aphrodite said. She put her hands behind her back.

"You will if he gets the ink in your soup."

They wouldn't let her go until she had cut all the squid up, squeezing the jellylike insides out and taking the tentacles off the reproachful heads. Then she had to make a soup with fish sauce and onions and the scallops and shrimp they had bought that morning from the fish vendor, while the barn cats came through the window after the squid heads and ate them messily under the table.

"There, now," Hera said. "Aren't you proud of yourself?"

"Aphrodite made this," Hera said to the family at dinner. "Isn't it lovely?"

"Delicious," the Aunts and Uncles said dutifully, considering that it was somewhat better than her previous attempts.

"Tastes like swill," Cronos told her, spitting it on the floor.

"I'll have more," Hebe said loyally. Aphrodite watched Hebe's eyes follow Heracles as he served her. Aphrodite sat back in her chair, thinking with revulsion about squid eyes. She wished she could lounge the way Ares was doing, but ladies were expected to sit up properly and not sprawl all over the place like strumpets, according to Aunt Hestia.

She glared at Ares. He had been kissing one of the maids in the dairy, and he needn't think she hadn't caught him at it just because the maid had run out the back door into the milking shed as Aphrodite came in the other way. If he was going to marry her, he had better watch out. She looked away from him, kicking her feet against the chair legs, to contemplate the painted dolphins on the wall. The house was a big one, built by Grandfather Cronos's ancestors and added onto over the generations. At its heart was the great hall, with its painted walls and tiled floor and a roof supported by pillars. Here the family dined and entertained guests, and family sacrifices were made on the hearth to the Goddess and the Bull. A skylight in the middle took up the smoke and let light in.

Her eyes slid to Ares again, who caught her looking and grinned across the table at her. Aphrodite
sniffed. He thought he could get away with anything
and she'd just come running back. He could think
again.

She told him so after dinner when he caught her
in the dimness of the back stairs and tried to kiss her.

"It didn't mean anything; you know that," he
said cajolingly.

"Well, it does. I don't know why you think I ought
to be faithful when you won't."

His arms tightened around her and his beard tickled her ear. He put his lips to the nape of her neck,
and shivers went down her spine. She could feel his
hands on her breasts over the tucks and pleats of her
gown. "Because you're mine, that's why," he whispered, and she knew he was right. She had been his
since she could toddle. It was just the way it was.
The others were for fun, but Ares was hers and she
was his.

The next morning, Aphrodite slid out of Ares's
chamber on silent feet and down the corridor to her
own before Hera and the Aunts could get up. She
dressed in her new gown with the ruffles at the hem
and the gold ribbons down the front, and put on her
bronze-and-gold girdle, in case anyone was going
into Tiryns and wanted to take her. It was coming
around to summer again, the air laced with bees and
the smell of flowers, and she felt restless and at loose
ends. She stood on the pillared portico breathing in
the warm air. Beyond the portico a vestibule led into
the great hall, where she could hear the morning bus-
tle. Along two sides were the sleeping chambers,

where the servants were turning out the bedding, and on the third the kitchen and the bathing room.

Aphrodite heard Aunt Demeter calling her name and circled the house to the kitchen. Bees were already busy in the kitchen garden, zizzing among the blooming tops of onions and garlic and the small pale flowers on the rosemary. At the door, Aunt Demeter met her with a pair of buckets. "Don't be all morning about it, please, dear."

"Yes, Aunt."

The one chore that Aphrodite did willingly was to fetch water from the spring. She liked to stare down into the depths of the pool and think. She set out along the road with the buckets. Her favorite hen was taking a dust bath, and Aphrodite stopped to scratch her feathers as a chariot bowled past them, and the hen flew up into a tree, squawking. It was Ares, his dogs lolloping after him. She shouted at him and he drew rein.

"Where are you going?"

"To wrestle with Leochares."

"You promised to take me on a picnic!" Aphrodite put her hands on her hips.

"I did not. You said you wanted to go on one, and I said, 'Mmmm.'"

"Then you said you'd take me!"

"No, then you asked me again, and I said maybe."

"Well, maybe means yes." He laughed and she said, "I want to go with you now then."

"You can't. We're going to wrestle. You get bored. And anyway, girls don't watch that."

I'm tired of what girls don't do, she thought, watching his chariot disappear down the road with the dogs behind it. She turned fretfully onto the path to the spring. A scattering of pale violets grew by the way, and she picked a handful for the altar there. There was water in the well by the house, but springs were sacred and had magical properties that Aunt Demeter used for the medicines with which she and Hebe doctored family and servants. Aphrodite knelt on the damp earth beside it and arranged her violets. Then she laid her arms on the edge of the pool and peered into the water. Sometimes she could see things in its depths, fish circling and the bones of things given to the Goddess long ago.

She thought of Adonis, who had been so spiteful, but who had looked at her with such angry yearning anyway. He sailed in ships over the sea to strange places, and she knew he would have taken her with him. She wondered what that would be like. Aunt Hestia said that people over the sea to the south had their heads at the bottom and their feet on their shoulders. Aphrodite thought she would like to see that. Ares wouldn't take her, though. All he wanted to do was go fight a war, if someone would just please start one. And then she'd be worried to death about him the whole time, waiting to hear he'd been killed, but he didn't think about that.

She peered deeper into the pool, studying her reflection. Just now she would have settled for watching Ares wrestle with his friend Leochares, but she knew, if she really thought about it, that that was just because he had said she couldn't. Aphrodite sighed and flicked a pebble into the pool to watch the ripples.

The spring was at the corner of the family land, where it butted against Leochares's father's holdings, and that of a third neighbor, so she wasn't surprised when she heard footsteps coming from the other direction. She sat up and shaded her hand against the morning sun. It glared brightly between the gray branches of the olive tree and the woods behind, making her squint. The sharp flash of a bird's wing crossed her vision, erupting from the trees, and a frog plopped off the bank into the pool.

When he came out of the woods, she saw it was a boy, a little older than Ares maybe, with hunting leathers on, his bow and quiver slung over his back. He had barley-colored hair and a muscular build. He wasn't very tall, but his hands were long-fingered and his feet, even laced into hunting boots, had a high, graceful arch like the feet of the bull dancers. He stopped on the path when he saw her.

Aphrodite stood up, brushing the leaves from her dress.

"I won't hurt you," he said. "Don't be afraid of me."

It had not occurred to her to be afraid of him, despite Aunt Hestia's dire warnings about strange men. Maybe it would be more maidenly to act as if she were. Aphrodite considered that, looking at him from under rose-gold lashes. "That's the path from Leochares's farm," she said. "Do they know you're hunting on their land?"

"I am staying there," the boy said. "I am Anchises, from Troas."

"Troas," Aphrodite breathed. Troas was a long way away, she knew. Farther than Crete, across the sea in Aeolis, where the big trading ships went.

"Who are you?" The boy kept staring at her.

"Aphrodite. I belong to Cronos's household. You'll have heard Leochares speak of him."

Anchises nodded. He had heard Leochares call Cronos an evil old cyclops, but thought it might be more tactful not to say so. This was the most beautiful girl he had ever seen. He wanted to marry her. He wanted to ravish her. He wanted to worship at her feet and bring her things. He shook his head, clearing the fog a little. She was still radiant.

Aphrodite smiled at him. "Do you want to help me carry this water back to my aunt?" she asked him. He was a friend of Leochares's so that made it all right.

Anchises picked up the buckets. He dipped them in the pool and saw her reflected there, looking over his shoulder into the dark water. He thought of nursery tales of young men who had met strange girls in the woods and loved them, and found them later to be goddesses in disguise. He wouldn't have been surprised. He picked up the buckets and followed her as she skipped, laughing, down the path ahead of him.

Anchises was a distant relative of Leochares. He had been sent here to find a suitable wife among the maidens of Mycenae or Tiryns, he explained when he and his hosts were bidden to dinner by Zeus. Even Ares had to admit that that made his presence unobjectionable. Anchises came of a wealthy family in Troas, and *suitable* meant also wealthy and of known parentage, both things which Aphrodite was not. Ares was at pains to point this out to her, and she smiled affectionately at him.

"You know I don't love anyone but you. How could I marry someone and go live in Troas, where I'd never see you?"

"I saw him looking at you," Ares said.

Aphrodite shrugged. Men always looked at her.

"You're mine," Ares said.

IV

❧

The Spring

Aphrodite meant to be faithful to Ares; she really did. She always loved him best. But it was so easy to love other boys, too, while they were there. She had half forgotten Adonis already; he wasn't there. But Anchises was, laughing with Zeus and the Uncles, complimenting Aunt Hestia on the dinner so that she preened, throwing spears with Ares and his half brothers to see who could send them the farthest. They got up a mock war between them, Ares, Hermes, and Dionysus on one side, and Anchises and Leochares on the other, with Heracles added to even out the numbers, and fought it across the stableyard and into the olive grove, ambushing one another behind trees until it was too dark to see.

Aphrodite watched from a chair on the portico, and Hebe came and sat down beside her. The boys galloped like young horses in the stableyard, flinging their padded spears at one another. Heracles was the strongest, but Ares was the fastest and the most dangerous. Anchises held his own, fighting back-to-back with Heracles. Leochares had taken a fair blow and was "dead" under a tree.

"You should ask Mother to let you marry him," Aphrodite said.

"And go all the way to Troas?" Hebe's eyes widened. "He wouldn't want me anyway," she added, dismissing that idea.

"Not Anchises, silly. Heracles."

Hebe's face flooded red. She shot Aphrodite a horrified look. "I don't . . . I never said . . ."

"You can't deny it," Aphrodite said. "I can see you do. *I* think it's romantic." She sighed at the romance of impossible love.

Hebe fled into the house.

Aphrodite thought about the problem. Considered from a purely practical angle, if Hebe were pregnant then Mother would probably let her marry Heracles, but the difficulty was in getting Hebe pregnant. Hebe acted as if she didn't know how it was done.

The boys left off their battle in the darkness and came trooping into the house, headed for the bath. Aphrodite could hear them splashing and shouting and forgot about Hebe, because there was a chink in the wall that she knew about and she wanted to see what Anchises looked like.

Anchises stayed at the house of Leochares for five months, into the turning of the year and the start of winter. After the first month, Ares went to train with the king's army at Mycenae. Aphrodite screamed and pouted at him, but he laughed at her, fitting on his greaves and the new breastplate that Hephaestus had made for him.

"Why are you *leaving* me?" Aphrodite wailed.

"This is man's business," Ares said. "I'll be back,

you silly chicken. This is a wonderful opportunity. The king doesn't take just anyone into his command."

"But there's no war."

"Doesn't matter. There will be soon. Troas is being unreasonable about our shipping coming past the Hellespont. We'll have to do something about it if we don't want to truckle to King Priam forever."

Aphrodite was uninterested in shipping. "Just don't expect me to wait for you!" she flung at him.

"I'll be back," Ares called, shaking out the reins, "before you know it."

Hera pulled her, screaming, into the house and told her to be quiet and stop making a scene.

But she did mean to be faithful. It wasn't her fault that Anchises was at the spring again the next day and that he just happened to have a bracelet of silver and dark pearls that he said he knew would look nice on her, and it did. And it wasn't that she thought she could get him to marry her. She didn't want to marry him—and go live somewhere away from Ares? But it was such fun to be in love. And Ares was being stupid. All of which had something to do with Aphrodite agreeing to meet Anchises at the spring again later, at night when no one was watching but the round silver face of the moon.

Hephaestus saw her go, and had a good idea of where she was headed. He had seen the way Anchises looked at her—with the starved look that men always wore when they first saw Aphrodite. If there was something wistful in his own gaze as well as he watched her white dress disappear in the darkness like a scrap of mist, he knew about that, too. He had spent a lifetime not having what he wanted, and Aphrodite had spent hers taking everything that she did. Maybe hers was the better way, but Hephaestus had found that he was too afraid of sorrow to run after joy. It came, he supposed, of an intimate acquaintance with sorrow. And if Aphrodite didn't know sorrow now, she would, he thought. She was courting it nightly.

It wasn't until Anchises had sailed away, bearing a betrothal contract between himself and a wealthy girl in Mycenae, that the household discovered that Aphrodite was pregnant. Aphrodite had known it for some time and had thought hopefully to herself that it would probably go away on its own if she didn't say anything. And if it didn't, she thought, cheering up, it might be fun to have a baby. She doted on Amphitrite's little boy. And she had loved the baby that Aunt Demeter had had five years ago, that had died when it was only six months old, poor thing. Nobody knew who the father had been, and Aunt Demeter wouldn't say despite Cronos's trying to beat it out of her until Zeus intervened. Ares would probably be angry, but he would come around. He shouldn't have gone off to the king's army and left her alone, so it was his fault anyway. Aphrodite watched her swelling figure with interest until Hera caught sight of it.

"Slut! Shameless!" Hera dragged Aphrodite by the arm out of the bath—which she had barged into without even asking if anyone was in there. "Put your clothes on!" Hera dragged her back into the bath and snatched up Aphrodite's mantle, flinging it over her. She hauled her out again into the corridor, which was rapidly filling up with onlookers drawn by Hera's shrieks. "Slut!" Hera slapped Aphrodite across the face.

Aphrodite jerked away from her, holding her damp mantle around her, back to the wall.

Zeus waded through the crowd of interested faces. He took in the red handprint on Aphrodite's cheek and the swelling of her belly under the wet cloth. "Whatever you are supposed to be doing, go and do it!" he bellowed, and the crowd scuttled away about its business. It didn't scuttle any farther than it had to, however. Aphrodite could practically feel the ears pricked on the other side of the kitchen wall. Only the family members were left, the Aunts looking shocked, Hebe reproachful, and Hermes and Dionysus uneasily interested.

"And you!" Hera shrieked at Zeus. "Are you responsible for this?"

Zeus looked affronted, since he had not in fact actually slept with her, not strictly speaking.

"No!" Aphrodite said. It seemed only fair to defend him. She had heard the rumors about the father of Aunt Demeter's baby, and everyone knew that Hermes and Dionysus were his. He shouldn't be blamed for this one, too, and besides, Hera would be even madder than she was already if it were Zeus's.

"Whose is it?" Hera demanded. Hermes and Dionysus faded out of sight. Cronos and Rhea, who were drawn by any altercation as if by a magic spell, stumped around the corner from the great hall, where they had been sitting in their web, Aphrodite thought, waiting for flies. "She's with child!" Hera shrieked at them.

"Slut," Rhea seconded Hera's judgment.

"Beat her," Cronos said. "That'll shift it."

"No!" Aphrodite wailed, frightened now.

"No," Zeus said. He stared at his father and managed to stare him down, but the loathing flowed between them like lava.

"I'll take care of it," Hera said.

Zeus laid a hand on her arm. "You are not to hurt her."

"Certainly not," Hera said. "Come with me." She held out a hand to Aphrodite, and Aphrodite went with her because Cronos and Rhea frightened her so.

Hera led her none too gently down the corridor to her chamber. "Stay there."

Aphrodite huddled on the bed, wondering what would happen next. What if they made her marry Anchises? She would have to leave Ares, and anyway, Anchises was betrothed already. But Aphrodite's experience of Zeus was that he could make anyone do nearly anything.

Hera returned after a lengthy disappearance with a cup full of something, which she held out to Aphrodite. "Drink that."

Aphrodite sniffed it. It was dark green and it smelled like swamp water. "What is it?"

"Just drink it."

Aphrodite took a sip and made a face. Hera took a step toward her, hand raised. Aphrodite swallowed the contents of the cup and gagged. "What is it?"

"Medicine," Hera said grimly. Her face softened a touch. "I'll stay with you. You probably aren't going to feel very well."

Aphrodite huddled on her bed. Maybe it was for the best, she thought miserably, already a little wistful about the baby they weren't going to let her have. Her stomach cramped, and a wave of nausea overcame her. She vomited into the basin that Hera held out.

Aphrodite was violently ill for the rest of the day and most of the night, but nothing else happened. In the morning, Hera gave her a dose of something else that made her head swim and think she saw owls sitting on her clothes chest, but the baby didn't budge then, either.

"Owls," Aphrodite said. They waved their wings at her in sequence, like a line of dancers.

"It's too late," said Aunt Demeter, called into consultation.

Hera got the household snake out of his basket, which he didn't like, and walked him widdershins around the chamber twice, his tail snapping in annoyance, but nothing happened. The owls didn't seem to mind him. Hera walked right through them and they didn't budge.

Aunt Demeter bent over Aphrodite, her face floating just a little off her neck. "Get up, dear."

Aphrodite stood up and slid gently onto the floor. Aunt Demeter and Hera took her under the arms and lifted her to her feet. They propelled her along the corridor and through the great hall, where Cronos and Rhea sat. They looked comically like pigs, and Aphrodite stuck her tongue out at them. Outside, Hera and Aunt Demeter stood her on an upturned feed bucket and had her jump off it. After she landed in a heap the first time, Aunt Demeter stood there to catch her once her feet had hit the ground. Aphrodite's teeth rattled in her head and she twisted her ankle, but the baby didn't go anywhere.

"I told you it was too late," Aunt Demeter said. "She's young and strong. She's going to have it."

The irritated noise that Hera made sounded like a duck quacking, and Aphrodite giggled.

"Whose is it?" Hera asked, snapping her head around suddenly at Aphrodite.

"Anchises's," Aphrodite said, startled into truthfulness. She glared at Hera, vexed. She hadn't meant to tell. What if they sent her away to him?

Hera threw up her hands. "What were you thinking? You knew that boy wouldn't marry you! And why didn't you tell me before he sailed?"

"Don't want to marry him," Aphrodite said wearily, leaning on Aunt Demeter.

Hera gave up. They dragged Aphrodite back to her chamber, put her to bed, and left her alone.

Once the effects of Hera's medicines wore off, Aphrodite found that being pregnant was not unpleasant. Her breasts got becomingly bigger, for one thing. She spent her days lazing in the sun, thinking about the baby and what fun it would be to have one. She went to the Goddess's pool and looked into it to see if she could see the baby's face, and thought she saw it just behind her own. She smiled and the baby smiled back.

Ares returned from the king's army at Mycenae and got into a shouting match with her. "You are mine!" He drew back his fist.

"Don't you hit me!" she shrieked.

"You belong to me!" His fist caught her in the jaw. "You've been sneaking around with dirty foreigners!"

Aphrodite backed away, holding her jaw. She picked up a rock and hefted it.

Hephaestus heard them from the forge and came at a limping run across the yard. "Enough!" He took Ares by the shoulder. Ares glared at Aphrodite, his chest heaving in fury.

Aphrodite tossed her head. "I don't want to see you again!" she said to him, and proceeded to ignore him for the rest of her pregnancy. When he spoke to her she pretended he wasn't there.

When she was nearly due, Aphrodite took her blue evil-eye bead that Adonis had bought her, and asked

Hephaestus if he would make her a rattle with it to keep the baby safe.

Hephaestus looked troubled, as if he were going to say something, and then thought better of it, his mouth downturned under his dark beard. But then he changed his mind and held out his hand for the bead. He smiled, and as always the smile changed his whole face. His dark eyes were a warmer shade of brown, and his mouth was nice—wide and quirked at the corners. Aphrodite hadn't really noticed before, because Hephaestus so rarely smiled. His arms were muscular from working at the forge, and his legs from carrying himself on his twisted feet. He was really very handsome in a solemn way, if you didn't look at his feet. There must be some nice girl who would like him, Aphrodite thought. No one had really tried because Cronos and Rhea, despite the fact that they hated all their offspring, never thought anyone outside the family was good enough for them. It was the same with Hebe and the Aunts. Aphrodite decided she would look around for someone for Hephaestus.

"I can put it in a bronze cage," Hephaestus said, bringing her attention back to the rattle. "So the bead will be able to look out, but the baby can't get it out and swallow it. Will that do?"

Aphrodite smiled back at him. "Yes, please." She patted her swollen stomach, feeling the baby's foot rippling under her hand.

V

❧

What the Goddess Gives and Takes

The pains came suddenly in the middle of dinner. Aphrodite clutched her stomach, eyes wide. The next pain doubled her over. She howled, and Hera got up and took her by the arm.

"Hush! It's just the baby coming."

"It *hurts!*"

"Did you think it wouldn't?"

"It's early," Grandmother Rhea said with satisfaction. "Wouldn't be surprised if she dies."

"Be quiet!" Hera snapped, and Rhea mouthed her teeth at her and spat.

Another pain ground its way across her belly, and something wet gushed from between her legs, splattering the floor. Aphrodite howled again.

"Gods! Get her out of here!" Zeus said, revolted.

Hera cast him a baleful glance. A servant, Dionysus's mother, Semele, scuttled up with a cloth and a bucket. Aunt Demeter got up from her chair and went with them, waving her arm at Semele to come along, too. They took Aphrodite down the corridor to her chamber and undressed her. "Lie down and let me look at you," Hera said.

Aphrodite felt mortified letting Hera look up between her legs and prod at her, but it hurt too much to argue. "It will be a while yet," Hera decided. "You'll feel better and it will come more quickly if you walk around."

"Noooo!" Aphrodite curled into a ball as the next pain came.

"Now, now." They got her up again regardless and walked her around the room.

"Owwoooo!"

Semele brought in two braziers and lit them for warmth against the spring chill. Hermes's mother, Maia, came in carrying the birthing stool. They set it on the floor and plopped Aphrodite on it. She sat, knees and feet splayed apart, belly so big she wondered how she could see over it. "I want to lie down!"

Hera was fussing with clean sheets and sponges and flasks of oil. "It will come faster sitting up. Let the earth pull the baby out of you; don't try to push it up, you silly child."

"Owwoooo!" Aphrodite fixed frightened eyes on Hera. No one had said it would hurt *this* much. Not counting Grandmother Rhea, of course, who had followed her about telling her awful stories of women torn in half and babies that never came out. Aphrodite wondered now if maybe they had been true.

Aunt Demeter sat on the floor and squinted upward between Aphrodite's legs. "It's coming."

Aphrodite gasped and panted and felt something shift.

"Good girl," someone said.

She stared at the octopus painted on the wall and

gritted her teeth. The octopus looked back at her with a mad eye like Grandfather Cronos's winking in its bulbous head.

And then the baby was there; she could hear it squalling as Aunt Demeter kneaded her belly. "Stop that!" She batted at Aunt Demeter's hands.

"The afterbirth has to come."

"Ow! No, it doesn't. I want to see my baby." Her head felt floaty.

"Yes, it does," Aunt Demeter said relentlessly. "It can't stay in there; you'll be dead in two days. Push now."

Aphrodite pushed, glaring at her, and the afterbirth slid out, revoltingly.

"Be glad you aren't a cow," Aunt Demeter said. "You'd have to eat it."

Aphrodite gagged. "I want the baby," she whimpered.

A look passed between Hera and Aunt Demeter, and then Hera shrugged. "As soon as we get you clean, then."

Maia and Semele washed her with oil and warm water and tucked her into clean sheets with a wad of rags between her legs. Hera, her face expressionless, put the baby in Aphrodite's arms and stalked out.

"He's just beautiful," Semele said.

"Is it a boy? Is he all right?" The baby's head was red-faced and lopsided-looking.

Semele unwrapped him. "He's perfect. That's just from the birth."

Aphrodite admired him. He was a perfect baby; Semele had said so. She wrapped him up again and closed her arms around him. He was *hers*.

When she woke the sun was coming through the

window over her bed, and the baby was fussing. She put him experimentally to her breast, and he fastened his mouth over it like a pump. His splayed fingers kneaded her skin like a kitten. *Mine*, she thought again, flooded with happiness. She took the rattle Hephaestus had made from under her pillow and shook it. The blue bead chimed against its brass cage.

Two mornings later they came and took the baby away. Hera had a strange woman with her, a big, round-breasted woman in a rough wool dress.

"Where are you taking him?" Aphrodite tried to hold on to the baby.

"To his father," Hera said, handing the baby to the strange woman.

Aphrodite flung herself out of bed and winced at the pain. "No! Give him back!"

"He can't stay here," Hera said. "You aren't fit to care for him."

"I am! He's mine!" Hera and the strange woman left the room with the baby, and Aphrodite ran after them, pulling at the woman's arms. Aunt Demeter and Aunt Hestia were in the hall. They grabbed her, and she fought loose, smacking Aunt Hestia in the eye. "Give him back! He'll die!"

"The wet nurse will care for him."

"*I'll* die! He's mine!" Aphrodite ran after them again, shrieking. Zeus stepped in front of her.

The whole family seemed to be milling in the great hall. Ares was there, and Hebe, and the Uncles as well. "Ares! Stop them!" Aphrodite screamed at him over Zeus's shoulder, but Ares didn't answer her.

"Stop it!" Zeus shook her by the shoulders. "That child cannot stay here."

Hephaestus had limped through the doorway from

outside, as if the commotion had roused him from his forge. He saw the wet nurse and pushed his way through to Zeus. "This is cruel. Let her keep it."

"It can't stay," Zeus said again. "Its father is from Troas. I won't give the king a reason for his eye to light on me when he wants a pretext for war with Troas, or King Priam, either. It's going back to its father, and we are staying out of their quarrel."

Hera returned. Outside Aunt Demeter was settling the wet nurse in a wagon with Heracles at the reins. Aphrodite leaned against Zeus's chest, howling. He patted her ineffectually.

"Be quiet," Hera said. "You should have known the trouble you were causing with that foreign boy. Furthermore, we could have exposed the child, but Zeus has decided to spend a small fortune to buy it *and* the wet nurse passage to Troas. You should thank us."

"That's asking a bit too much of her, Mother," Hephaestus said angrily. "You didn't expose it for fear someone would pick it up and learn where it came from and who its father was, and then make use of it. We are not as altruistic as you paint us."

"Oh, please give me back my baby." Aphrodite was weeping uncontrollably. "I'll never tell whose he is. I won't!"

Hera gave her an exasperated look. "When you are married—which had best be soon—then you can have babies."

"I want this one!" She tried to push past Zeus again, but they held her until the wagon rattled out of the yard. When they let her go, she chased it down the road until she collapsed in a bloody heap in the dirt. She buried her face in the road, shaking violently, the sky spinning around her.

Hera started to send a servant after her, but Hephaestus glared at his mother. "I'll get her. You leave her be now."

"Oh? And who are you to take charge?" Ares demanded now, stepping in front of him.

"Someone more interested in whether she lives or dies than in who she sleeps with," Hephaestus snapped at him. Ares looked startled. He backed away and shrugged.

Hephaestus limped after the wagon to the small heap of bloody nightdress in the road. He planted his twisted feet apart for balance, lifted Aphrodite, and began to carry her, lurching as he walked. Her face was red and slick with tears and dirt. She shivered. "I want my baby," she whimpered. He knew that she did. When Aphrodite loved someone, she loved them, no going back. The trouble was that she could love so many people at once.

"I'm sorry," he whispered. "I tried to tell them."

She nearly died of it. Running after the wagon had started her bleeding again, and it didn't stop. Aunt Demeter, white-faced, came and went from her chamber all night, while Ares lurked frantically in the corridor.

"Go away!" Aunt Demeter hissed at him.

"I want to see her!" He had dark rings under his eyes. Hephaestus said he hadn't slept. Ares had spent the night at the forge, sitting in its red glow, talking wild talk.

"Well, you can't." Aunt Demeter shoved him out the door and slammed it. Hephaestus took him by the shoulder and led him away.

"Good thing if she does die," Cronos said. "No more running about with her skirt over her head."

Zeus knocked his father from his chair with his fist and sent him sprawling in the hearth.

Ares laughed, Grandmother Rhea screamed, and Hephaestus limped to the old man and dragged him clear.

In the end both Cronos and Aphrodite survived.

Aphrodite grieved with the same passion she gave to loving. She stayed in her chamber, turning the bronze rattle with its blue bead over and over in her hand, staring at the painted fish on the walls until they began to swim; swimming into the distance, toward Troas. When Hera tried to take her to the Goddess's spring she refused to go. The Goddess had let her baby be taken away, so what did the Goddess care if she was clean or not? Hebe tried to talk to her, but Aphrodite didn't seem to hear her. She sat with the rattle cradled against her aching breasts, and rocked back and forth on the bed, arms about her knees. She had never lost anything before, not anything that mattered, and she was bereft and bewildered and vengeful. When Hephaestus came to see her she threw the rattle on the floor and turned her face to the wall.

He picked it up. "Shall I make something else out of this?" he asked her gently.

"I don't care." The small voice was almost inaudible. "It didn't protect him, did it?"

"Nothing can protect against some things," Hephaestus said. "We just make our little charms and magics—and act as if they might work."

"Why make them then?" she asked miserably. Her eyes were red and puffy, and her hair hung in limp strings.

"For hope's sake," Hephaestus said.

"Yah! That's useless." She smacked the bed with her fist. "Hebe has been in here telling me I will have more babies when I marry."

Hephaestus breathed out a long, sad breath. "Hebe has never had a baby. She doesn't understand."

"Neither have you."

"No."

"Then why are you here?" she spat at him.

"I don't know." He did, though. They were going to make her marry him. He had thought of simply refusing. You could make a girl marry someone just by giving her to them, but the bridegroom had to consent. But whom would they marry her to if not him? Zeus wanted her kept in the family; he would never send her somewhere else. Aphrodite was like some enchanted talisman that no man who saw it could ever part with.

Ares wanted her, he knew, but that would be a recipe for disaster. Hermes and Dionysus were as flighty as she was. That left him. At least he would be kind to her.

"Hephaestus will make you a good husband," Hera said. Ares had heard of their plan and was raging outside, challenging Hephaestus to fight him. Aphrodite could hear him in the yard behind the forge. Hephaestus's low voice was a steady murmur against Ares's shouts.

"I won't marry him." Aphrodite folded her arms. "I want to marry Ares. You can't make me."

"I can make you," Hera said grimly. "But listen to me for once, child. Ares wouldn't make you a good husband. He hit you, remember."

"He was just mad about the baby," Aphrodite said.

"And he'll get mad again. He fights with everything. You don't want to be his wife." Ares was too like his grandfather, Hera thought, a lightning bolt condensed into human form, ready to lash out.

"He loves me."

"Love is not the best foundation for a marriage," Hera said. Certainly she had learned that from Zeus, who had loved her. Hephaestus knew better than to expect or want love. Hephaestus was the steady one, the solid one in a family given to wild flights of passion and impulse. "Hephaestus will give you respect, which is worth more."

"No, it's not." Hephaestus was kindly and brotherly. *That* wasn't love, surely. Love was the wild wind at the heart of a storm, the green recklessness that sent you wheeling out over the clifftops like the swallows in their mating flight. *That* was love.

Hera snorted with amusement. "You'll change your mind about that when you are older."

"When I'm dead!" Aphrodite wailed. She looked up at Hera pleadingly, her embroidery crumpled in one hand. They were on the portico, letting the evening breeze cool them, stitching linens for the marriage Aphrodite had thought was to be to Ares. He had asked Zeus again last week.

"You will be dead if you marry Ares. Or hurt in some way I can't heal. I am not joking. Ares is dangerous, even to you, even though he loves you. *Because* he loves you."

"He wouldn't really hurt me. He was just angry about Anchises," Aphrodite said again. Ares was always sorry afterward.

"If you were married to him and you were unfaithful, he would kill you." Hera was absolutely certain of that.

"I wouldn't be unfaithful!" Aphrodite protested.

Hera shook her head. Aphrodite was as capable of being faithful as she was of sprouting feathers to fly. "You will marry Hephaestus."

"Come on. Come on. You can have the knife, and I'll fight you with my bare hands. Come on." Ares crouched, circling Hephaestus. He threw the knife at his brother's feet.

Hephaestus kicked it back at him awkwardly. "If I want a knife, I have one. I won't fight you."

"You can't have her!"

"Tell Father that. It's not my decision."

"He won't talk to me." Ares's face was agonized, his eyes wide and wild. "She's always been mine. He knows that! Everyone knows that."

"It's no good fighting him," Hephaestus said. "I tried. Father will have this marriage, and I can't go against him."

"I'll kill you!"

"Then Father will exile you." Hephaestus felt his own anger getting the better of him and squelched it. "And you can't kill me, you idiotic puppy. I'm stronger than you are, even if I can't run. Don't try it."

"I'll have her," Ares said. "You'll see." He turned and ran toward the stables. In a few minutes Hephaestus saw him on his best horse, thundering through the stableyard. Ares jerked the horse's rein savagely, and they jumped the paddock fence and swerved into the barley fields, leaving a path of wrecked stalks behind them.

"Drink up. Last night as a single man." Hermes waved the wine flask under Hephaestus's nose. Dionysus lounged on his other side, settled into a chair, feet in the warm ashes in the hearth. They had come when the rest of the household had gone to bed, to drag Hephaestus out of his chamber and make merry whether he wished it or not.

"Loosen up, brother! *I'd* smile if I was marrying that!" Hermes plopped himself down on the hearth's edge, facing him.

Hephaestus took the flask and drank from it glumly. "Be glad you're not."

"You'll change your mind." Dionysus dug him in the ribs with his elbow.

"Oh, he'll sing a different tune after the wedding night!" Hermes chortled. "Poor old Hephaestus— *forced* to marry that gorgeous little bundle. He doesn't know what he wants!"

"I know that no one has asked Aphrodite what *she* wants," Hephaestus said, "and nor are they likely to."

"Doesn't matter what she wants," Hermes said cheerfully. "It's what Father and your mother want that counts."

"I expect so. And how often have you liked something that someone did to you for your own good?"

"Not often," Hermes admitted.

"Never," Dionysus said.

"You see," Hephaestus said. "Oh, give me the wine." He tipped the flask up and drained it.

VI

The Wedding

In the morning Hera and Aunt Demeter and Uncle Poseidon's wife, Amphitrite, took Aphrodite to pay her wedding-day respects to the household snake, and then to the spring to dedicate her girlhood to the Goddess. She looked rebellious and tearful, but she dressed and came with them when she was told to. She brought a small bronze horse and chariot to toss in the spring, symbolizing the dedication of her girlhood toys to the Goddess, along with her about-to-be-lost virginity, a polite fiction that was maintained for the sake of decorum. It was midsummer, and the bronze sun blazed above them already, but it was cool in the Goddess's grove. Aphrodite dropped the toy into the dark water and watched its gleam sink from sight, the ripples spreading across the water's surface as its depths closed around her childhood.

They had dressed her in a new gown with layers and layers of blue ruffles down the skirt, and a tightly pleated bodice laced up with red cords. Her rose-gold hair was pinned in a knot at the back, the front strands twined into a few loose curls. Hebe had made her a wreath of yellow lilies, and the stray curls shone against their petals. She was breathtaking, and she knew it. *I will be dignified,* she thought. *Dignified and tragic. They will be sorry they have done this to me.*

Ares had ridden back to the king's army at Mycenae, to everyone's secret relief, but the rest of the household was gathered in the great hall, with assembled friends and neighbors, when the little procession returned to the house. Zeus had declared a holiday for servants and household alike, and the smell of roasting meat from the sacrificial bull already filled the air. The household snake had been given an egg and a bowl of milk and honey, and Maia and Semele had decorated the hall with garlands of greenery and flowers. A cage of cooing doves, the Goddess's birds, rested on a three-legged table beside the great hearth.

Hephaestus stood waiting for her there, leaning on his cane. The grandparents had been settled where they had a good view of the proceedings, and the household wore its festival best. Hephaestus, generally seen in the leather skirt he wore at his forge, was resplendent in a fine white wool tunic bordered in purple and belted with soft red leather. His dark hair was dressed with sweet oil and his long-fingered hands scrubbed clean of the grime of the forge. He wore a gold cuff chased with hunting lions on each wrist, and a collar of gold links. His expression was somber, more in keeping with a funeral than a wedding.

Aphrodite sniffled loudly enough for people to hear and scrubbed her face with the back of her hand while Hera glared at her. She had been trying not to cry, but it wasn't easy when everything was so tragic. She hadn't expected Hephaestus to look miserable, though. That seemed insulting somehow. She studied him while Zeus was making the prayer to the Goddess to bless their union and give them a long life of harmonious agreement together. Hephaestus looked like he had a headache.

After the gods had been appealed to, Zeus opened the doves' cage. They fluttered out, circling the guests in surprised flight, and then found the open door. They soared into the clear sky, a flash of pearly feathers against the blue air. She was married. She was fifteen.

The ceremony ended with a banquet. Aphrodite sat at the table with Hephaestus, with Hera and Zeus on either side of them. *To keep us from running off,* Aphrodite thought. She had hardly seen Hephaestus since he had tried to comfort her over the baby. Once they had told her that she had to marry him she had refused even to look at him. It had not occurred to her until just now that he might be as reluctant as she was.

The table before them was laden with dishes of spiced fruit and fish and a soup of crabs and scallops. Meat, rarely eaten, made the main course, roasted and spiced with rosemary and garlic. Its source, of course, was the wedding sacrifice. The gods ate only the smell, the essence of an offered animal. The priests of the temple, or the household making the offering, ate the rest. The first dishes were followed by others, and by the wedding wine, well watered but plentiful, and many dishes of small, sticky sweets. Hephaestus ate sparingly and drank only one cup of wine. Aphrodite drank three and would have had four if Hera had not waved Heracles past her with the pitcher and poured her cup full of plain water instead. Hebe was still mooning over Heracles; Aphrodite saw her following him with her eyes. *I will do something about that,* she thought. *Someone ought to have what they want.*

Hephaestus stirred at her side, reaching under the table. He brought out a bag of pale blue cloth tied closed with white ribbons, and handed it to her. Aphrodite blinked at it. "It's my wedding present to you," he said.

Aphrodite reached for the bundled shape, curiosity getting the better of her. It was hard to be tragic enough to refuse a present. She loosed the ribbons and the cloth fell away from something that gleamed gold. Aphrodite's jaw dropped. It was a necklace of gold spirals with lapis lazuli eyes at the center of each one. Even Hera didn't own anything half so fine. Even the queen at Mycenae didn't have a necklace like that.

Hera was apparently of the same opinion. "That is disgracefully extravagant," she said.

Hephaestus raised an eyebrow at her. "You said a gift was appropriate. I always listen to you in these matters, Mother."

"Did you make this?" Aphrodite whispered, but she knew he had. No one else could do work that fine.

"Where did you get that much gold?" Hera demanded.

"The king wished for several pieces of new armor," Hephaestus said. "It appears he wants to be well equipped if he happens to start a war with Troas."

"Ought to have gone to war years ago," Cronos

grumbled from the other end of the table. "No right for foreigners to keep their shipping lanes bottled up like that."

"What is this gift? What did he give her?" Rhea demanded.

Aphrodite held it up. Everyone was craning their necks to see.

"She can't keep that!" Rhea said. "Much too fine."

Aphrodite glared at her and put the necklace around her neck.

Hephaestus bent his head near her ear. "If you don't like the idea of a gift from me, you can wear it to spite Grandmother." He fastened the catch for her.

They ate and drank to the bridal couple's health until all the guests were bleary eyed and Cronos had gone to sleep. A good deal of drunken singing accompanied them finally to the house that had been built for them. It stood next to the big house, on the outer point of a small spiral of dwellings that included the Uncles' houses and the houses shared by the upper servants. All were built of the same limestone and stucco as the big house and linked by flagged walkways so that the farm had become a small city in itself. Hera and Amphitrite, the married women of the clan, escorted Aphrodite to Hephaestus's threshold and put her hand in his. It felt cold to her fingers, but he smiled gently as he drew her through the doorway and shut the door in the revelers' faces.

"There, then. That's enough of them. You're tired; you ought to be in bed." He yawned and limped across the central hall to the chamber that Semele had gotten ready for them. "I know you don't want to be here," he said, tossing his cloak on the oaken clothes chest at the foot of the bed. "But you needn't think I'm going to pursue you. Get in and go to sleep. I'll be along in a while."

Aphrodite stared at him. He didn't want to make love to her? She had spent the day thinking of how noble and tragic she would be, doing her duty although her heart was broken.

He was gone before she could say anything. Feeling a little drunk, she pulled off the new dress and draped it on the clothes chest with Hephaestus's cloak. There was another chest across the room, which must be hers—it had fine carvings of flowers and birds and was bigger than her old one—but it was too much trouble to get there. . . . She put the lapis lazuli necklace on top of the dress, and the gold spirals shimmered there. The spiral was the Goddess's path, the oldest pattern anywhere, shaped when the cosmos was born, the way into the womb of the world. She wondered whether Hephaestus had thought of that when he gave it to her for a wedding gift.

Aphrodite lay down on the bed, settling into the summer mattress of fragrant straw and watching the moon riding the sky just outside the window. She could hear Hephaestus fidgeting with something in the other room, and the tears started again. That should have been Ares. They had decided with just no reason at all that she couldn't marry Ares. Of course she would have been faithful once she was married. And Ares wasn't dangerous. He just had a temper, but she knew how to manage him. Aphrodite sniffled, lonely in a bed big enough for two. And *he* didn't even want her, she thought dolefully.

It was quiet in the next room, except for a faint, deep breath that might be someone snoring. He wasn't even going to sleep in here, she realized. Aphrodite sat up. That was *too* much. That was insulting.

She thought a moment and then put the wedding necklace back on, and rummaged among her possessions, which had already been put into the new chest by Maia and Semele. She drew out the girdle and fastened it about her naked hips. Then she wrapped Hephaestus's cloak around her and padded into the next room. Hephaestus was asleep in a chair beside the hearth, his broken feet sprawled out at odd angles, his cane on the floor beside him. Aphrodite blew in his ear.

Hephaestus sat up with a snort. She giggled.

"What are you doing up?" He rubbed his face.

"I couldn't sleep."

"You had enough wine to fell an ox."

"It's lonesome in there," she said plaintively.

"You always sleep alone." He watched her suspiciously as she sat down on the floor at his feet. The cloak slipped from her shoulders a bit, displaying a patch of breast. In the moonlight her skin had a silver shimmer.

"I didn't expect to sleep alone when I got married." She sniffled.

"You didn't want to marry me."

"I am prepared to do my duty," Aphrodite said nobly.

Hephaestus laughed. His hands tightened on the arms of his chair. "You have no idea."

Aphrodite sat up, facing him, hands on his knees, driven by stubbornness now. She could make him want to sleep with her. She only had to call on the Goddess a little bit, turn her shoulders just this way, move her hips inside the girdle, and she could feel the Goddess's power flowing through her; it always happened. It was what she knew how to do, something she was aware that other women didn't, mostly, not all the time. Aphrodite had found that she could always do it, no matter who the man was. Maybe she could teach it to Hebe, she thought, remembering the way Hebe's eyes had followed Heracles at dinner. She had never tried to *show* someone.

The cloak fell away from her shoulders so that her torso rose naked and silver out of a pool of dark fabric, like a living statue humming with some dark, secret energy. He had gone to sleep in all his clothes, but she could feel him stirring. She put her hands on his thighs.

"Stop that," Hephaestus said. "I am not a eunuch."

"Then come to bed with me," she whispered.

"Tell me why, then. You don't want me."

"I'm lonely." That was true.

"You're a child. You want whatever you see at the moment."

"They made me marry you. Are you just going to abandon me?"

"These things have lasting repercussions," Hephaestus said. "Ripples."

"I don't care." She leaned forward, pressing against him.

"You will."

Aphrodite began to cry, burying her face in his lap. She felt all of him stiffen at that. "Love me," she sighed. Someone had to love her tonight. She felt his hands begin to stroke her hair.

After a moment he stood, lifting her to her feet, the cloak abandoned on the floor. "I will think better of this in the morning," he said. He picked up his cane and limped toward the bedchamber, one hand on her bare shoulder, tangled in her hair.

Aphrodite unbuckled the girdle and the necklace. She lay down on the bed and watched him pull off his clothes. She had never paid particular attention to his body. How odd that he had grown beautiful. If you couldn't see the twisted feet, the rest of him was muscular and sleek, his skin unmarked by the scars that Ares bore from his quarrels and sword-play. Like most of the men, Hephaestus went half-naked in the summer heat when he wasn't at the forge, and his skin was a golden tan. Only an old burn scar marred it, a white streak halfway up one arm. He hobbled to the bed and stood looking down at her. She stretched, curling her arms invitingly over her head.

"You know you're drunk," he said.

She smiled at him, a slow, conspiratorial smile. She wiggled her toes and arched her hips. "Everything works."

He lay down beside her at that. She turned to him, and he put his hand on the cool mound of her breast. Her lips parted and he put his mouth over hers. The morning could take care of itself. He was married to her, after all. Surely this was the thing to do, then. Surely he wouldn't ache from it in the morning.

VII

❧

Eros

He did, of course. In the morning, Aphrodite looked so sad that the thought of touching her again knotted his stomach. He went to the forge and pumped the bellows until he blew the fire up so hot that Hermes and Dionysus, who had been inclined to hang about and leer at him, were driven off.

As soon as Hephaestus left, Aphrodite dressed in her wedding finery and went to the sacred spring. When she got there she lay on the ground beside the omphalos stone and stuck her arm into the pool up to the shoulder, fishing for the bronze horse and its chariot.

"Give it back!" she said between clenched teeth. The water was icy. "Give it back. I don't want to be married."

The water swirled around her arm, soaking her sleeve. She couldn't feel the bottom of the pool. Something soft and slick brushed past her elbow, and she shrieked and jerked her hand out. "Give it back!" she said furiously.

The water darkened until she couldn't see into it at all.

"Give me my toys back; I'm not going to be married!"

The gurgle of the spring filled the silence. A pointed silence, she thought. She knelt and looked into the depths of the pool, but no one looked back at her but her own face. Aphrodite slumped against the omphalos stone. A clatter of hoofbeats on the stony path jerked her to her feet.

It was Ares on a horse.

"What are you doing home?" Her heart hammered in her chest.

He got down. "I had to see you. I'm sorry I didn't stay for the wedding. I just couldn't bear it."

She ran to him and buried her face in his chest. He wrapped his arms around her. He smelled of horses and leather and his own sweat, a deep, dear, familiar smell.

"I thought you hated me," she said in a small voice.

"My love, no. Never. But I couldn't bear to see you married to my brother."

"They made me."

"I know." He pressed his cheek against the top of her head. "I will make them sorry one of these days; I swear it."

That sounded very satisfactory in theory, but it didn't ease her heart. "How long can you stay home?"

"A ten-day. Then I have to be back to the king's camp. Things are brewing. Troas is blocking our shipping, and we'll have to teach them a lesson."

"Father says King Agamemnon is just looking for an excuse. That's why he sent my baby away."

"You can have another baby," Ares said. He didn't understand why women made such a fuss. There was always another one along, and the first one hadn't been his anyway.

"I don't want *his!*" Aphrodite wailed.

"You won't have it, either," Ares said, suddenly angry, as if Hephaestus had been responsible for the first one. His thieving brother or that foreign pig from Troas, it didn't matter. "This time I'll give you mine." He gripped her shoulders and pushed her down on the soft earth by the spring. His chestnut hair hung in his eyes. Their pale blue faded to gray with fury, and his hands hurt her. She clung to him, taking it all in, feeling every grip and thrust so she could keep it, remember it; keep him. He was hers.

Ares stayed for a ten-day, and if Hephaestus saw Aphrodite disappear with his brother in the evening or slink into the woods in the dappled afternoon shade, his mouth tightened but he didn't say anything. When Ares left, Aphrodite was despondent. She moped about the henhouse, sitting on the stoop with her pet hen in her lap, stroking its feathers, eggs rolling from her overturned basket. She hunched by the hearth of the new house she shared with Hephaestus, her spindle trailing from her hand, wool snarled in its basket. She had a cook of her own now and was supposed to be overseeing that inexperienced servant's efforts in the kitchen, but lost interest after the first day. Then a ten-day after the midsummer Festival of the Bull, when Ares had gone back to his army, she developed a ravenous hunger and returned to the kitchen and ate half a loaf of bread with olive oil and cheese. After another ten-day she knew she was pregnant again.

"That will keep her busy," Hera said with satisfaction.

But now terror overtook Aphrodite. She was almost certain the baby was Ares's. Hephaestus wasn't stupid; he no doubt thought so, too. What if he took this one away from her? What if he killed it? She put on her best dress and ordered the cook to make something splendid for dinner. "Anything. I don't care. What men like. Put that rabbit Uncle Hades brought us in a stew. And lots of wine."

She served her husband dinner solicitously, which produced only a perplexed expression on his face. In the month since their marriage she had slept in the same bed with him and never tried to so much as touch him, or he her. At meals she ate and disappeared about some household chore, real or imaginary, as quickly as she could bolt her food. Now she sat smiling across from him, playing with her wine cup, pouring more into his.

"Have some more of this stew. Uncle Hades gave us the rabbit, and Cook has put onions and apples in it."

"Aphrodite, what do you want?"

She sighed prettily. "I want to be a better wife. I'm sorry I have been so cross."

He took a sip of wine and raised his eyebrows. The wine was nearly unwatered. "You're a terrible liar."

"I am not!" She looked indignant.

"What I meant was that you don't do it very well," he said.

"Maybe you should give me lessons!" she snapped, resenting being seen through. Men always believed what she told them, except for Hephaestus.

"When have I lied to you?" he inquired.

"Oh, I don't know. You must have. Everybody does. And if I can't tell, then you must be good at it."

He burst out laughing. "Circuitous but interesting," he managed when he had stopped.

She smiled at him, sunny again now. "At least I amuse you."

"You do." She reached to pour some more wine into his cup, but he put his hand over it. "Aphrodite, why are you trying to get me drunk?"

"I'm not. But this is very nice wine. I ordered it from that wine merchant in Mycenae specially, because I know you like it."

That was true. It was a vintage from Argos that he was very fond of. And much too good to get drunk on. Despite the fact that he had felt like getting drunk ever since his wedding. "You're looking very nice," he offered. "Pregnancy suits you."

Her face paled. She had meant to get him drunk before she reminded him about the baby.

He narrowed his eyes at her, intent now. "Aphrodite, what are you afraid of?"

She wrapped her arms about her belly.

"Is it the child?"

"It's mine," she said fiercely. "This one is mine. You have to promise me."

Hephaestus sat back in his chair. He let out a slow breath. Of course. He could see the terror on her face now. "What do you think I'm going to do?" he asked her.

She knew what Ares had told her about babies, and now that she was older she had seen it happen. Leochares's brother had exposed his last child because he said they couldn't afford another girl. She shook her head, afraid to say it aloud.

Hephaestus's eyes went to his feet, splayed awkwardly under his chair. "Grandfather and Grandmother would have exposed me," he said.

Aphrodite shuddered. "They are horrible. Like spiders."

"Mother fought them. I owe a life back to someone, I think."

"Even if . . ." Her voice was a whisper, trailing off.

"If it's not mine?"

Aphrodite was too terrified now to answer.

"If it's mine, it might have feet like these," Hephaestus said gently. "Have you thought of that?"

She nodded. That just gave people another reason to take it away from her. "Promise me you'll let me keep it."

"Even if it *is* mine?"

"Promise." Her arms went around her belly again, and her voice held a fierce urgency. This baby was *hers*. Whatever it looked like, maimed or whole, Ares's or Hephaestus's, or fathered by some god in a shower of sparks. It was growing inside *her*. It was *hers*. They had taken the other one away.

Hephaestus pushed away the table with its plates and litter of food and took her hand. "I promise. By the Goddess."

"Thank you!" Aphrodite's face glowed with triumph. You couldn't break a promise made before the Goddess.

It was like watching a fire blaze up suddenly in kindling, Hephaestus thought. It had been such a simple thing to give her. It was a shame it was all she wanted.

When the baby was finally born, there seemed to have been no need to worry. It might have been

Ares's or Hephaestus's—they were much alike in the face—but its feet were straight, and it was a boy. Aphrodite thanked the young snake that lived in her new kitchen, with a bowl of quail's eggs, and named the baby Eros on his fourth day of life. This time Hera and the Aunts seemed to approve, even if they had their suspicions. It had been a hard birth, harder than the first, and the baby was turned the wrong way, Aunt Demeter said. They sent for a midwife from Tiryns, who came and wrestled the baby out of Aphrodite's body still alive, but something tore and she bled the way she had the last time.

"She won't have any more," the midwife said to Hephaestus. "Good thing this 'un's a boy."

Aphrodite didn't care. She sat in the sun on the portico with Eros in her lap, counting his fingers and toes, curling his tuft of honey-colored hair around her finger, laughing at the way it stuck straight up like a cock's comb. He was a sunny baby, quick to smile and coo, with clear blue eyes and long, thick lashes like a girl's. Hephaestus watched her and thought he had never seen a woman dote on a baby as Aphrodite did. Even when Ares came home the first time, she paid him scant attention, sitting with the baby to her breast, singing little songs to him. When he began to toddle she refused to have a wet nurse, and kept him by her until he was nearly two.

She also turned her attention to Hebe, who now looked at her wistfully while they sat weaving at the looms in the courtyard garden between the houses. Aphrodite realized it was her marriage that Hebe envied. "You will have to take matters into your own hands," she informed Hebe.

"I couldn't," Hebe whispered, looking down.

"Hebe, how old are you?"

"Five and twenty." At five and twenty women had given up expecting to marry and hoped their brothers would support them.

Aphrodite stood up. "You come with me. I'm going to show you some things."

It was fun teaching Hebe how to seduce Heracles. Aphrodite couldn't think why she hadn't done it before.

"Father will send me away," Hebe whispered.

"No, he won't. If he didn't send me away, he won't send you. Father never lets anyone leave; that's why you haven't married. We're just going to force his hand. He'll be happy about it when he has time to think it over. He actually likes Heracles; he just has to look at him differently. As eligible."

Hebe looked dubiously into a polished silver mirror, lacing the bodice of her dress the way Aphrodite had showed her, so that it displayed just a little more than it looked like she had meant to. Aphrodite lent Hebe her girdle, too, the one that Hephaestus had made her so long ago, that always made her feel beautiful. She fastened it around Hebe's hips. "What if he doesn't want me?" Hebe said.

"Looking like this?" Aphrodite deftly arranged an elegant curl behind Hebe's ear. The face that stared back at them looked startled by its own rouged lips and kohl (restrained but elegant) around the eyes. "You have a very nice shape, too." Aphrodite tightened the girdle just a bit about Hebe's hips, to emphasize their curve. "Besides," she added practically, "marriage to you will mean a big step up in the world for Heracles. Now what sensible man would turn that down?"

Thus Hebe found herself in the kitchen garden, where Heracles was building a fence that Cook hoped might keep the deer out of the lettuces. His muscular back was toward them, bare and shining with sweat. Aphrodite gave Hebe a little push. "Go on."

Hebe turned to her, panic warring with determination. "Are you sure he'll—"

"Trust me. He'll discover that he's been in love with you for years."

And indeed he did, since Aphrodite had laid a little groundwork there, too, pointing out to Heracles, just in case he hadn't noticed, what a good figure Hebe had, what dark eyes, and, most particularly, that a wholly fictitious young man from Tiryns was rumored to be courting her. As a result, the marrige was celebrated in midsummer during the Festival of the Bull before Hebe's belly began to swell too noticeably. Hera looked startled, as if she didn't know how this had happened, but Hebe was so happy she couldn't bring herself to be angry. Heracles, for his part, paid his respects to the Goddess for his good fortune (a substantial dowry from Zeus, a house of their own, and a herd of cattle) by giving a black bull to the sacrifice.

"Interestingly arranged," Zeus said to Aphrodite. "One wonders how my daughter became such a siren so suddenly. Poor Heracles was quite startled. He took pains to tell me that, for fear I harbored ill will."

"People just need a little encouragement," Aphrodite said, holding little Eros up to see the bull leapers.

"Be careful who you encourage," Zeus remarked. "You seem to be very good at it."

They all agreed, however, that her attention was

better focused on others' love affairs than her own, and it was remarked with relief and optimism that the baby was what she had needed to settle her down.

With Eros walking and talking, Aphrodite did begin to take over the running of her house, as if the baby's growth had pushed her toward womanhood in spite of herself. She spun and wove and supervised the maids as they made cheese from the milk of Hephaestus's goats. Sometimes when Hephaestus slid into bed beside her, she even turned to him and started something, but not very often. He never approached her. It was an unspoken rule between them that Aphrodite initiated lovemaking. When Ares was on the farm, on his infrequent leaves, Hephaestus closed his eyes if he saw them together. Ares was rising in the ranks of the king's army, still predicting war anytime now, although the war never seemed to materialize. Envoys were sent back and forth between Mycenae and Troas, and diplomats made offers and counteroffers over civilized cups of wine while their kings blustered. After one of Ares's visits, when Eros was four, Aphrodite demanded of Hephaestus what it was all about. Hephaestus was knowledgeable about the world, about what governments really meant when they said things. Ares just knew he wanted to fight a war.

"Money," Hephaestus said. They were eating dinner, and Eros had escaped from the nursery in search of his mother. Hephaestus scooped the boy up and set him on his knee, and Eros grinned. "Troas sits on the strait of the Hellespont, which is the only way into Propontis and from there through the Thracian Bosporus to the Euxine Sea and the lands of the Scythians." Hephaestus drew a map on the table with a finger dipped in his wine while Eros said, "Tross . . . Hespont . . ." thoughtfully to himself.

"A geography lesson for you," Hephaestus said to Eros, who leaned back against his chest and bounced his small feet in the air. Eros was a sunny child; no one could help loving him. He was nearly as beautiful as his mother.

"What are the Scythians?" Aphrodite asked.

"A mysterious and barbaric people. I have never seen one, but our traders bring back marvelously wrought gold from them. And horses, when we can get past Troas and King Priam's ships. Or are willing to pay him his price to let us through. That black stallion of Uncle Poseidon's, the one that was such a demon, was a Scythian horse."

"I remember him. He bit Hermes once." The horse somehow fixed the Scythians in her head as real. Aphrodite had only a vague picture of the world outside Tiryns and Mycenae. There was enough in the comings and goings of the king and his family and the scandals and diversions of her own to fix her interest. People and their passions seemed far more interesting to her than shipping lanes.

"All his colts bite, too," Hephaestus said, laughing. "But they run like the wind."

"And we want more of them? That is why we are going to fight a war?"

"We want more of everything," Hephaestus said dryly. "We always do."

Eros slid down off his lap and climbed into Aphrodite's. She cuddled him. When they talked of Troas she always thought of her lost baby, but Eros had dimmed that memory. He was here now, in her lap, and her heart overflowed whenever she looked at him. Men were all very well, but left you, and fought wars, and were unkind or afraid of your husband. Eros loved her unconditionally. As for the mysterious Scythians and their gold, jewelry was nice—she liked presents; any sane woman did—but as far as Aphrodite was concerned, what you really needed more of was love. Wherever you could get it. She turned to Hephaestus. She didn't understand what he was talking about half the time, and suspected him of being condescending at her lack of knowledge, but he ought to have some pleasures; the Goddess knew she had run him a ragged dance. And he loved her. She had grown almost certain of that in his kindness, as certain as she was that he would never say so. Which was just as well, since it absolved her of certain requirements for faithfulness, by her reckoning. She stood to take Eros off to bed, and his small, warm body flooded her with affection for Hephaestus as well. When she had tucked the boy in, and sung him a song, and told him a story, and explained that where the sun god went at night was across the underside of the world in a boat, she went back into the hall and found Hephaestus lingering over his wine. She draped both arms about his shoulders from behind and nuzzled her lips against his ear.

The next day she fell in love with the muscular driver who brought a load of wine jars to the farm, and the week after that with a juggler in Tiryns at the sacrifices that marked the turning of the year before the descent into winter's darkness. Fortunately (from most points of view) she had Eros with her both times and couldn't do more than enjoy their admiring stares, the way their lips parted and their eyes grew intent when they looked at her.

When Eros was six, he began his lessons with a

tutor, and Aphrodite was at dangerous loose ends again. That was when Zeus decided to take her with him to the king's court at Mycenae, where he and the king's advisers were called for a council with Paris, prince of Troas. Paris represented the next round of diplomatic negotiations, sent by his father to demand certain concessions in exchange for freedom of the Hellespont.

"You are mad," Hera said flatly.

"I'm not," Zeus said. "Ares will be *here* on leave in a ten-day, and Aphrodite will be *there*, which is all to the good. Furthermore, Agamemnon has summoned his brother Menelaus up from Laconia for this meeting, and Menelaus will bring his new queen. This girl, Helen, is Menelaus's claim to the throne; her father was the old king. She'll be young and lonely and will need a friend. It won't hurt for that friend to be our Aphrodite."

"Her elder sister is Agamemnon's queen," Hera said. "Why should she be lonely?"

"It's said they don't care for each other."

"Well, Clytemnestra won't welcome Aphrodite," Hera said. Agamemnon's queen was known to take an interest in political affairs. "She won't want a guest to entertain."

"She won't be entertaining her sister Helen, either. That's where Aphrodite comes in."

"She won't like her. Women never like Aphrodite." Hera sighed.

"They don't like Helen, either," Zeus said. "She's reputed to be the most beautiful creature anyone in Mycenae or Laconia has ever laid eyes on, so naturally the women at her husband's court despise her. That makes our Aphrodite the ideal candidate for friend and confidante."

"It doesn't matter. Aphrodite will make trouble somehow. Trouble flows to her like water."

"Menelaus is quite protective of his bride, I'm told," Zeus said. "Aphrodite will be shut up in the queen's quarters most of the time."

"Have you asked Hephaestus?"

Zeus smiled. It was a crafty smile, one that Hera recognized as appearing whenever he thought he had been clever. "I did just mention the possibility to him. If you ask me, he looked relieved."

Hera gave up. But she saw them off to Mycenae with some misgivings. It wasn't that Aphrodite tried to make trouble; Hera had to give her that. She always meant well. But her well-meaning was like a volcano that was trying to be polite. She had meant well when she had shown Cook's wife some things she could do in the bedchamber to regain Cook's instant attention, and they had worked so well that Cook was convinced his wife had been unfaithful with "foreigners," people who knew things that weren't decent, and dinner had been spoiled for a solid ten-day until Hera had gotten to the bottom of it and sent Zeus to explain things to Cook, who was quite straitlaced and would have died before he heard them from the mistress's mouth.

Something would go wrong, Hera thought, watching Aphrodite bouncing in excitement on the driver's seat beside a stableboy, the wagon bed loaded with the luggage she felt necessary for a visit to the palace. Zeus rode beside them on his horse.

VIII

❧

Helen

The year was two mornings from the summer Solstice, when the day would stretch to its longest
length and Helios, the sun god, rode high in a blind-
ing blue sky, glowing like a brass bowl. A pair of
linnets, gleaming yellow in his light, danced overhead. It was a half day's travel to Mycenae by cart,
and once the road had passed the citadel at Tiryns,
it climbed slowly through a sloping coastal valley,
divided into plowed fields like a draughts board, up
into the low hills. The way was thick with traffic:
oxcarts and flocks of goats, couriers on the king's
business riding lathered horses, and troops of soldiers on the march. Aphrodite looked to see if she
saw Ares among them, but their faces were always
shadowed by their helmets, expressionless and stern
as warriors on a carved frieze.

Mycenae was even grander than Tiryns, towering
above the usual outer warren of huts and shops
where the soldiers drank wine and pursued more
dubious pastimes. Aphrodite held her nose against

the smell of the drains that emptied from inside the citadel and the output of the huts outside it. The road here was paved with flat stones, and at the top it passed through a narrow passage between high rock walls and under the great Lion Gate. Above the lintel, two carved stone lions rested their paws on a pair of altars and guarded a pillar that Zeus said held inside it by magic the kingship of the city. Their heads faced outward, watchful and grave. Below them, massive wooden doors faced with bronze ornaments stood open to the day's traffic, with a forbidding-looking guard at either side. The stable-boy maneuvered the cart between the soldiers into the citadel proper. Inside were more houses, better ones built of stone, and a market where merchants were hawking weapons, fine wines, oysters brought that day from the coast, jewelry, and charms to ward off curses and lung disease or madness. Aphrodite gaped about her with delight.

Just beyond the gate a cobbled road sloped up toward the palace, buttressed by a stone retaining wall. It ended at a portico so high and grand that Aphrodite got a crick in her neck looking up at it. Here Zeus handed off cart, driver, and horse to a palace servant who seemed to have been expecting them, and escorted Aphrodite through the portico. Inside, a shifting crowd of people flowed through a cavernous hall, its ceiling supported by red and blue pillars. All seemed intent on their own errands: scribes, soldiers in varying uniforms, officials conferring in low voices as they walked, a clerk with an armful of clay tablets tottering nearly higher than his head.

Aphrodite wanted to see where they were all going, but Zeus escorted her instead up a set of wide

steps to a doorway screened by embroidered hang-
ings, where he handed her over to a large eunuch
who stood just outside it. The eunuch wore indoor
robes of light green, and was pale and soft-looking,
like a large, homely woman. Aphrodite looked at him
curiously. She had never seen one before, although
Hephaestus said they were common in the East.

She looked back over her shoulder, but Zeus had
already disappeared. "Madam should come this
way," the eunuch said. "My name is Elpenor, and
my function is to make certain that my lady's guests
have everything for their comfort." He smiled at her,
a friendly expression indicating that they shared
some deeply satisfactory mutual jest.

Elpenor escorted her to a room in which a carved
ebony bed was overlaid with a blue coverlet embroidered with a pattern of white waves, laid over a
down mattress that smelled of crushed mint. Her
clothes chest had already been brought in and set
beside a table with a silver mirror and a clay lamp
painted with leaping fish. Elpenor lifted a hanging
at the rear of the chamber discreetly, to display a
toilet with a clay seat, rather than the chamber pots
they used at home. "Madam is bidden to dinner with
Queen Helen's household when she has freshened
herself," he said. "Just ring that bell." He pointed
with a graceful wave of his hand to a small silver
bell on the table beside the bed.

Aphrodite wandered about the room, trailing her
fingers along its elegant furnishings—ebony chairs
and a table inlaid with ivory—before she touched the
bell. At its sound, a trio of serving maids appeared
like a flock of birds landing, and began to wash and
brush her. A basin appeared and a bowl of soft

sponges, and oil and a strigil. A fresh gown was unearthed from her clothes chest and taken away, to reappear freshly pressed and starched, its flounces rustling. A brazier appeared with hot tongs to curl her hair. When they were finished they delivered her through the door to Elpenor, who escorted her down a short flight of stairs, and along a beautifully dressed stone passage lit by painted lamps in sconces, to even grander quarters.

Here a woman with pale blond hair like sun on water sat in an armchair playing with a small gold ball that ran up and down a string. She smiled when she saw Aphrodite.

Aphrodite smiled back, smitten as everyone always was. The queen of Laconia made strangers smile just to look at her. She was the most beautiful woman Aphrodite had ever seen—maybe even more beautiful than herself, she thought, undismayed—and radiated a force that was sheer beauty, unadulterated by appetite. It would make men want to worship at her feet, put her on a throne, and look at her. Aphrodite bowed her head as Hera had instructed her. "Your majesty. I am Aphrodite of Tiryns."

"Please come in. I am so glad to have company. I am Helen." The golden woman gestured to a chair beside hers. "It's very large here and I got lost yesterday, and my husband says I am to stay inside. I might as well be back in the schoolroom." She gave Aphrodite a friendly frown. "Very vexing."

Aphrodite sat, since Helen seemed to expect it of her. "My husband dislikes the city," she said. "But he let my father bring me. My father is here for the council with King Agamemnon over Troas, which I don't understand at all."

Helen looked sympathetic. "Nor I," she confided. "But I saw Prince Paris, and he looks like a painting on a vase. Extremely handsome."

"Perhaps you might pay more attention to matters of state than to handsome faces, and understanding might arrive," a voice said from the opposite doorway, and Aphrodite turned to see a woman who looked a bit like Helen, but overlaid with the same stern quality that Hera exuded. She recognized Queen Clytemnestra and leaped to her feet.

"Oh, sit down, child. You are entertaining my sister, which is a boon to us all." Clytemnestra gestured at Aphrodite's empty chair, which Aphrodite was too afraid to sit back down in. "It was kind of Zeus to bring you."

"And delightful of you to join us," Helen said.

"I shan't stay," Clytemnestra informed her. "There are matters of state to attend to. I have ordered a supper sent in for you, since politics bore you."

She vanished again, and Helen stuck out a tongue at her retreating back, startling Aphrodite into a surprised snort of laughter. Helen looked at her solemnly, and when she caught Aphrodite's eye, Aphrodite fell back into the chair and they both dissolved in laughter.

Zeus had been right. He might have been dismayed to know how right. Helen and Aphrodite were made to be friends, and that friendship was a novelty that made Aphrodite giddy. Women didn't like her as a rule—except for Hebe, who was far too nice to be jealous—but Helen was even prettier than Aphrodite was. Aphrodite liked just looking at Helen. They compared notes on children—Aphrodite had a son and Helen a daughter—and joked about betrothing them. They ordered a lady's chariot from Agamemnon's stables and rode out together, with Helen driving and a groom to see that they were safe. They picnicked by the river, and compared impressions of Prince Paris of Troas, whom Aphrodite had now inspected and pronounced handsome indeed.

"He is smitten by you, too," Aphrodite told Helen. "I saw how he watched you at dinner last night. Didn't you?"

"I was afraid to look up," Helen said, "for fear my husband or my sister would decide I was doing something wrong. Clytemnestra can always find something I am doing wrong. I eat shrimp the wrong way or drink too much wine, or not enough, or my dress shows too much bosom. You have no idea how delighted I was when Father gave her to Agamemnon and she went to live in Mycenae."

Aphrodite giggled. "She reminds me of Mother."

Helen played with a bunch of grapes, rolling them about on the cloth. "So Prince Paris was watching me?" she asked.

"The whole way through dinner. Your husband asked him how they tax farmland in Troas, and he said something about the dinner wine and his compliments to the vintner instead. You could tell he hadn't been paying attention."

"Do *you* like your husband?" Helen asked her.

Aphrodite thought about that, startled. "I suppose I do. He's kind. He's good to our son." She sighed. "I wanted to marry his brother."

"Oh, that's tragic," Helen said, and Aphrodite nodded.

"Ares, the one I loved, is in the king's army now.

I only see him once in a while. I think Father brought me here to keep me from him when he goes home on leave."

"I think you're brave," Helen told her. "Father married *me* to Menelaus because he only had daughters after my brothers were killed in a stupid brawl. He thought Menelaus would do the best job of ruling the country, and I went with it. And he wanted an alliance with Mycenae. I wish I had a tragic love affair to look back on. It would be more interesting than that."

"What about Prince Paris?"

"I think about him all the time." Helen poked at the grapes.

"Really?" Aphrodite asked.

"I really do. He looked at me when we first met and my heart just went thump in my chest."

Aphrodite looked cautiously at the groom, who was propped against the chariot's wheel, apparently asleep in the shade of a plane tree. "What are you going to do?" she whispered.

"What can I do? You're the only one I've told. I just want a chance to talk with him alone a little bit. It wouldn't do anyone any harm. But Clytemnestra would tell my husband if *she* ever found out."

"Well, I'll never tell. This is so exciting." Aphrodite scooted closer to Helen. "Elpenor told me the prince goes out for a ride every morning before breakfast. We could just *happen* to meet him, and I could stand lookout for you while you talked to him." Aphrodite's eyes gleamed.

"Would you? Would you come with me? I'll have the nerve to do it if you come."

"Of course. It will be an adventure."

"I'll do it!" Helen clapped her hands together. "I

never have any fun. We'll get up very early tomorrow, but don't tell Elpenor. He's sweet, but he takes orders from my husband. Menelaus brought him from the East just to guard me because he doesn't trust *any* man around me."

"That's terrible," Aphrodite agreed. It must be dreadful to be a queen. At least she had the freedom to go where she chose even if she got lectured for it afterward. Menelaus had a sour, closed-up look, like a dog with its paw on a bone. Poor Helen deserved to have a little fun. And Prince Paris, too. You could tell he had eyes for no one but Queen Helen—he hadn't even seemed to notice Aphrodite.

And it was really so easy. They rose early, dressed, and tiptoed out of the queen's quarters, past the room where Elpenor was snoring softly, and across the polished marble floors of the great hall, where two soldiers stood guard at either end. Aphrodite had dressed Helen's hair, because they didn't want to call her maids, and lent Helen her wonderful girdle, "for luck," because it had worked for Hebe. Now both were bundled in a pair of Uncle Poseidon's old cloaks that had been used to cushion Aphrodite's clothes chest in the wagon bed. They drew the folds up over their faces. "Such a to-do, turning us out of bed so early, and all for the sake of fresh eggs," Aphrodite grumbled as they passed the guards. "Wish *I* could sit around all day having my hair dressed and eating eggs."

"Watch your grumbling, missy," one of the guards said. "The queen will set you to work in the laundry instead if she hears that."

Aphrodite made a repentant gesture of putting her fingers over her mouth, and Helen followed suit, her eyes dancing. Excitement made the fine gold hairs on Aphrodite's arms stand up and her skin prickle. A cold little wind was blowing across the portico as they slipped outside. It was barely dawn, and the birds were busy with their morning conversation in the trees. The king's stables were at the rear of the palace compound, near the road that led through the north gate of the walled city. They passed no one else but a sleepy stable boy with a shovel over his shoulder before there was a rattle of hooves on the road and Paris clattered toward them on a bay horse.

"Quick! Take off that mantle!" Aphrodite whisked the folds from Helen's head and bundled the threadbare garment under her own. She pushed her toward Paris. Paris drew rein and stood gaping at the queen. Helen took two steps toward him, and he leaped from his horse.

Aphrodite watched the road behind and before them for anyone approaching, her heart pounding with excitement, while they talked softly in the shadow of the stable wall, and the horse, unattended, snatched at tufts of grass growing between the cobbles. Helen's face shone, and Paris's eyes were intent on hers. Aphrodite felt just like a secret go-between in a ballad. This was as much fun as an assignation of her own. She watched until a blossom of red flamed over the mountains in the east and the tramp of Agamemnon's night watchmen thudded along the road below them. Then she called softly to Helen. Paris turned back to his horse, mounting it in one muscular leap, and reined its head toward the North Gate, where the guards would be drawing back the bars.

"Oh, Aphrodite," Helen breathed. "He loves me!"

IX

The Horns of the Bull

It was even more romantic than Aphrodite had thought it would be. Helen's first assignation with Paris was followed by several more. Aphrodite grew adept at disguising the Laconian queen and slipping her past the guards. There wasn't much else to do. The men were all talking politics, and Queen Clytemnestra, who attended these councils, made it plain that Aphrodite and her sister Helen were too ignorant to be more than an annoyance. Only occasionally did Clytemnestra retire to the women's quarters, with her daughter Iphigenia. Iphigenia was a shy, sweet girl betrothed to her father's general Achilles, a muscular soldier twice her age, whom she had never met. More often though they were alone and they would sit in Helen's chamber and play draughts, or play catch with the gold ball Helen carried on its string. Helen would tell Aphrodite what Paris had said to her that morning in the dawn shadows. And Aphrodite would give her ideas on how to make him tremble with wanting her. It was as much fun as a romance of her own, until the morning that Zeus came roaring into the queen's quarters before dawn with a frantic Elpenor at his heels.

"Where is she?" He shook Aphrodite awake while the maids flocked into the corner and cowered.

"Who?" Aphrodite rubbed the sleep from her eyes.

"The queen of Laconia! And don't pretend you don't know anything about it. You two have been thick as thieves for weeks."

"You said to make friends with her!" Aphrodite said indignantly.

"What are you doing in my quarters?" a furious voice demanded. Zeus snapped his head around. Clytemnestra swept through the doorway, pulling a wrap about her.

"The queen of Laconia is gone," Zeus said, giving Aphrodite an awful stare. "And so is Paris of Troas. His ship sailed before dawn with both of them on it!"

"How do you know this?" Clytemnestra's face had gone rigid with anger.

Elpenor was pale as a sheet. "The king went to her chambers early this morning. He couldn't sleep; he is afflicted with insomnia. *He* found her gone, and all her jewelry." Elpenor moaned miserably. They could hear shouting outside in the halls now.

"What about her clothes?" Aphrodite asked.

"No one sneaks out with a trunkful of clothes!" Zeus snapped. "Pack your own clothes. You are going home!"

"What have I done?" Aphrodite wailed.

"I don't know yet, but you're going home. There will be war over this, as like as not."

"And my husband will have his way, thanks to my slut of a sister." Clytemnestra turned on her heel.

Aphrodite sat up in bed, the bedclothes pressed to

her mouth. "I didn't think she'd run away," she said into their folds.

"What?" Zeus snapped. "Take that blanket out of your face."

Aphrodite raised her head. "She has a little girl. Are you sure she's gone? How could she leave her child?"

The maids had fled, and Elpenor had followed Clytemnestra. Zeus sat down on the end of Aphrodite's bed. "Aphrodite, you are an utter mystery to me." He ran his hands through his coppery hair in exasperation.

"Well, I wouldn't have done it," Aphrodite said stubbornly.

"You haven't been faced with the choice," Zeus said.

"No, it was done for me!" Aphrodite snapped. "That's how I know how it feels!"

"Not everyone's . . . attachments have the strength of yours, obviously. Most of us find that more practical matters rule our lives."

"So I've noticed." Aphrodite sniffed. "I just wanted her to have a little fun," she said softly. "Women don't have much fun, you know. Maybe that's why they aren't practical."

Zeus rolled his eyes but he gave a snort of rueful amusement. "You seem to manage."

Aphrodite looked sorrowful. "I just managed a little bit for Helen. I didn't think she'd *leave* with him. Or him with her. He was here to be diplomatic, wasn't he?" She smiled hopefully at Zeus, in the fashion that still turned his loins over. She wasn't wearing very much.

"Put your clothes on," he said. "You aren't going to get in my good graces that way. And I'd better get you out of here before Menelaus decides to send for you."

"All right," she retorted, frightened at that idea. She wrapped the bedclothes about her. "What will happen now?"

"Menelaus is in Agamemnon's chambers convincing him to go to war with Troas."

"The queen doesn't want war. Can't she stop him?" Clytemnestra struck her as a woman who could stop nearly anything.

"She's been stopping him for years. She won't stop him now. Menelaus is insane with anger, and his brother is bound by honor to back him up."

Honor. Aphrodite mulled over that concept while she packed her clothes. Whenever something came down to some man's honor, there was always fighting involved. Going off to get killed was apparently always the honorable thing to do. Exactly what she had set in motion halted her now, frozen. *Ares*. Ares was in the king's army.

"Of course there will be war!" Ares said. He was there when Zeus and Aphrodite arrived, pacing about Hephaestus's forge, drawing a design for a new breastplate in charcoal on the forge wall. "I need this as quickly as you can make it."

"You will have to be patient," Hephaestus said. "Everyone needs armor as quickly as it can be made, and there is no copper for bronze just now because the king has already bought it all for his own armorers. I have a shipment arriving this month, and when it is here, I will make your breastplate."

"Don't make it for him," Aphrodite said. "You have all gone mad. If you make him new armor he will go fight this stupid war in it."

Ares ignored her. Hephaestus gave her a long look. "This stupid war is because Menelaus's queen ran away with Priam's stupid son. Maybe you should have thought of that when you were helping her to assignations with him. That story is all over Argolis by now."

"I'm sorry," Aphrodite whispered. "I didn't think she would do that. She left her child."

"What has that got to do with it?" Ares demanded.

Hephaestus said, "The trouble is that you don't really *think* about what other people might do. You think they're all like you."

That stung. She retreated to the house and cuddled Eros, who had missed her and who seemed to have grown just in the last month. "You are *not* to go away again!" he said.

"You had your lessons to occupy you," she said. "Tell me what you've learned."

"I learned to count to ten, and Father taught me to make a blade for my little spear. Well, he did most of it, but I banged on the blade."

"Very impressive. This is information you will need," she told him with a solemn face.

"For when I go to war?"

"Certainly not. You are not ever going to do anything so stupid."

"Father says I can help him make the bronze for Uncle Ares's armor when the shipment of copper comes. Father says it is coming all the way from Cyprus, where they mine it out of the ground. I should like to see that."

"It isn't as interesting as it sounds. It's just rocks when it comes out of the ground." As a girl, Aphrodite had envisioned shiny bars of copper being lifted out of holes, and Hephaestus had laughed at her.

"He says the ship's captain just inherited his father's shipping business and thinks he can hold us up for high prices, but he has another think coming," Eros reported.

"Who says? Your father?" Eros was like a talking raven, repeating anyone's ill-advised remarks.

"He's a Cypriot thief, but Father supposes we'll have to ask him to dinner when his ship docks, just to be polite. He's named Adonis. Father says that's a foreign name."

Adonis? Her eyes widened. "I suppose we shall. And you are not to repeat the things your father says like that." She had almost forgotten Adonis. It must be the same one. She wondered if he knew whose family he had sold his copper to. Surely after all this time, no one would still be mad.

If Hephaestus wondered why Aphrodite felt inclined to put herself out to organize dinner for a guest she had never met, he didn't ask, supposing it to be a matter of boredom. No one, least of all Ares, spoke of anything but the war, and other orders besides his brother's kept Hephaestus's forge hot.

Hephaestus brought Adonis back with the cart that delivered his copper ingots, and Aphrodite peeped at him from the portico as they walked toward the forge, Ares falling into step beside them. It had been a long time, but it *was* him, she was sure of it. He was even more beautiful than he had been as a boy.

She had devised the menu for a splendid dinner. She would be the perfect hostess, witty and lovely and laughing graciously. He would remember her, and remember also the evil things he had said about her when Hera and Zeus had come to fetch her from his boat. He would be tongue-tied and repentant. She would never admit to knowing who he was. It would be wonderfully romantic.

She oversaw the setting out of the meal, arranging the dishes artistically. The dining room had been painted to her liking, with a mural of an olive grove and doves flying like a white mist across the sky above it. On the other wall was a vineyard with fauns cavorting among the grape leaves. She wore her best dress, with a skirt of starched white flounces and a blue bodice and red laces. She put gold combs in her hair and wore the girdle and the necklace of gold and lapis lazuli that Hephaestus had given her at their wedding. She was overdressed for a family dinner, and Hera and the Aunts immediately cast her suspicious looks, but Ares and Hephaestus didn't notice. What they wanted to know, judging by the conversation at dinner, was what Cyprus intended to do about the war between Mycenae and Troas, if anything.

"It's not our affair," Adonis said. "Hadn't heard about it until we docked."

"Then you don't intend to sell copper to Troas?" Ares demanded.

"We're copper merchants," Adonis said. "We sell to the city that can pay us. If we worried about their politics we'd starve." He kept sneaking looks at Aphrodite, his expression uncertain. She gave him a slow smile and dropped both eyelids modestly.

Ares caught her and his brow furrowed in puzzled suspicion, but Aphrodite looked back at him blandly.

"I expect King Agamemnon will try to blockade shipping between Cyprus and Troas," Zeus said pointedly. "It might be more profitable to sell one's copper elsewhere, just now."

"Perhaps," Adonis said, noncommittal, eating the fish that Aphrodite's cook had spiced with rosemary and garlic sauce. "This is excellent. A pleasure to eat a real meal ashore. And kind of you to take me in," he added with a bow of his head to Aphrodite.

"We try to make our guests feel at home," she told him. Spurred by mischief, she asked, "Is this your first visit to Argolis?"

"No. No, I made the voyage several times with my father . . . as a boy." He hesitated.

"That must have been exciting," she murmured.

"What do you do for amusement?" Ares demanded before he could answer her. "When you are ashore? Do you hunt?"

"Yes," Adonis said, looking relieved. "I am very fond of hunting."

"Perhaps if your host and hostess will excuse us to follow more active pursuits, we might go out tomorrow," Ares said. "Before you have to travel on. I had hoped to spend a day or two in the chase myself before I'm called back to the army. There have been reports of a wild boar in these woods. They don't often come so close to civilization."

"That would be pleasant," Adonis said, but there was something in Ares's expression that Aphrodite didn't like.

She thought of telling Hephaestus, but she didn't know what he could do. And if Ares didn't recognize Adonis, then it would be a very bad idea to do anything that pointed him out. Ares was never home, she thought grumpily, but he still acted as if he owned her. Let them go hunting. Ares wouldn't recognize him after all this time. And Ares would wear himself out and sleep at night instead of wandering around the farm like a lion, pacing and grumbling because the war wasn't starting soon enough. Adonis would be alone in their guest chamber. If he didn't remember her now, he would. It served them all right for blaming her for Helen. *She* would never go off and leave her own child.

In the morning Ares set out with Adonis as the dawn was breaking. He had given Adonis his second-best horse, hoping, Aphrodite suspected, that it would throw him, but Adonis appeared as comfortable on horseback as on the sea. He mounted the horse, a wild-eyed roan, with an expert leap, and he rode lightly. The roan, after a snort and sideways slew like a cart with an off wheel, tossed its head and settled down. They disappeared down the track to the spring in the dawn mist, with Ares's hunting dogs like gray shadows at their heels.

Aphrodite watched them go uncertainly.

"You ought to resist the urge to prod at Ares," Hephaestus said.

"I wasn't!" Aphrodite said. "I was—"

"Prodding at Adonis?" Hephaestus asked.

"Why does everyone always suspect me of things?" Aphrodite demanded.

Hephaestus sighed. "Because you amuse yourself with other people. You play with them."

Aphrodite started to say that Hephaestus didn't know anything, when it occurred to her that that might not be wise. Hephaestus always seemed to know too much. Just as well not to give him the idea that there was something else to be known.

"You've gone too far this time," Hephaestus said, and limped off toward his forge, but whether he meant with Helen or with Adonis, she wasn't sure. She looked after him uncertainly as Eros came and tugged at her skirts.

"Teacher says I am to have the morning off, because I have given him a headache," he announced.

"Poor boy. And I don't mean you," Aphrodite said severely. Teacher was a pale young man from Tiryns, of good family and no money, who had been engaged to see Eros into a reasonably well-educated adulthood. His gaze followed Eros's mother like a wistful puppy.

"So you can play with me," Eros said.

Aphrodite knelt and wrapped her arms around him. Eros was the one person who loved her unconditionally, and never criticized her. "We'll go to the spring," she said, "and get water to make tonic with. And then we'll go see the chickens about some eggs for a custard. All right?"

She got the buckets, and they went along the path to the sacred spring, Eros zooming back and forth in front of her like a dragonfly. The woods were dappled with pale light, and the birds murmured sleepily in the branches overhead. At the spring he disappeared into the woods while she drew the buckets full. She heard him rustling in the dry leaves and shouting. He was playing two roles, judging by his comments—the boar his uncle had gone after, and the hunter.

"Did you catch yourself?" she asked him when he reappeared.

"I did. But I was very fierce first."

"Did you roar?"

"Yes, very loudly. I heard something in the woods, though, roaring back at me, so I caught myself quickly and came back to you."

Aphrodite cocked an ear. She hadn't heard anything over Eros's play, but now the woods seemed unnaturally still to her. The birdsong that had accompanied them had silenced. She strained her ears. Something hung in the air with no sound, like a silent echo. The water gurgled softly in the pool. She laid a hand on the smooth curve of the omphalos stone and then jerked her fingers away as if they had been burned. *Lost.* The word had come into her head from the stone.

"Come!" She grabbed Eros's hand and fled back up the path toward the house, the buckets abandoned.

"Mother! Wait!" Eros stumbled after her, over the roots whose interlaced fingers knotted the path.

"Run!" she said to him, pulling on his arm. They fled from the woods onto the wagon road, stumbling past a sleepy farm dog dozing in the middle.

No one was in the yard when Aphrodite reached it, gasping, dragging Eros behind her.

"Hephaestus!" She screamed for him, and he came running from the forge, lurching along without his cane. He hobbled to them and picked up Eros, who was crying now. "What happened?"

"I don't know!" Aphrodite said. "We were at the spring. I heard her speak—the Goddess. Where is Ares?"

"Gone hunting with young Adonis. You saw them go."

"They aren't back yet?"

Hephaestus looked at the sky. "It's not midmorning."

"Something has happened to him!" Aphrodite's face was terror-stricken.

"The Goddess spoke to you?" Hephaestus set Eros

down and put his hands on her shoulders. He looked at her intently. "Be still. Tell me."

"She . . . Eros heard something in the woods; the birds went quiet. I . . . I put my hand on the stone—when I was a child I used to think I heard things there. I thought sometimes she talked to me, but this was different, this was awful, it—"

"I believe you," Hephaestus said. "Calm down." If anyone had a direct connection with the Goddess, it was his wife. She was generative birth and lust and disaster in one. "What did she say?"

" 'Lost.' " Aphrodite whispered the word.

"Just 'lost'?"

Aphrodite nodded, her eyes still wild. Eros whimpered at her side. The farm dogs began to bark, and she whipped her head around. Two of them stood in the road now, barking at nothing. At something. They turned worried eyes to her, as if she could intevene in whatever was coming. A roan horse burst from the vineyard that bordered the woods and thundered toward them. It was the one Adonis had been riding. The rider raised his whip and brought it down on the roan's flanks. Hephaestus could see a still figure facedown across its withers.

"Ares!" Aphrodite screamed his name and began to run. Hephaestus limped after her, but she met the rider in the road before he could catch her. He saw her step back from the horse then and begin to shout.

"Wicked! I thought it was you! Wicked, wicked! I don't believe you!"

Ares's hunting dogs trotted from the vineyard, their tongues hanging. The rider kicked the horse forward, reining it around her, and he saw that it was Ares. The body on the horse was Adonis, and his blood smeared the roan's shoulder and the saddle girth.

"Help me," Ares panted, sliding off the horse. "He's been gored." He dragged Adonis down and hefted him over his shoulder. "Boy! Get my horse!" He didn't wait to see if anyone did, but set off for the main house with Aphrodite dancing around him, berating him.

Eros stood terrified where they had left him, and Hephaestus took him by the hand. Eros's teacher came flying from the house at the commotion and halted, panting in fright. "Thank the Goddess. I thought—"

"No, this is adult mischief," Hephaestus said. He handed Eros over to Teacher and limped behind Ares to the house as a stable boy came running.

Ares had laid Adonis's body on a couch in the hall of the big house, and it was clear that he was dead. His eyes were sightless and staring. A great hole was gouged in his chest, and the blood was beginning to coagulate.

Ares looked up at Hephaestus as he came in. Ares's hair was full of dust and leaves. His face was streaked with dirt and sweat, and his hunting leathers were sliced down one arm and across the skirt. "The thing was on him before I could throw my spear," he said. "It was monstrous, came out of nowhere. A great, evil thing with tusks as long as my arm. It must have been driven out of the hills by drought."

"You're lying," Aphrodite said between her teeth. "The Goddess spoke to me; she told me someone was dead, and I thought it was you, the more fool I. You killed him."

"Don't be ridiculous."

"You killed him." Aphrodite knelt beside the body on the couch and brushed its bloody hair from its face.

"He was a foreign little pig," Ares said. "Why would I kill him?"

"What happened to you, then? Someone has sliced your jacket with a knife. And where is *his* knife?" Aphrodite felt at the empty sheath on Adonis's belt.

"How do I know? It fell out. Maybe he tried to use it on the boar before it got him."

"You murdered him." Aphrodite looked Ares in the eye and knew he had done it. His eyes were cold and gray, and his hands were smeared with blood. He had recognized Adonis.

She began to cry, and Ares turned on his heel and left. One of his gray hunting dogs stuck its muzzle in her hand, whining.

They buried Adonis on the farm, and Aphrodite planted anemones on his grave. She didn't speak to Ares.

Hera leaned against Zeus among the collective family gathered around the grave dug on a windy hillock, a respectful distance from the grave mounds of their ancestors. "I never thought I would see the day when I would be afraid of my own child," she said. Ares stood a little distance away, cold-eyed, leaning on a spear, as if he thought the body might get up again.

"It's the war," Zeus said. "It makes everyone insane."

Hephaestus had sent Adonis's ship home with the price of the copper and a letter for his family. Ares had suggested that there was no need to pay for the copper now, and Hephaestus had offered to hit him. Now they laid Adonis in a round chamber in the earth, with a flask of wine and a jar of oil for his journey.

Zeus spoke a few prayers to the Goddess and the Bull, and asked whatever gods Adonis had worshiped to look kindly on him on the other side of death. Then Heracles and Uncle Hades filled it in, and Aphrodite took her basket of anemone corms and poked them into the loose earth.

Ares watched her, grim-faced. When she stood up, he said, "I told you: You belong to me."

The rest of the family had gone already. No one liked to be around Ares right now, she thought. She looked at Hephaestus hobbling down the track to the farm, with Eros by the hand. She felt desolate. Everything she touched gave heartache. "Will you kill my husband next?"

"I wanted to. When they first gave you to him."

Aphrodite was silent. Ares had gone out after the boar again the day after Adonis had died, and had brought it, too, home across his saddle. She knew he would never tell her whether he had killed Adonis himself or had let the boar do it, but it didn't matter. She started back toward the farm.

"Wait!" Ares caught up with her. "What do you expect of me? I love you."

She stopped and looked at him. His eyes were gray-blue and sullen with hurt. He wore his soldier's tunic and the padded leather jerkin that he and Heracles played at arms in. His chestnut hair hung over his scratched face, marked by whatever had happened with Adonis. She had loved him for so long she had ceased to wonder why. It should have brought her joy.

"You'll be leaving soon. Once Hephaestus has made your armor."

He nodded. "The king's fleet is nearly ready to sail."

"Why must you go?"

"For the honor of Argolis."

"Helen is from Laconia."

"To fight." His eyes gleamed at that, and he grinned suddenly, showing his teeth. "To fight the Trojans. Maybe I'll kill that other one you were unfaithful to me with."

"You like that best, don't you?" she asked him. "Fighting. Better than me. I was just your excuse." She shouted her question at him in the teeth of the wind: "Did you kill Adonis over me or because you wanted to kill someone?"

Ares looked annoyed. "That was different."

Aphrodite knew there was no turning him, that he would never see what she saw. He wanted to fight; he yearned toward battle like a drunkard to wine. When he fought, she thought, he knew he was alive. She ought to have been able to show him that, but it hadn't been that way. When they made love, when he was astride her, she thought that he fought her, too.

X

❧

Aulis

Hephaestus said nothing more about Adonis or Ares, but that night when he found her weeping over a single anemone corm she had found in the folds of her dress, he took her into his arms in bed and cuddled her and sang to her, some old lullaby with half-forgotten words, and didn't try to do anything else.

In the morning he turned his attention to Ares's armor, sweating in the shimmering heat of the forge while Ares watched and paced and gave directions and changed his mind on the design of the greaves or the thigh guard.

"Father says I am allowed to pump the bellows," Eros informed Aphrodite proudly.

She looked across the yard at them, where the forge's heat glowed through the open door, its red light licking the limestone walls. She sighed. "Then I will go with you. There are too many ways to burn yourself in there." Ares wouldn't watch him, and Hephaestus might forget about him when he wasn't pumping the bellows. Zeus was right: The war had made everyone insane. Despite his gentleness last night, this morning Hephaestus worked grimly, furiously, mouth snapped shut, pounding the bronze on his anvil as if he were killing it.

Aphrodite sat down on a wooden block to watch Eros, who stood on a stump between Hephaestus and Ares, his hands working the bellows. She wondered which of them had fathered him. They looked much alike, with bony faces and wide mouths and winged eyebrows. They both wore their beards trimmed close in the military fashion, Hephaestus because, as he said, it was very unpleasant to catch your chin on fire. Hephaestus's hair and eyes were dark; Ares's eyes were the changeable color of seawater and his hair the same chestnut as Hera's. But if you saw them drawn in black paint, they might be the same man in different moods.

And if they looked that much alike, she thought, why did she love Ares and not Hephaestus? It wasn't the feet. She ought to be able to make herself love Hephaestus. Maybe it would be enough if she just loved him, *too.*

Ares stopped pacing and picked up a spear Hephaestus had been fitting with a new head. He lunged with it, striking and parrying with an invisible enemy.

"You are a fool," Hephaestus said.

Ares paid him no attention.

"I have made you a new sword." Hephaestus grunted, his eyes on the anvil.

"Brother!" Ares laid down the spear and planted himself before Hephaestus. "Good man! Where is it?"

"In the chest yonder," Hephaestus said. He nod-

ded at a scarred wooden box that sat against the
rear wall.

Ares lifted the lid, took out the sword, and hefted
it. It was fine bronze, with a hilt laced with silver
wire and a grip of turned wood cushioned with
leather. The pommel was a wolf's head. He swiped
the air with it. "She's perfect!" He swung it again,
back and forward, a backhanded stroke and a quick
cut to an imaginary head. "You are the prince of
armorers!"

"See that it brings you home alive," Hephaestus
said.

Ares darted into the yard and swung the sword at
a chicken that scuttled, squawking, into the henhouse. He laughed. He swung it against the blue sky,
and Aphrodite thought it could cut the air to ribbons.

"I took it down to the spring," Hephaestus said
quietly to her. "I put it in the water and asked the
Goddess to send him home again. Maybe she
listened."

"Why should she? He hasn't ever listened to her."

"Maybe because she knows you want him," Hephaestus said softly.

"Aries only listens to the Bull," Aphrodite said.

"Then maybe the Bull will guard him."

Aphrodite shook her head. "That isn't the Bull's
business, guarding. The Bull's business is running
and goring."

And that was what Ares liked best. He always had,
but with the war coming, his eyes gleamed with it,
and even Aphrodite was uneasy around him. He
looked splendid and terrifying in his new armor,
with his red shield painted with its single great eye.
Hephaestus had embossed his bronze breastplate
with a wolf's head to match the pommel on the

sword, and the same snarling face adorned his greaves. His helmet was crested with a scarlet horse-hair brush, his eyes a dark, dangerous glitter behind the eyeholes. When the king's fleet sailed she felt a sort of queasy relief.

It wasn't until two months later, at the start of winter, that they got word that the fleet had stalled, becalmed, at Aulis on the coast of Attica. A seer there pronounced King Agamemnon in disfavor with the Goddess's Attic incarnation, for having killed a stag in her sacred grove while waiting for a favorable wind. Now there would be no wind until she was propitiated. The king's courier, sent to Queen Cly-temnestra at Mycenae, brought a message from Aga-memnon ordering her to bring their daughter Iphigenia to Aulis, to solemnize her previously ar-ranged marriage with his general, Achilles, in the hope of pleasing the Goddess and raising a wind for Troas.

A royal wedding required royal ceremony, and Queen Clytemnestra, grumbling but pleased—Iphigenia had wanted to be married before they left, and Agamem-non hadn't allowed it—sent for all the king's coun-cilors and their families to sail for Aulis with her. That included Zeus and his household.

"You may come," Hera said to Aphrodite. "A royal wedding is something the boy shouldn't miss. But for the love of the Goddess, keep your distance from the queen."

Hephaestus, who said he could think of nothing he wanted to do less than sail all the way to Aulis to watch a day of ostentatious royal display, was ordered to accompany them anyway.

"This is not an invitation from the third assistant secretary for wheat tariffs," Hera informed him.

"This is from the queen. We do not turn down invitations from the queen."

They all sailed in the boat in which Zeus shipped cargo from the farm, decorated for the festivities with ribbons fluttering from the rigging, and a silken tent on the deck to sleep under. Zeus and Hera took the only cabin. The grandparents, pronounced too feeble to make the journey, stayed at home, to everyone's collective relief. Without their corrosive presence, the journey took on a festival air. Aphrodite had sewed Eros a new tunic and cut his blond curls into an aureole about his face. She regaled him with accounts of the many horses there would be in the procession, and the cakes that would be served afterward.

The wind was fair half the way and then it died, caught perhaps in the Goddess's net that had becalmed the king's fleet. Zeus and his brothers and sons put their backs to the oars, following the queen's ship, which, rowed by thirty oarsmen, easily outdistanced them.

As they made their way along the coast of Attica and up the strait of Euripus, the idiosyncratic current in the strait forced them to row against it, and then suddenly reversed, propelling them onward, as if the Goddess had finally softened her wrath. When they reached the harbor at Aulis they could see the king's fleet riding at anchor under a still, cold sky and the queen's ship tied up at the dock. Zeus maneuvered their smaller craft between the warships of the fleet and followed those in attendance on the queen. As they neared the dock, Aphrodite could see the Princess Iphigenia with a garland on her head, being led off the ship by six of her father's soldiers. Aphrodite had met the queen's children in Mycenae and remembered Iphigenia as a small, shy girl of fifteen, generally in attendance on her mother. Now she would be married immediately, it seemed—the need for a wind to Troas was crucial—and then her husband would sail away with the king's fleet.

Aphrodite was scrambling with the rest of the family to disembark before the festivities started without them when there was a shout from the queen's ship and they stopped.

"Get back on board!" Zeus said. He set himself to an oar. "Back water, now!"

Aphrodite gaped at the queen's ship. There was no bridal procession. It wasn't a wedding the goddess had demanded. Queen Clytemnestra was shrieking, thrashing in the grip of her husband's soldiers. The six who had come for Iphigenia were dragging the princess up the path from the dock toward the top of a small hill crowned with the white-columned temple that had awaited, she thought, her marriage.

Hephaestus hesitated at his oar.

"Row!" Zeus said. "You can't stop this!" He swung the tiller hard about. "Get us out of here before they decide their goddess wants anyone else!" Hephaestus swore and bent his back to an oar with the rest. All around them was chaos: shouted orders, the thunder of row on row of shields being raised, a single staring eye glaring from each one, and over it all the sound of the queen screaming.

Aphrodite saw the soldiers drag the girl up the hill, the shield wall closing behind her. In a moment the struggling procession had climbed above the heads of the soldiers, and she saw her again, fighting in their grasp. A figure in a golden breastplate waited at the top, beside the altar. The soldiers threw the princess on it and held her down. A priest in a white robe stood over her, and Aphrodite could see the glint of the low sun on the raised knife in his hand. She heard the princess scream now, a terrified, pleading shriek, and saw the king—it must have been he—drop his arm. The knife came down with it.

Aphrodite stared in horror as their ship came slowly about in the crowded harbor. She turned so that she could still see what was happening on the hilltop. The priest was chanting a hymn to the Attic Goddess. The figure in the golden breastplate had buried its face in its hands, and the sinking sun caught it in a flash of fire before it dropped behind the mountains. The queen's wailing carried across the water into the deepening dusk.

A wind came up, and Poseidon and Heracles raised the sails and set them into it. Aphrodite wondered if the king's ships would leave her bones there and sail now, too, following the fleeing wedding guests out of the strait, before they turned east to Troas. She leaned against the rail and cried as the boat wallowed in the rising sea, salt tears evaporating in the salt wind. Eros came to her, puzzled by their flight, and she wrapped an arm around his shoulders, holding him fiercely to her side.

"Didn't they get married?" he asked her. "Aren't we going to eat cakes?"

Aphrodite shivered. "No, darling. No." The men left their oars as the wind strengthened. Zeus took the tiller and set a course for home, while Hera stood beside him, ashen faced. Even Hermes and Dionysus looked somber.

"There is a curse on that family," Hera said quietly. "There has always been."

"The king's?" Aphrodite asked her. No curse could take away the knowledge that this was her doing. If she hadn't encouraged Helen about Paris, given her

romantic notions . . . She should have told her that
romance wasn't fun, not afterward.

"On the House of Atreus," Hera said. "King Agamemnon's father, King Atreus, murdered his brother's children to ensure the succession of his own.
Stories say he fed them to him, but that may be just
fancy. The murder was real enough. They murder
easily in that family. Agamemnon killed Queen Clytemnestra's first husband and their baby, with her
father's consent, in order to marry her. She won't
forgive him for this."

Aphrodite shuddered. "No one could forgive this.
And all for a wind, because some seer told him to."

Hephaestus came to stand beside her, on Eros's
other side. "We had best stay away from the queen's
court," he said grimly. "She will have some evil
greeting awaiting Agamemnon's return. Best we be
out of it."

"Best I be out of it, you mean," Aphrodite said.

"That, too."

She buried her face in her hands, and remembered
the king having done the same. Did he really feel
remorse? Or had that been for show's sake. Did she?
It had seemed so much fun at the time, helping Helen
have a romance. But what about the child Helen had
abandoned? And the one Agamemnon had just murdered? She leaned against the ship's rail, racked with
misery, and threw up her supper.

XI

✦

The Cat's Kitten

By the time they reached Tiryns, Aphrodite was sicker than she ever remembered being. The waves nauseated her, and food refused to stay down. She spent the journey leaning over the rail, or burrowed into quilts inside the tent, arms wrapped around her rebellious stomach. She felt as sick as she had when she was pregnant, but there would be no baby to show for it. Iphigenia's wailing rang in her ears, and in her dreams the cries of the seabirds were translated into her voice. Hephaestus, who had been grimly angry at first, although he had never spoken a cruel word to her, took her ashore and put her to bed with the servants in attendance, and went to his forge, where she heard him hammering into the night by torchlight.

Misery settled over her like a cloak. Aphrodite had never thought much about her adventures afterward, but now there were horrible things to think about that would not leave her be. In her waking dreams she saw Ares's face among the soldiers who had

dragged the princess to the altar. Could the Goddess
of Aulis be the same as the Goddess of Argolis? She
supposed so. The Goddess was death as well as birth.
She was the whole wheel of life, of death and new
birth. But why take Iphigenia when the fault was the
father's? Aphrodite thought of the foal that Uncle
Poseidon had slaughtered because its dam had developed a wasting disease and he said the foal would
have it, too. The world ate its children. It had taken
her firstborn. He would be a boy now, but she
thought of him always as an infant, forever lost to
her. She turned over and buried her face in the bedclothes and dreamed of lost and murdered children.

Eros came to her in the afternoons when he had
finished his lessons, and she petted him and cuddled
him. They made wooden boats and sailed them on
the Goddess's pool, and built a palace together in a
tree above the spring. Aphrodite tied her skirts up
and climbed into the twisted branches, dragging a
bag of scraps of wood, and a hammer and bronze
nails filched from Hephaestus's forge. Together they
fitted and banged and went home satisfied, with
hammered thumbs. The next day they pulled cur-
tains and a lunch up into their refuge in a basket
and pretended they were pirates on the sea, and then
King Minos who had ruled at Knossos long ago. No
one felt much like being King Agamemnon and
Queen Clytemnestra. Eros's presence raised her spir-
its while he was with her. When he was not, she
imagined awful things befalling him, wild dogs to
tear him apart, floods to drown in, bandits to cut his
throat for the little money he carried; and then be-
rated herself for conjuring these images up and so
perhaps giving them substance. Her secret terror was
that the queen would send for him, would demand

to give him to the gods in exchange for her lost daughter. Aphrodite crept into the kitchen each night and gave the snake a saucer of milk and honey to keep that thought from the queen's head.

Gradually her terror subsided in the spring when no messengers came from Mycenae. No word came to anyone from the queen, who had sent her sister's household back to Laconia and lived in her palace in solitary bitterness and rage. It was rumored that she had sent for Aegisthus, who was half brother to her murdered first husband, and a survivor of the massacre of children perpetrated by Agamemnon's father, Atreus. No one thought any good would come of that, but no one dared to send word to the king, encamped outside the walls of Troas.

"It is never wise to interfere in the affairs of kings," was Zeus's pronouncement. Aphrodite thought he had regrets of his own over fostering the friendship between herself and Helen. And it was clear that his parents had finally begun to die that spring, which gave him preoccupations of his own.

Cronos and Rhea had existed since any of the next three generations could remember, and no one had loved them. That seemed immeasurably sad to Aphrodite now that they had lost their power to frighten her. Without love there was nothing left but horrible things, randomly overtaking the hapless, swallowing them down like the maws of dragons. If someone loved you, then you could think that the dragon might stay away, just for that day.

Cronos and Rhea did not end their days gracefully. As they grew more feeble, their tongues grew more vicious. Zeus could not enter their bedchamber without a flung accusation of filial neglect, or a condemnation of his children's and his own manners, morals, and worth. He assigned the family to their care in turns, dutifully taking his own, rather than leave them to servants. The tic under his left eye was constant, and he snapped at anyone who came near him.

"Leave them to the servants," Hera said. "You will make yourself ill."

"They're mine," Zeus said grimly.

Only Aphrodite, oddly, could tend them without anger. She had been afraid of them for so long, but now the sight of them reduced to this, sitting in the great bed together like bony gorgons, spewing malevolence, just made her sad. They were both pitiful and vituperative, soiling their bedclothes and demanding endless things to eat that they never consumed but, more often than not, threw at their caretakers.

Once Aphrodite, to see what would happen, threw a handful of gruel back at Cronos. He jabbered at her, sputtering, and she left him till late afternoon before she came and cleaned him off. After that he cowered a little when she entered the room, and she found that gratifying and guilt-inducing at the same time.

"Attagirl," Hermes said, smacking her on the backside as she left the room carrying an armload of dirty bedding. "We all owe the old monster one. Strike a blow for freedom!" He laughed.

"Stop that," Aphrodite said, irritated and ashamed of herself. She looked back into the chamber. Cronos was asleep now, his toothless mouth gaping. Rhea's head nodded back and forth like a toy. Spittle dripped from her lips. "There's nothing left for us to strike," she said to Hermes.

"No, he's just too weak to hit you. He still wants to," Hermes said. "He left such a welt on my back once I thought he had broken my ribs. Called me a bastard son of a sow to my mother's face. I'm going to enjoy this while it lasts."

"That's wicked."

"Not half so wicked as the old man."

Dionysus and the Aunts and Uncles seemed to be of much the same opinion. Only Hephaestus showed no satisfaction at their passing.

"They were crueler to you than to anyone," Aphrodite said to him, when he came to their kitchen for soup for Rhea.

"Maybe that's why I take such satisfaction in being decent to them now," Hephaestus said. "What you put into this world you will get back out in one way or another, and sometimes in ways you won't like. I have no idea whether my feet are my own ill fate or my mother's."

"And whose ill fate was Princess Iphigenia's death?" Aphrodite asked quietly, speaking the question she had been afraid to give voice to.

"Her father's, I think. Or it will be. Things like that bring nothing but horror after them."

"It was my doing." She said what had been in her mind since the voyage to Aulis. "It all goes back to me. What dreadful thing will come to me in return?"

Hephaestus put the bowl down. "I thought that, too, when it happened, but I have had time to think since. The king has wanted war with Troas for years. It would have come no matter what. And if he thought the Goddess wanted his daughter in exchange for a wind, he would have given her. I should have said that to you. Helen was an easy pretext— Menelaus's obsession with her drove him to war. That's what he'll tell Clytemnestra when he comes home."

"When will they come home?"

"I don't know. News travels slowly. All I have heard so far is that they have begun to besiege the city. Troas could hold out for years."

"Ares never sends any message," she said quietly. It was no use pretending to Hephaestus that she didn't care.

"He is in the army. They don't let junior officers use their couriers, child."

"I am not a child!" She flared up at him.

Hephaestus considered her. "No. Not now."

"Your grandparents have aged me," she said briskly. She picked up the bowl. "I'll take this to her. Go and talk to your father. He's hated his parents his whole life, and when they die, no telling what it will do to him."

She went out the kitchen door and set out across the courtyard to the big house. Hephaestus looked after her with a raised eyebrow. She was suffering from a newly acquired wisdom, he thought, hard bought and uncomfortable. It had manifested itself in nightmares since their return from Aulis, and he had thought it was only fear. Now he thought it was knowledge that made her afraid to sleep.

How did you live with the knowledge of things you couldn't undo? Aphrodite wondered, spooning soup into Rhea's mouth. Did Agamemnon begin every morning thinking for that brief moment between sleep and waking that his daughter was alive, and then remember the knife coming down? Did Clytemnestra watch it all happen again and again in her head, and wonder why she hadn't been suspicious? Did she think of how it might be if she had refused to sail for Aulis?

Rhea spat soup at Aphrodite, staining her dress.

Hah! You old harpy, Aphrodite thought. *That's why I wore an old one.*

"Swill!" Rhea mouthed the last drop of soup. "Poison me, as like as not."

"Could, but wouldn't," Aphrodite said, mopping the front of her dress with a rag.

"No nerve," Rhea said with satisfaction. "None of you ever had any nerve. *We* knew how to take care of what needed doing."

Aphrodite remembered the rumors that Cronos had murdered his father. "You can think that over later, I expect," she said. There was reputed to be lots of time for thinking in the afterlife.

Rhea's head nodded down to her chest, and her breath rattled in her throat. The skin was stretched tight over her face, and the malevolent glitter in her eyes was fading behind rheumy skin. Aphrodite picked up the tray and took it away.

She encountered Zeus outside the door. "They're failing," she told him.

"It won't be long now," Zeus said. "They'll go together."

"How do you know?"

"I just do." The tic beneath his left eye jumped under the flesh like something trying to escape.

He was getting old himself, Aphrodite realized. His fiery hair and beard were half gone to gray now. She put her arms around him, standing on tiptoe to kiss his cheek. "You couldn't have made it any different," she said.

She wondered if that was really true, while she put the dishes in the kitchen to be washed and played with the snake, who liked to coil around her arm and nestle his head in her collarbone. If Zeus and the Uncles had done as Cronos had done they

would have had that to live with. That would have
been different. Worse. But now the old ones were
dying, and once they were dead there would never
be any hope that they would someday love their children. Their children would have no last chance to
love them back. No chance even to ask them why
they were not loved.

It took all through the summer, while the old pair
slowly wasted, looking at the end as desiccated as if
they had been corpses long since. Cronos cursed all
his children with his final breath. Rhea sat up, looked
straight at Hebe, of all people, said, quite clearly,
"Slut," and died.

The Uncles dug their tomb on the hill where their
ancestors lay, and the family buried them at the fall
equinox, when the day and night balanced each other
like weights on a scale. Into the round chamber in
the earth they put wine and olive oil and bread for
the journey, a bronze chariot fashioned by Hephaestus, and a team of bronze horses to pull it. (Aphrodite thought of her toy, long sunk in the Goddess's
pool.) Rhea wore the necklace of gold leaves that had
been her finest possession, and Cronos a twisted collar of silver and gold. Aphrodite wondered what
they would do with them in the underworld, who
would admire them, and if the necklace and collar
would be more real than the shades who wore them.
She imagined the necklace and collar walking in
stately fashion among the halls of death, inhabited
by pale mist.

Eros clung to her skirts as the Uncles set a roof of
timbers across the top of the rock lining of the tomb,
an arm's length below the surface.

"What will they do down there?" he whispered
to Aphrodite.

"Darling, I don't know."

"Can they get out?"

"No," she said firmly. "You mustn't worry about that."

"I shouldn't like them to get out," Eros said thoughtfully. He had spent his babyhood dodging their clawed hands and barbed tongues. Dead they would be even more frightening.

Zeus shoveled the dirt excavated from the tomb's core onto the top of the timbers until it nearly reached the surface. Then the bull set aside for sacrifice was led to it, and Poseidon cut its throat beside the tomb, catching its blood in a basin to pour onto the turned earth. Hera and the Aunts laid a fire on the bloodied dirt, and they burned the bull's leg bones in it for the Goddess and her consort. The meat was piled on a cart to be dragged back to the farm and eaten.

Eros wrinkled his nose at the smell. "Do I have to eat some?"

"Just a bite." Hephaestus stood on his other side. "Enough to be respectful to the gods." He sounded as if he found the whole idea amusing, but Aphrodite had never quite known what Hephaestus believed. He did the proper thing at festivals and funerals, but she thought it was only for form's sake.

When the bones were charred, Hera filled a clay cup with wine and said a prayer. She poured it on the bones and smashed the cup. Then the Uncles and Zeus piled the rest of the dirt on the bull's bones, burying them with the shards of the cup until a small, squat mound rose above the grave. Hermes and Dionysus heaved a capstone onto the top. It looked raw and white among the worn, mossy stones of older graves and the low, crumbling wall that surrounded them. It had been carved by Hephaestus with marks signifying the grandparents' names and their final prayers to the gods of the underworld.

Eros thought it looked heavy enough to keep them inside.

After the funeral of Cronos and Rhea, Zeus took the fishing boat out and didn't come back for a month. Everyone else walked gingerly, as if they expected the grandparents to reappear at any moment. But by winter there was an odd feeling of freedom in the air, of a window having been suddenly opened. It was frightening. *We are all like caged birds,* Aphrodite thought, *terrified to fly out the open door.* Naturally they started to quarrel among themselves, but it was halfhearted, more for something to fill the space than anything else. Zeus, although he was the youngest of them, had been running the farm for years, and no one challenged him now. Uncle Poseidon had the horse herd to manage, and Uncle Hades the selling of grain and wine and olive oil and the buying of the luxuries they supported—cloth from the East, copper from Cyprus, painted pottery from the kilns on Crete. It should have been a golden time, and in many ways it was except for the war with Troas in the distance and the rumors that the queen had taken the king's cousin Aegisthus as her lover and something dreadful would happen when Agamemnon came home. Whatever it was held the same hint of future dreadfulness that Aphrodite had felt at the grandparents' death, but when nothing actually happened she put it at the back of her head.

Eros, who grew up in the shadow of the war, seemed unmarked by it. It was all happening a great way away, and Eros's preoccupations were closer to home. Like his mother, he was a sunny child of an affectionate disposition. So much so that by the time he was twelve it was clear that he shared a number of her proclivities.

"Those are sluts," Aphrodite said to him firmly when she heard reports of his cavorting with the girls whose mothers washed laundry for the merchants of Tiryns.

Eros gave her a repentant smile. "They are very friendly," he offered.

"I don't doubt it!" Aphrodite snapped. "You stay away from friendly girls."

Eros put his arm about her waist. "No one is prettier than you, Mother," he said, cajoling her.

"Flattery will not get you around me," Aphrodite said reprovingly, but she smiled at him anyway. That was still true, and she knew it.

"You will have to let go of him," Hephaestus said to her when Eros was, theoretically, memorizing poetry in his chamber, as befitted a young man of good family. "He will chase girls; it's the nature of the beast."

"He's too young!"

If his mother thought so, Eros apparently did not. At fourteen, he would slip away and come home with the dawn, and Aphrodite would be enraged. She still dallied with men who took her fancy, and Hephaestus still ignored it, but she didn't do it as often—she was really quite well behaved—and in any case, it was different. She belonged to no one—except Ares, who wasn't here—and Eros belonged to her.

"That is a dangerous way of looking at it," Hephaestus said when she voiced the last part of that sentiment to him.

She went away in a huff, and Hephaestus went back to his forge. Eros, who had been listening quietly just around the corner, slipped past on silent feet, hurrying by the kitchen door, where he could hear his mother banging pans about and arguing with her cook over how to boil eels. He didn't come back all night.

Aphrodite, wakeful in the early hours, went out to feed the chickens at dawn, just as the farm dogs and the barn cats were slinking home from their nightly wanderings. Her son was among them, wearing much the same expression.

"Where have you been?" Her voice snapped like a trunk lid slamming down, and he jumped. The chickens flew into an agitated cloud of squawks around her.

"Just out," he said airily as she fixed him with an outraged eye.

"You are far too young to be 'just out,'" she informed him. "You will get into some kind of trouble with a girl, or worse, you'll be robbed and killed."

"Between here and Tiryns?"

"Aha! Is that where you go at night?"

"Maybe. Sometimes. Anyway, I am fleet of foot, which ought to get me out of both difficulties." He slipped his arm around her waist, but she wasn't mollified.

"Eros, I mean it. You are not to go chasing that sort of girl."

"What sort of girl?"

"The sort that will let you chase her!"

"Well, I don't want to chase the sort that wants to get married," he said. He gave her a smile, beguiling and unrepentant. His hair hung in golden curls over one eye, and it had hay in it.

Aphrodite gave him a look that she was ruefully sure Hera had given her. "You'll end up married to the other sort if you aren't careful," she said. "Or her father will be here complaining to Hephaestus. It doesn't do to take advantage of the peasant girls." Peasants' morals were generally stricter than their own family's. They had to be; poor girls had nothing to sell to a prospective husband but their virginity.

Eros looked annoyed. The thought that went across his mind was so plain that it might as well have been painted on his forehead. He had heard the rumors about his mother, and they had never bothered him. Good for her for having had fun, was what he had thought then. That was what they gave you a body for. But she certainly didn't own the right to act now as if she had dedicated her body to the Goddess. He opened his mouth to speak. *Don't do it*, a cautionary voice in his head told him. *Don't say it. That's your mother.* Aphrodite glared at him abruptly, and he bit his tongue.

"I mean it, Eros."

"I am fourteen, Mother. I expect you don't remember what it's like to be fourteen," he suggested.

"I am clearer on that subject than you might think," Aphrodite said. The corners of her mouth twitched. The trouble with Eros was that he could charm her. He had always been able to talk her into anything when he was a child, even when Hephaestus warned her that she was spoiling him: a new pony, a pup from one of Hermes's hunting bitches, a small boat of his own, which she lived in certainty that he would drown himself in, a play sword with which he hacked the heads off her roses but never hurt any living creature otherwise. The pup, Follow, was full-grown now, and leaned against his master's legs, tongue lolling, as Eros cajoled her. *And where have you been all night yourself?* she thought. "You are supposed to be getting an education with Teacher," she said firmly to Eros. "There will be time for girls later."

"I give Teacher a headache," Eros said. "They're getting worse, I think. He says he may retire."

"He isn't old enough to retire, thank the Goddess," Aphrodite said. "If he feels you have learned all he has to offer, you may help your father with the forge."

"I do," Eros protested.

"And you may keep me company."

"Mother . . ." Eros bent and patted Follow while he chose his words. "A fellow doesn't want to always be running about with his mother."

Aphrodite looked hurt. "We used to have such fun. Remember the house we built in a tree by the spring? We were pirates."

"I was little then."

"Well, of course. We can do more grown-up things now, you know. How would you like to come into Tiryns with me tomorrow and help me find someone really talented to paint my sitting room walls? I want a sea scene, I think. You can drive the horses," she offered.

"Mother . . ."

She turned away from him, hurt.

He kissed her cheek. "I'm going to bed. I'll take you into Tiryns some other day, all right? We'll make a plan."

They wouldn't, she knew, watching him disappear into the house, whistling softly, with Follow at his heels. He would have some other plan by then, and she would go into Tiryns with a servant.

It didn't help that Hephaestus had told her as much. Somehow she had just assumed that Eros would always want to be with her. She had loved him; she had been everything that the grandparents had not been to their children, even that Zeus and Hera had not been to her. She had indulged him, been his secret partner in misbehavior, his playmate. Now he preferred younger girls to her. She wasn't the most beautiful anymore. She knew that without being told; she wasn't stupid. These last two years she had seen the fine lines etch themselves about her eyes and mouth and the flesh of her upper arms soften, so that now she kept a shawl about her shoulders for vanity's sake. No one kept their beauty forever. She did know that. She still turned men's heads when she walked by, even young men's. But she couldn't match the girls that Eros was chasing after, the girls with the dewy skin of babies, and firm breasts and limbs.

She wondered dolefully what Ares would think of her when he came home. He had been gone seven years now. She had thought when he first sailed that she would know if he were dead, but as the years went by she had become less sure of that, too. She prayed to the Goddess and the Bull nightly for his safety, for so long now that it had become a routine. Sometimes they got news of the war, of battles fought and won, of the king's army still mounting the siege on Troas, whose walls still stood, whose inhabitants still rained arrows down on the invaders, who still sent spears flying over the walls and marched to do battle with the army that marched out to meet them. Neither side would give in, so they said. And if King Priam had been willing to send his son's stolen woman out to her lawful husband, it wouldn't have done any good. There were too many dead to avenge, too many bitter years gone into the war. Troas, it was said, was backed by surrounding kingdoms, none of which wished to have Troas in the hands of the Mycenaeans, and Agamemnon was forced to battle them first to cut off the supply lines allowing Troas to hold out.

This news came piecemeal to Argolis, on the lips of merchants and other travelers. The ground outside Troas, it was said, was dark red now with the blood it had soaked up.

The chickens fluttered about her feet, settling back to their breakfast with Eros and Follow gone, clucking disapprovingly. Aphrodite thought of her pet among them, long dead now. *Would* she know if Ares were dead, as far gone from her as that chicken? Had death swallowed him up years ago without her knowing? None of the travelers had met him, one captain among so many in the king's army. Many were dead, they had said. No, they didn't know their names.

She brooded on that through the fall. Since she had been small, she had felt the invisible cord that tied her to Ares. Now it was as if it had frayed and gone slack, and there was no knowing who or what was on the other end.

In the winter, after an oil merchant had come and gone, trundling the fall pressing to market in a line of carts and leaving behind him only scant news of the war, Hephaestus found her lying in the barn, her head pillowed on a farm dog's flank, sobbing into its brindle fur.

He bent over her, steadying himself on his cane. "Hush, what is it?"

"I don't know if he's dead!" Aphrodite wailed. "I don't know!"

"None of us know." Hephaestus sat down in the straw beside her.

"I thought I would know. Now I can't tell! And no one has seen him!" Aphrodite raised red eyes to his while the dog snuffled anxiously at her face. "I shouldn't be crying to you over him. I'm sorry."

Hephaestus sighed and put his arm about her shoulders, pulling her to rest against his chest. When Ares had first left she wouldn't have thought to be sorry, or even to say that she was.

"What if he comes home and I don't recognize him?" she whispered.

"We may not," he said quietly. "War does dreadful things to people." Maybe particularly to Ares, who liked it far too well. He didn't say that.

"What if he doesn't recognize *me*?"

"There is little danger of that, my dear." Even with lines in her face, she made any man's heart turn over. Even his, even now.

She snuffled against his chest. "I have been a dreadful wife."

"You have."

"I don't think I can be any better."

"No. You are who you are."

She laid her head against his shoulder in the dusty straw and he held her, rocking her back and forth gently while she wept.

XII

❧

When All the Heroes Are Dead

The soldiers of Agamemnon scurried among the dark tents spread out like a movable city on the plain below the walls of Troas. They swept back and forth like floods of ants, coalescing to charge the city gates with their battering rams, thudding them endlessly against the timbers with a sound like thunder. Aeneas watched them from his perch on the battlements.

"Look to your men," the general snapped at him, passing by on his rounds of the walls. "Don't be daydreaming; you'll find yourself with a spear in your eye slot, like as not."

Aeneas straightened his back and his spear and stood at attention, an act that served to straighten the row of bowmen up and down the wall. He had been in King Priam's army for three years now, the last three years of the unending war with the men from across the sea. Odd how clear those three years were in his head, and how he didn't really remember how it had been before the war started. He had been ten years old when his mother's people first attacked Troas. They had come in fleets of ships to demand that Prince Paris's whore be handed over to them. Aeneas's father, Anchises, was not flattering in his explanation of Prince Paris and his stolen woman. No thought to his duty, Anchises had said grimly. Duty was the most important rule in Anchises's household. It was what distinguished an honorable family from the lower classes. It was dishonorable behavior that had brought the Mycenaeans down upon them.

To Aeneas the men from Mycenae were both frightening and endlessly fascinating. He stared at their distant faces, trying to see something of himself in them. When he was small, he used to wonder why his real mother had sent him to Troas to be raised, but when he asked his father he always got the same sad look for an answer, and so he had given up asking. Aeneas's stepmother had also come from Mycenae, a plain and presumably more suitable girl than his mother, and she had been a dutiful wife who had given her husband a son and promptly died along with the baby. Anchises had buried her with the ceremony befitting the wife of a nobleman of Troas, and then, Aeneas thought, forgotten her. Anchises remembered Aeneas's mother, though; Aeneas was certain of that, although he never spoke of her. The only thing he had said, once, was that she had been more beautiful than Paris's Helen, and if Anchises could think of his family and his country first, then the king's son could have done so.

The king's son still refused, however, and King Priam and his councilors backed him up. Helen might have been the pretext, but now that they were here, everyone in Troas knew that what the Mycenaeans really wanted was the city itself and the strait it guarded, and they wouldn't go away until they had it. Even Anchises said so.

When Aeneas came off watch he went home to dinner in the small apartment in the palace guest quarters that was their last refuge. The army had overrun the farmland around Troas, and burned or taken captive everything in its way. Anchises, who walked with a limp from a twisted leg that a lightning strike in the high pasture had given him, sat by the fire, his scarred legs covered by a blanket, while Aeneas's wife, Creusa, and small son, Ascanius, tended a pot of stew, more broth than beans. Creusa was Paris's sister, but not even kings' daughters had more than a handful of beans to eat these days. Or a servant to cook them. Most of the men were dead, fighting the invaders before King Priam had ordered those who were left back inside the gates to try to outwait the army they couldn't drive off. Half the stable hands were women who had been cooks before.

"What of the battle?" Creusa asked him, looking up from the pot.

Aeneas shrugged. "They are still out there. Did you think they had evaporated?"

Creusa wiped her face with her apron. "No. I suppose I hoped they would see that they can't get in and give up."

"Eventually they will get in," Anchises said.

"Not without traitors inside, Father," Aeneas said. "They can beat at that gate all they want, while we drop stones on them. It has held so far."

"And we are eating thin soup," Anchises said. "Our wells are finally going dry. While they sit outside the walls with the spoils they have taken, ten times our number. They will be here when Ascanius is old enough to fight them, but we will never drive them off. We have no one left to send out to fight them. Hector is dead, all our heroes are dead." He sighed and turned away from the fire, his gray head bent over the blanket in his lap.

Creusa shook her head at Aeneas. It did no good to talk to the old man; he was too despondent to be argued with. And likely he was right anyway.

Helen half slept, listening to the tramp of the sentries outside the women's quarters. As long as she could hear those, she was safe, but it wouldn't be long. She had always wondered why King Priam hadn't simply given her back; Paris couldn't have stopped him. Or killed her and thrown her body over the walls. Paris's sister Andromache would have done that if they had let her, when their brother, Hector, died. Menelaus's men had dragged Hector's body behind a chariot until the stones and rough ground had battered it to a bloody pulp. Old King Priam had gone out himself under a flag of truce to beg for it back. They had given it to him, laughing, and Helen had seen it before they burned it. Now she dreamed about it, bloody hands waving their stumps in front of her eyes, or the ghastly head with its eyes pecked out by birds. She used to dream about Paris. Now she dreamed about death. It wouldn't be long before Menelaus came for her. They might as well have killed her. Menelaus would.

But in the morning, when Helen woke, pushing away the bloody shreds of her dreams, she heard happy shouting in the corridors outside. She pulled her mantle around her and went to the window.

In the guest quarters, Aeneas was strapping on his breatplate and Creusa adding water to the remains of yesterday's broth when the voices began in the courtyard, carried from the street below the palace walls. Creusa put her spoon down.

"Stay here." Aeneas belted on his sword and picked up his spear. He jammed his helmet over his head. Outside, a breathless soldier stopped him. "Captain! They have gone away!"

"What?"

"Their fleet has sailed. They are gone!"

Aeneas clattered through the maze of the palace to the outer wall. The palace itself stood higher than the city walls, and from its topmost walkway the morning sun lit the plain below Troas and the harbor beyond it, scoured bare of tents and ships. The detritus of a decamping army littered the scarred ground. He turned and ran for the stairs.

A sentry inside the city gates held a single struggling Mycenaean soldier by the scruff of the neck.

"There's a thing outside," the sentry said to King Priam, who arrived with Aeneas, buckling his armor over his nightclothes.

"What sort of a thing?"

"A horse thing. A big statue. This fellow"—the sentry shook the soldier and shoved him toward the king—"says it's an offering to their gods for a good wind. He says they've gone off and left him because he was drunk and didn't wake up."

"Why did they leave?" Priam demanded. He stuck his face in the Mycenaean soldier's. Aeneas could see hope warring with suspicion in the king's eyes.

The soldier muttered something. "He says the seer told them their own cities will be destroyed if they take Troas now," the sentry said. "He says they were told to make an offering to the sea god for safe passage and go home."

Helen, wrapped in a cloak, watched from the palace walls. Her heart began to pound in her chest.

"They're gone!" Paris appeared beside her, unshaven, his hair a greasy tangle, his helmet in his hand.

"They can't be," Helen said faintly. Not after all this time. She had known for years that an evil fate was waiting for her. Was it possible that it had packed up and sailed away? Was she really going to be allowed to stay in Troas? She looked at Paris, puzzling over what had possessed her to go with him in the first place. There had been beautiful young men in Menelaus's court. Why had she risked everything for this one? Now she didn't know. It had seemed so inevitable, the only thing to do at the time. But ten years of war and hiding had ground that down until now she just didn't know.

"Open the gates," Priam said in the courtyard below them.

"Father, is this wise?" Cassandra, Paris's youngest sister, huddled next to him in a voluminous shabby mantle and bare feet, keening under her breath.

"Hush, child." Priam patted her arm distractedly.

"It's evil," Cassandra insisted.

"It's a gift for their gods. We will honor ours with it instead, and maybe theirs will sink their fleet." Priam nodded. "Go and tell your mother."

Cassandra trudged away, her mantle trailing behind her in the courtyard mud. Aeneas watched her dubiously. She was the royal family's embarrassment, given to wild-eyed ravings and pronouncements no one could understand.

"Open the gates!" Priam said again.

*   *   *

Ares could feel the waiting of the others in the dark. It was like a smell in the air, closed up and redoubled inside the wooden belly of the horse. Odysseus, the general, had ordered silence until he gave the word, but they could have been banging on pots, Ares thought, and the stupid Trojans wouldn't have heard them. From the sound of it the Trojans had broken out the last of the wine stores and were dancing about the beast, singing and howling in drunken victory. Odysseus's men would all go home heroes if this worked, Ares thought. The king had given Odysseus the honor of wearing the armor of General Achilles, who had been killed in the last clash between the armies—before the Trojans had retreated into their city like a turtle into its shell. But this general was a craftier man than the dead Achilles. It was the general who had thought of the horse. Ares wouldn't have said the Trojans were that stupid, but the general clearly knew what he was talking about. Ares leaned back against the horse's wooden ribs and waited.

The city began to burn while the Trojans slept. Aeneas woke coughing and flung the bedcovers off. Voices erupted in the courtyard outside, and he slammed the door open to see flames rising from the direction of the granary and the houses that ringed the merchants' square near the city gates. A squadron of soldiers staggered by at double time, pulling at tattered armor.

He turned to his father. "They're in the city!"

"Fools," Anchises said. "Drunken fools."

Creusa pulled small Ascanius from his bed, wailing.

"Come! Now!" Aeneas grabbed her hand and turned to his father.

"Leave me," Anchises said. "I can't run."

"Get up!" Aeneas snapped. He dragged Anchises from the bed and hefted him over his shoulder. Beyond the wall the flames rose up toward the palace, and he could hear people screaming.

Before they were out the door the soldiers passed them running the other way, a ragged band of undisciplined terror. Outside, the flames roared like an army on the march. A terrified throng pushed through the streets, fleeing the fire and Agamemnon's soldiers, who had unaccountably come back in the night. The crowd bunched at the rear gates of the palace, struggling to push through and trampling one another in their panic. Behind them Aeneas could hear the sounds of futile battle and rout. He turned back, hesitating.

"This way!" Creusa screamed at him. "You can't go back and fight them! It's useless!" The crowd surged around them and swallowed her like an open mouth.

"Creusa!" Aeneas snatched at Ascanius's hand and dragged him back beneath a rearing horse's hooves, but Creusa had let go. There were enemy soldiers in the palace now. She disappeared in the bedlam and flames. Aeneas hoisted his father higher on his shoulders and struggled toward the gates, pulling Ascanius by the hand.

Something took hold of the war when Iphigenia died. Some dark hand reached out and held the men from Argolis and Laconia in its fingers, and something that ate souls enveloped them. Men who were decent men soaked it into their skin. Some had seen it coming. Achilles, the hero general of Agamemnon's army, had tried to hide when the ships sailed. Odysseus, king of Ithaca, had pretended to be mad. Now they had been here ten years, and Achilles was dead. Before he died he had desecrated the body of Hector, the hero of Troas, and with that act the dark fingers had closed the rest of the way around the invaders. They might have known it if they had thought about it, and so they didn't think about it. It grew easier every year to let the war envelop them, remake them into something they had not been before. Only Ares was conscious of the process.

The battle was a creature, breathing flame. Ares had always felt that war was somehow alive, and now he knew it. It was foe and lover at once. It roared and the flames rose up from Troas, swallowing the night. They found the thief Paris and shot him down, and they found King Priam cowering behind the altar in a temple and pulled him out, cutting his throat to the swelling cheers of the soldiers who were everywhere now, pulling what valuables Troas had left from its houses, and its priestesses from their altars. Ares saw one dragged from a temple of the Goddess and her legs spread open on the steps while three men had her one after the other. She shrieked curses at them, and Ares recognized her voice—the girl who had warned old Priam that the wooden horse was evil. He grinned at her as she lay sobbing on the steps now that they were through with her. And so it had been.

"That's Priam's daughter!" the general shouted. "Take her to Agamemnon!"

They plunged on into the palace. The last remnant of King Priam's guard stood with swords bared in the door to the queen's quarters.

"Keep them bottled up until we have the city under control!" Odysseus said. "Hold them there. The king will want them!"

Under control meant burned to the ground, with only the battered ruins of the walls standing, their gates hanging open. When everything else was as blackened and silent as the bodies in the streets, Odysseus gave the signal. His cohort, the favored ones who had been in the horse with him, fought their way past Priam's dying guard. Ares stepped across the bodies, laughing as the men scurried like hounds into the warren of the women's quarters.

It didn't take long. They found them huddled together, hiding in the queen's bedchamber, and dragged them out: Hecuba, Priam's queen; the princess Polyxena; Andromache, widow of Hector, with her baby son; and the faithless Helen. The soldiers leaned toward Helen like dogs on a leash, teeth bared and hungry, waiting to see what was done to her. Menelaus would kill her, Ares thought, watching them, but he would never throw her to the men. Not even now. She belonged to Menelaus even dead.

The king of Laconia was sent for, and Ares's mouth turned downward in a surprised scowl when Helen held her bound hands out to Menelaus like a supplicant and the fool took them and kissed her.

"Bah!" Ares spat in the blood-soaked dirt on the floor.

Odysseus clapped his hand on Ares's shoulder. "Not everyone loves death better than women," the general said. "You're an odd one. The old man just wanted his woman back."

"She was faithless," Ares said. "He should have killed her. I would have."

"That's what I mean," Odysseus said. "War makes

any man's cock rise up, but not more than a woman does. Except for you."

They threw Andromache's baby son, the last heir of Priam, off the battlements, a sacrifice to the Bull for their victory. Andromache screamed and fought them, biting Ares in the ear, until he hit her and she subsided in exhausted sobbing with Hecuba's arms around her.

"The peace is sealed between us and the city of Troas," Agamemnon pronounced. There was nothing left of Troas; his army had dragged from their houses and killed everyone whom the fire hadn't taken. But it was the land that mattered. Mycenaean administrators would see to the rebuilding and the management of trade through the Hellespont.

In camp, they divided the captive women among themselves. King Agamemnon gave Andromache to Achilles's son Neoptolemus, and the queen, Hecuba, to Odysseus. He kept the princess Cassandra for himself. She gave him an evil look from her bloody, battered face and told him it would be his death. Agamemnon laughed. Everyone in the army knew the Trojan princess was crazy, but she was beautiful, so it didn't matter. A crazy woman could warm your bed as well as a sane one. Then they sacrificed her sister Polyxena at the grave of Achilles, because he had been their hero, and he ought to have a woman, too.

Aeneas saw it. He watched them from a thicket in the hills above the ruined city. They were only tiny dots on the wrecked plain, but he knew what they were doing. He gagged and turned away from his mother's people, and huddled in the thicket, waiting for nightfall.

XIII

❧

Blood and Love

Aphrodite huddled by the fire. It was early fall and hardly cold yet, but there was something in the air that made the skin rise in little bumps along her arms and the fine gold hairs stand up. *A goose walked on your grave,* old Rhea would have said. *Or on someone's grave,* Aphrodite thought. She had had a grisly dream full of dead bodies and fire and blood, with Princess Iphigenia's face looming over all of it. The princess had been dead for ten years, and her face was almost all bones, with dark, staring eyes sunk deep in their sockets. Aphrodite had wakened, weeping, and Hephaestus had held her and whispered to her until she was fully awake and knew for certain that the princess was not in the room with her. Now he was at the forge, making a bronze brazier for her chamber that he thought she didn't know about yet. It had doves and roses and apples around its base, and the legs were three swan's necks, curving down. She had sneaked out to the forge two days ago and looked at it, even though she knew it was supposed to be a surprise. Aphrodite had never been good at waiting for surprises.

She sniffled and pulled her mantle closer about her, but it didn't warm her, and she knew the brazier wouldn't, either. Something awful was happening. The household snake wouldn't come out of his basket in the kitchen even when she brought him an egg, and all the onions in the cellars had suddenly rotted overnight. A tinker had come offering to mend pots and told a tale in the kitchen of ships sailing home from Troas with crews of dead men, until Hephaestus had shouted at him that he could mend his own pots and driven him off with a curse.

"Fool!" he had snorted and stalked back out to the forge. Later when Aphrodite had gone to the Goddess's pool she had found a black slick on the water. She had siphoned the water down and scrubbed it clean but the stain of the black slime didn't come out of the stones.

Hera had seen it and looked pale. "Stay at home," she had said. "There is something bad coming that we have no need to be part of."

Aphrodite would not have left the farm for a cartful of gold.

And Hera was right. They heard about it afterward, the news spreading like a black wave that couldn't be stopped, black news on black wings, telling you things you didn't want to know. And it didn't matter how tightly she shut her eyes; Aphrodite could still see it.

She saw the ship coming into the harbor, and the column of soldiers with their spears flashing, the blue eyes on their shields triumphant, and the king riding at their head with the girl beside him on a red horse.

They clattered up the road to the Lion Gate under

a gold sun, and the gates swung open. The queen had seen them coming—she was waiting for them in the great hall, at the end of a purple carpet, the bright sun splashing the red and blue pillars and the gold collar around her throat.

Agamemnon stopped at the edge of the carpet. He eyed her hesitantly. Clytemnestra smiled at him. "So long gone," she said. "So long missed, my lord." She held out her hand.

He nodded, relieved. "Come along, then," he said to the girl behind him; and to his wife, "I have brought someone to wait on you and keep you company."

"I had heard that. How thoughtful." Clytemnestra's smile was icy.

Agamemnon started down the carpet toward his queen. The girl shrieked and ran the other way. Agamemnon whirled about and snapped his fingers at a soldier, who caught her and held her. She wailed something in a foreign language, struggling frantically. She tore at her hair, and her mouth gaped open.

"A princess of Troas, so I have heard," Clytemnestra said. She eyed the thrashing girl with disdain.

Agamemnon stopped a few paces from the queen. "I . . . have heard that my cousin has offered you his aid in my absence. I don't see him."

"He has other duties," Clytemnestra said.

Agamemnon looked about him at the household guards standing at attention in their shiny armor, the red crests of their helmets like waterfalls of blood. Their faces betrayed nothing. Outside, his own bedraggled men waited for him to dismiss them.

"We will speak of him later then," Agamemnon said. "It was kind of my cousin to lend his assistance, but we must release him now to return to his own lands."

"Of course." Clytemnestra held out her hand again. "Let us greet each other in some not quite so public place." This time her smile was beguiling, her eyes gentle.

Agamemnon left his soldiers behind and went with her. No one saw what happened after that, but shortly a servant of the queen came out of her quarters and told the soldiers waiting outside that the king had sent for his captive. They handed the girl over, and the queen's servant dragged her, still screaming and tearing at her hair, through the doorway and down the passage to the queen's apartments. The screaming echoed off the stone walls and stopped abruptly.

Shortly thereafter the bodies were put on display.

Agamemnon was buried with suitable pomp, the dead princess of Troas with less so, and Queen Clytemnestra and King Aegisthus ruled Argolis for a month.

The queen issued a proclamation decrying the murder of her daughter by Agamemnon, and public feeling was marginally on her side. The elders of Mycenae found themselves with other things to do, such as tend to their farms in distant valleys, and the ruling couple made a tour of Argolis to show themselves to the people and cement their loyalty. They came to Tiryns in the spring for the Festival of the Goddess.

Hera cast a cautious eye on the courier sent to bring a royal invitation to the court, and pleaded a cold in her chest. "There is a curse on that house," she said to Zeus when the messenger had gone away again. "I told you they murder easily in that family."

"It isn't over," Zeus said. "There are two children left. Aegisthus will get them, or they will get him."

Aphrodite thought of the queen's youngest, Prince Orestes and Princess Electra. They had been small when she had seen them years ago at the court, younger than Iphigenia, and due to be sent to be fostered in the court at Phocis, according to royal custom.

"Will they come home now?" she asked Zeus.

"Very quietly, I expect," Zeus said. "We will stay away from Mycenae."

On Festival Day the family stayed home and honored the Goddess at her spring instead, but the commotion on the road lured them down to the lower barley fields to watch.

The royal couple rode by in a gilded chariot, waving regally. The queen wore a gold collar set with rubies, and the new king's armor was of bronze and silver, not so fine as Hephaestus's work, but studded with gems so that he outshone the queen. Their heads were crowned with wreaths of flowers. The parade of chariots behind them carried their retainers, and everyone's clothes were very grand, fluttering with red and blue and purple ribbons. All the same, a darkness flew above them like a crowd of black crows, not so much seen as sensed. It was as if the queen and the new king had some disease, Aphrodite thought, some doom hanging about their shoulders, so that no matter how they justified what they had done, how they scrubbed it, as she had scrubbed the sides of the sacred pool, it didn't quite come clean.

She watched the procession as it climbed toward the city to meet the priestesses of the Goddess. Surely the Goddess was tired of so much blood. The roads outside Tiryns were crowded now with homecoming soldiers as well as with holidaygoers. The ships that had sailed ten years ago from Argolis were returning, bearing men who were ten years older, too. They looked weary, and their armor was dented and tarnished, their shields battered. They carried boxes on their shoulders or trundled carts with bags of looted treasure. The officers would have gotten the best of it, but each man had carried off what he could. They weren't exactly dead men, not as the tinker had described them, but something wasn't right with them, either. Their eyes were dark and unreadable and their laughter brittle. Aphrodite could hear the same flutter of dark wings that had flapped around the queen's head.

"What about Ares?" Aphrodite whispered to Hera. "When will he come home?"

"Best not to interest yourself in that," Hera said. She looked at the soldiers swarming along the road. "You may not be glad to see him."

I will always be glad, Aphrodite thought rebelliously. Surely he wouldn't look like these men on the road, not once he was with her again.

"I'll be glad to see Uncle Ares," Eros said. "I barely remember him."

"He taught you to shoot a bow," Aphrodite told him.

"That's right!" Eros laughed. "He set up targets for me, and wouldn't let me have supper until I could hit them."

Aphrodite smiled at him proudly. "He'll be happy to see how you've grown." Eros was seventeen now, as good a horseman as Uncle Poseidon had been in his youth, and a dead shot with a bow. "You'll have to show him what you can do with your bow now," she said. They would hit it off, she was sure. After all, Ares might be his father and knew it. Eros could hear his adventures, and they could hunt together, and Eros would have no time for chasing girls, particularly not the one in Tiryns whom he had been sneaking off to see, thinking he was fooling his mother.

Everything will be better now, she thought. *Ares will come home and everything will be the way it used to be.*

The young Prince Orestes came home before Ares. When news reached across the water to Phocis, he sailed with a retinue who were better armed than they looked. His mother let him in and he cut her throat. Aegisthus died without the help of his household guards, who had recognized Orestes and had no love for their current master. All this news came to the farm outside Tiryns on the same black wind that had brought news of Agamemnon's death.

Mycenae began to fall to ruin. From the outside, nothing looked so very wrong at first. The palace and its treasury belonged to Orestes one day, to whoever might challenge him for it the next, to yet another noble who could raise an army on the next. The common people went on much as they had. Then it was said that Orestes had gone mad. The nobles of Mycenae squabbled among themselves, forming alliance and counteralliance, pitting their troops against one another. Then the gates sagged open, and the returning army looted its own city.

Zeus and Hera stood in the farmyard and watched the black smoke that rose in the distant hills—breath of each new funeral pyre that lit the sky above Mycenae.

"Will he come back, do you think?" Hera whispered.

"Do you want him to?" Zeus kept his eyes on the distant smoke.

"He's my child." Hera took a long, deep breath. "But I have always been a little afraid of him."

Zeus nodded. His beard was more than half gray now, and Hera's chestnut hair was streaked with a silver that was not unbecoming. *We are getting old,* he thought. It had been peaceful without his parents and without Ares. The farmyard had seemed enfolded in a buttery light, in which the chickens muttered happily outside their henhouse and the goats coming in to be milked waggled their beards like old councilors arguing philosophy under a tree. "I worry what that war has done to him," he said at last. "About what Ares may bring home with him from it."

Hera looked surprised. She laughed a little. "I have never heard you speak so disrespectfully of war. That is a woman's thought."

"I grow old," Zeus said. "And less inclined to settle my quarrels with a spear than I was in my youth. And"—he looked at the smoke again—"there is some poison in this one, like a wound that festers. I don't want it spreading here."

Hera nodded. The cities of Argolis had done well enough each within its own walls, before the House of Atreus had brought them all under one rule. They could do so again. Kings were not necessary. But their quarrels might be catching. She could see the black cloud spreading out from Mycenae, lapping at the walls of Argos and Tiryns. Ares would bring *that* home with him. "I hear that Helen has gone home to Laconia with Menelaus," she said. "Perhaps he will go to serve that army, now that Agamemnon has fallen." Ares would want to be in someone's army. She couldn't envision him tending goats at home. "Aphrodite has done so well without him here to distract her," she added.

Zeus laughed, a bellow of amusement that startled a she-goat nibbling at the withies that fenced the kitchen garden. "What you mean is that Aphrodite hasn't misbehaved under your nose since he's been gone."

"She has seemed very content with Hephaestus," Hera snapped.

"Have you asked Hephaestus?"

"Not every marriage is happy all the time. I should know that," Hera retorted. "But there has been no more scandal."

"You have motherhood to thank," Zeus said. "She's too worried about what young Eros is getting up to, to look for mischief herself. It's a shame she didn't have a few more to keep her thoroughly occupied."

"Certainly," Hera said, as the subject of their conversation came around the side of the barn, trailing a handful of wild mint and an unraveling skein of wool with a barn kitten pouncing after it. As they watched, she stopped to braid the mint into a wreath for her hair and dropped the wool. The kitten tumbled it into a cowpat while she set the wreath on her head. The rose-gold aureole of her hair shimmered around the green leaves. "And how many fathers could they count among them if she'd had more?" Hera inquired tartly.

Zeus sighed. Several, probably. Possibly himself.

But he had been the one who had ordered the first baby sent away, and now no doubt it was dead in Troas, and he was feeling old and guilty.

Aphrodite was not as moony as they thought, wandering among the goats and braiding mint. She was waiting for Eros. Eros had been sent to Tiryns to fetch her a twist of red embroidery thread and a pot of mustard from the apothecary and told to come right back. That had been this morning, and it was now nearly dusk. The last rays of the sun limned the western hills like a line of fire to match the fire in her eye. It was close to full dark when she heard his horse's hooves clopping softly on the dusty road.

She waited while he came whistling up through the twilight, and stepped suddenly out in front of him, a vengeful figure in a white gown. The horse shied.

"Mother! Is that you?" Eros peered down from its back while it danced nervously in the road. Follow, who had been trotting at his heels, knew who she was and stuck his head happily in her hand.

"Yes, you wretched boy. Where is the mustard for Cook's back?"

"Right here." Eros patted the bag slung over his shoulder. "What are you doing out in the dark? I thought you were a ghost."

Aphrodite glared at him. "Waiting for you. I should have known better than to send you into Tiryns."

"It took a while to get the mustard," he said placatingly. "The apothecary was all out, and I had to wait for it to be made up."

"And where did you wait?"

"Well, this girl I know—"

"Just happened to ask you in? I told you to stay away from that slut!"

"She isn't a slut!" Eros said indignantly. "Not this one. She comes from a good family, and her two sisters were there the whole time! Mother, you should be ashamed of yourself!"

"Indeed?" Aphrodite eyed him speculatively. It was hard to see his face in the dark, but she thought he looked suddenly uneasy.

"Never mind!" Eros said. He kicked the horse and reined it around her. "I'll just take this up to the house for you," he called over his shoulder.

Aphrodite stood in the road looking after him. His horse's tail was a smoky flicker that vanished as he rounded the barn. *This one is serious*, she thought. And then, *He is much too young!*

XIV

❧

Joy Sometimes

Eros plopped the pot of ground mustard down on the kitchen table and rooted in the pantry for something to eat. He emerged with a loaf of bread and half a cheese as his mother came through the door from the kitchen garden. A cool onion-scented breeze blew into the kitchen with her. She eyed the mustard pot with annoyance.

"That is for Cook's back, and now the poor woman has gone to bed and it will have to wait until morning."

"Sorry," Eros said with his mouth full. "There's no olive oil in the crock," he added plaintively. Follow stuck his nose in the snake's basket and backed off when the snake hissed at him.

"That is because you ate the last of it," Aphrodite said. "It's like trying to feed a lion."

"How do you know what lions eat? You never saw a lion."

"I have heard of them. They eat a great deal."

"They kill their prey." Eros advanced on his

mother with bared teeth. "They don't eat bread and cheese."

"They would if their mother happened to have some handy," Aphrodite retorted.

"Then they would want olive oil." He sniffed at a tray of pastries on the shelf above the oven. "Are there apples in those?"

"And where is my embroidery thread?"

Eros patted his tunic as if the thread might have unaccountably attached itself to his person. It hadn't. "In the bag?" he suggested.

Aphrodite picked up the leather pouch in which he had carried the mustard, and felt inside. "Eros, it isn't here. What have you done with it?"

"Well, I bought it."

"Does that mean you think it's come home by itself? When did you buy it?"

"In the morning. First thing."

Aphrodite gritted her teeth. "And where do you think you might have left it?"

Eros gnawed the last of the bread reflectively. "At Psyche's house?"

"And Psyche is the little tart you—"

"Mother, don't!" Eros set the remains of the cheese down on the table. "She's a nice girl from a respectable family, and I won't have you insulting her."

"Tell me about this nice family." Aphrodite folded her arms across her chest. She was aware that she did not have the moral high ground in insulting Psyche, but it was hard to keep that in mind.

"Well"—Eros picked the cheese up again and gnawed it as he talked—"her father's a leather merchant. Sells sandals and boots and so on. Nice ones. Her mother's from an old family in Laconia. Related to the queen even, I think."

"That is not precisely a recommendation these days," Aphrodite said. She thought of Helen, taken back to Laconia. After all that struggle and death.

"Not a close relative," Eros said. "Well, stands to reason she wouldn't be if they're selling boots in Tiryns. But a nice family, that's all I meant. There are two sisters, but Psyche's the pick of the lot."

"Eros, have you promised this girl anything?"

"No!" He looked shocked.

"Oh, for goodness' sake! A respectable family, the girl will want you to marry her!"

"You said I was too young," Eros said innocently.

"That's my point." Aphrodite glared at him. Talking to Eros was like trying to make conversation with the wind. Every time she tried to settle a point or get a straight answer from him, he blew on past it, smiling charmingly and patting her shoulder with such obvious affection that it was hard to keep a grip on her anger.

"I'll see what Father thinks," he said now. "How about that? Father always gives good advice." He popped the last of the cheese into his mouth and departed, plucking a pastry from the shelf as he passed and tossing a bit of it to Follow.

"I don't care what your father thinks!" Aphrodite said to his disappearing back. Hephaestus would back up Eros; he always did. For a man as cynical as Hephaestus was, Aphrodite suspected he had a secret belief in love. It was why he understood her so well. A rustling by her feet caught her attention, and she bent to give her respects to the snake. She poured some goat's milk into a saucer, and the snake flowed over the top of his basket to drink it. "Talk to the Goddess for me," she whispered. "Ask her to tell him how much trouble love is."

*   *   *

In the meantime, Aphrodite went into Tiryns her-self to buy a new pair of sandals. There were three shops in Tiryns that sold leather goods, but she knew she had found the right one when she saw the girl behind the counter.

"Can I help you, my lady?" The girl was about fif-teen, Aphrodite thought, with full, pouty lips that gave her a perpetually surprised and delighted look—no doubt she turned that look on Eros—and hair the color of pale wheat. Her eyes were an odd, speckled blue, like a bird's eggs, and her hands long and graceful. She was breathtaking. The shop was full of people, nearly all male, and not more than half of them buying boots. The rest had found some reason to lounge about where they could look at Psyche.

"I want a pair of sandals," Aphrodite informed her. She was pleased to note that the men all swung their heads around and looked at her, too, with a good deal of interest. But she also knew she was a bonus. They would talk about how they had seen two of the most beautiful women they'd ever laid eyes on today, but it was the young one who would be in their dreams.

"We have some very nice ones in red leather." The girl's voice was soft and mellifluous, like a sweet, sleepy bird. "Father just made them yesterday, and they're lovely."

"Let me see them, then."

The girl called to someone beyond a leather curtain that hung behind the counter, and another girl came out with the sandals. She was clearly Psyche's sister and just as clearly no match for her. A sister like Psyche would be a constant aggravation for a plain girl, Aphrodite thought. She slipped her feet into the

sandals and admired them. They were lovely work-
manship. *And my son can do better than a cobbler's
daughter. Leather merchant, indeed!*

She went home to inform him—and Hephaestus—
of that in no uncertain terms.

"Well, they're very nice sandals," Hephaestus said.

"Are you taking his part in this?"

"I'm not taking anyone's part. Love has a way of
being inconvenient. We should both know that."

"It's not love. He's too young."

"How old were you?"

Aphrodite looked at the sandals, rather than look
at him. "I don't think I've ever been old enough,"
she offered. "It just happens." Her gaze fell on the
bronze brazier with its swan's-head legs. "I don't
know why you're so nice to me," she added.

Hephaestus chuckled. "Where did that thought
come from? I thought we were arguing about Eros."

"We were," she said fretfully. "I just keep thinking
that if I were a better person, then he wouldn't be
so much trouble."

Hephaestus threw his head back and laughed. She
blinked at him. He hardly ever laughed. He was still
laughing when he went out to the forge. He spent
all his time there, but he always had. In the evenings
he came home and sat by the hearth with her and
let her tell him about whatever had happened that
day, and acted as if it really mattered to him, which
no other man she had known ever did. Dionysus, for
example, who was still living on the farm and hadn't
ever married and was half-drunk most of the time,
had listened while she had explained to him very
carefully why the new goslings must not be let out

of their pen, and then he had let them out and an owl had gotten them.

Aphrodite put her new sandals away, buckled on the ones she wore to feed chickens, and went out to console the goose, which, it turned out, had already laid another clutch of eggs. Geese were optimists. She was thinking that it might be simpler to be a goose when she saw a cart rattling up the track that ran out to the main road to Tiryns. Aphrodite shaded her eyes with her hand. It was a covered cart, with a driver sitting on the seat and two good horses harnessed to it. She wiped her hands on her apron and went out to meet it, since no one else was in the yard. She could hear Hephaestus's hammer in the forge. Everyone else was in the fields or the dairy.

The cart clanked to a stop, and she eyed the horses curiously. They snorted at her and stamped their feet. They were clearly not cart horses. Nor was the woman who climbed down out of the covered back a peddler's wife. She put her veil back from her head and Aphrodite gawped.

"My husband is in Tiryns with an army, deciding whether to besiege Mycenae and try to get his father's throne back," Helen said. "I am allowed out with my ladies, to visit other ladies, so I came to see you." She looked uncertain of her welcome, but she stood her ground. The two attending ladies peered uneasily from the cart.

The war had marked her; Aphrodite could see that. It wasn't just ten years' worth of lines in her face—Aphrodite had those, too—but ten years' worth of sadness and death. She looked beautiful and mournful, like a carving on a tomb. Aphrodite put her arms out and pulled Helen into them.

Helen sniffled against her ear. "I wasn't sure you'd let me in."

What could you say to that? Aphrodite was silent because she didn't know. She put her arm around Helen's waist and led her into the garden. The ladies followed discreetly.

Aphrodite's garden had a paved floor and a wonderful border of flowers and blooming herbs. She picked a few medicinal leaves from it, but mainly the garden was for flowers, a useless extravagance and a waste of land, according to Hera. At the center was a bronze sundial Hephaestus had made, balanced on a pedestal like a leaping dolphin, and bronze chairs cushioned with pillows, around a pool of darting silver fish. Aphrodite settled Helen and her ladies in it and called out to Cook, who was in the kitchen garden hoeing the beans, to bring them something to eat. Helen and her companions were silent while they waited, Helen looking at her toes. Cook produced a tray of small pastries and a flagon of good wine, and tried—unsuccessfully—not to gape at the visitors, who were grander than anyone Cook had seen. Their gowns were bright with ribbons and their hair was curled in the latest style. The ladies sat at a discreet distance from Helen and Aphrodite, but were plainly on guard.

"I thought you would have Elpenor with you," Aphrodite said at last.

"My husband blamed him for my leaving. He is dead. Something else on my conscience," Helen said.

Aphrodite fell silent again. All she could think about were the picnics and the adventures they had had in Mycenae and what fun it had all been and how she had never thought that it would end in a war. "Where is your daughter?" she asked Helen finally, because that was the thing she kept coming back to, how she could have left her in the first place. But she knew that not everyone thought about their children the way she did. Agamemnon, for instance. Or, most likely, Clytemnestra, just before her son cut her throat.

"She is in Laconia," Helen said. "She was to have married Orestes when they were grown. Now . . . I don't know. My husband"— Aphrodite noticed that she never called him by name—"wants to force the marriage, but we have heard—"

"Nothing good of Orestes," Aphrodite said. "No. But what does your daughter want?" Not that it would matter, probably.

"I don't know. She was nine when I left. Now I don't know her at all." Helen looked down again. "It was all such a muddle. I loved him so. And it was such fun. My husband was an old man even then, you know. I hadn't . . . Well, there had never been a *young* man. Now I am the woman who wrecked the world. Our economy is in ruins in Laconia, with my husband gone so long, and so much money spent on the war. I don't know what I thought would happen. That he would just let me go and forget about me, maybe. He had the kingdom, after all. I didn't think I was really important."

"Men are odd," Aphrodite said. That was all she had been able to figure out about men in the course of her lifetime.

"Are you happy?" Helen asked.

Aphrodite looked about her, at her garden, and the forge with the sound of Hephaestus's hammer ringing from it, and at the vineyard where Eros was supposed to be pulling the weeds that grew up around the young vines, and was probably asleep under them instead, and tried to think about that. Ares was still an empty place beside her, but he was like an old scar now, flattened and pale, and only itching occasionally. "I have had joy," she said finally. "I don't know about happy."

"Maybe joy sometimes is all we get." Helen smiled a little. "I did have that. But I thought it would last. I thought love was joy. And then the warships came. And the siege. And I knew it was my doing."

"It was Paris's doing!" Aphrodite said, indignant now. "He was the one who coaxed you to run away with him. He was the prince of Troas." Helen's ladies looked at her curiously, and Aphrodite lowered her voice. "Who are they?"

"Warders," Helen said dryly. "Ladies of good Laconian families fallen on hard times. All times are hard times in Laconia just now. They are to watch me and make sure I don't run off again. I am not allowed out without them."

"But he treats you well otherwise?" Helen's gown was of fine cloth, the skirt flounced with three ruffles and the bodice laced with sea-green cord. Her hair was pinned with gold combs, and her fingers had enough rings to weigh them down, so that they fluttered languidly like moths when she moved her hands.

"I am his proudest possession," Helen said.

Aphrodite made a face, the face they used to make at each other when they found something revolting and almost funny at the same time, so many years ago.

"He could have killed me," Helen said. "I think he nearly did. He said he was going to, over and over, through all those years. He said all he wanted from the sacking of the city was the chance to kill the faithless bitch. One hears these things. There is a certain amount of coming and going between besiegers and besieged. But in the end, he didn't. I don't know why."

"What of Paris?" They had heard conflicting tales from travelers: He had been killed by Menelaus. He had thrown himself from the walls when the army broke through the gates. He had been rescued by the Goddess and carried off by an eagle.

"I never saw him die," Helen said. "It happened when they sacked the city. They hunted him down just before they came for us. My husband often tells me about it."

Aphrodite put her hand to her mouth. Menelaus was evil. No wonder he had let his brother kill his child for a wind. She looked at Helen's finery and at her own farm wife's gown and the sandals she had put on to see to the geese. Not even being able to wear clothes like Helen's all the time would be worth having Helen's marriage.

"I did come to bring you news," Helen said.

"Ares?" Aphrodite leaned forward in her chair. "Ares?"

"No," Helen said. "I never saw him, or if I did, I wouldn't have known him. But I saw your son."

Aphrodite froze in midmovement. "My son."

"Anchises's boy. I remembered how you'd told me how they took the baby from you and sent him to his father in Troas. When I got to Troas, he was there. Anchises and your son. They owned a lot of land outside the city, and Anchises was one of Priam's councilors. He took good care of the boy because he never had another. Priam married your son to Paris's sister, Creusa, so we were . . . related, I suppose. I thought of you every time I saw him."

"Is he still living?"

"I don't know."

"What was his name?" Aphrodite asked softly.

"Aeneas."

"I would have called him Photios." She turned the name over in her mind. "I always thought of him that way. Aeneas. I'll have to get used to that."

"Some of them lived," Helen said. "He may have. It was dreadful. My husband's army sacked the city and set fire to it and killed everyone they could find, old men, and women, and babies. It's beginning to be said that what has happened in Laconia and Mycenae is because of what they did in Troas. I don't know. Are you all right here?"

"Yes. We stay away from Mycenae, and mostly from Tiryns, too, and just work our farm."

"The roads are full of bandits," Helen said, "with no troops patrolling to stop them. My husband brought a whole phalanx with him to guard us on the way."

"Will he try to take Mycenae, do you think? My mother says the House of Atreus has a curse on it."

"If it didn't, it does now," Helen said. "My sister . . . How could I marry a daughter to Orestes after that?"

One of the ladies stood abruptly and inspected the sundial. She looked at Helen. "It grows late," she announced.

"Of course." Helen stood. "And there are certain things I am not to speak of." She hugged Aphrodite and gave her a small smile. "I may not be able to come back again. But I haven't had many friends in my life, so I'll be glad if you can still think of me as one."

The ladies stepped up, one on either side of her,

like jailers, and escorted her out of the garden, back to the cart, where the driver was dozing on his seat. One of them spoke sharply to him and he jerked awake.

Aphrodite watched the cart turn in the farmyard and rumble down the track. The chickens flocked around her, clucking for their evening grain, and she saw Eros coming down from the vineyards in a pool of sunlight, walking with Follow at his heels, the low sun making long shadows across the rows. A lark perched on a branch by her head and cocked a bright eye at her. Hebe came out of the dairy with a pail in each hand. The clang of Hephaestus's hammer stilled, and she heard him shuffling as he put his tools away. *Joy sometimes*, she thought, and went to feed the chickens.

Eros watched Aphrodite carefully as he came down from the vineyard. Dinner would be ready soon, and then Mother would expect him to sit about the hall afterward and recite poetry or play the lyre. There would be no one there but Mother and Father, and possibly Teacher if Mother had invited him to dinner. Teacher would moon after Mother, Father would show every sign of going to sleep when the poetry began, and Mother would beam at Eros proudly, and keep him by her side until she went to bed.

"I can't face that," he informed Follow. "A fellow's got to have some fun." Follow gave him a look indicating perfect agreement. Eros listened a moment at the kitchen door and then slipped cautiously into the house past Cook. Aphrodite was no doubt in her chamber changing for dinner, and so he swiped a few more pastries behind Cook's back, took a skin

of good wine from the pantry, and collected his lyre
on tiptoe from his own chamber. He had every intention of playing it tonight, but not for his mother.

Eros whistled softly to Follow and they slunk out
to the stable together. Follow watched with interest
while Eros saddled his horse. When they trotted
down the track, the moon was up, full and silver as
a coin, bathing the barley fields in opalescent light.
Eros began to whistle again.

Psyche lived with her widowed father, Leonidas,
and her two sisters in a house behind the shop. The
shop itself was boarded up for the night, but Eros
went around to the back and knocked on a door
there. Leonidas's one servant opened it and peered
out at him.

"Master Eros! Good evening."

"Are the ladies at home?" It was polite to pretend
you wanted to see the homely sisters, too.

"Indeed. The family has just finished dining and
they'll be glad of company. I'll put your horse up
and you go right in." The old servant clattered off
up the alley with the horse, and Follow went after
them on errands of his own.

Eros slung his cloak and the bag with his lyre in
it over his arm, and went inside. Leonidas and his
daughters were sitting around the hearth, the girls
industriously spinning, and they brightened when
they saw him. They had hopes for Eros. The family
was well enough off by a cobbler's standards, but
clearly not so wealthy as Psyche's suitor.

Psyche ran to fetch a cushion for his chair, and
Chloris and Alecto smiled at him. They weren't
homely exactly—he could see that when he looked
carefully—but anyone in the room with Psyche was

homely by comparison. She was really more beautiful than his mother, which was why he knew it would be a bad idea to take her home.

He unslung the wine and pastries and put them on the table. "I've brought something to sweeten my welcome," he said with a grin. "Master Leonidas, I remember that you liked these."

"Ah, indeed. Not that your welcome needs sweetening, young man. Not in certain quarters." He winked at Psyche, who blushed. The sisters rolled their eyes at each other at that.

Eros took out his lyre and played a tune while they ate, and then, as Eros had suspected he would, Leonidas rose and beckoned to the sisters. "Come, girls, I have a job waiting that needs your small hands to stitch. We shan't be gone long." He beamed at Psyche and Eros.

"Father, that's not respectable!" Chloris hissed at him as they left the room.

"If he's going to marry the child, I don't care what's respectable," Leonidas shot back. "He brings her fine presents, and he's clearly a man of means. He's not going to come to the point with us breathing down his neck."

Eros took Psyche's hand and kissed it as if he hadn't overheard that. "I brought you something else, too." He reached into the bag and brought out a smaller leather pouch, dyed red. "Open it."

Psyche turned the contents out on her palm and gasped. It was a set of small gold rings set with opals, one for each finger of her hand. Eros watched her expression with satisfaction. They had cost him most of his monthly allowance, and Aphrodite would be furious if she knew what he had spent it on, but it was so much fun to make Psyche happy. She looked up at him, smiling, and he kissed her. "Can we take a walk? There's a full moon out," he whispered.

She looked around, and since her father didn't seem to be available to ask, she nodded. She put the rings on, and they went out into the spring night. The moon had washed the whole city with milk so that it seemed nearly as light as day, but with all the colors leached out, the landscape limned in black and white and Eros's face finely etched and mysterious. He smiled at her, and his lips and eyes were silver and his mouth dark when he pressed it down over hers.

His arm tightened about her and she thought she would faint. "Isn't there a garden somewhere in this city that hasn't fallen to ruin yet?" he whispered. "Someplace with grass and nice tall bushes?"

Psyche's eyes opened wide and she nodded. "Behind the Temple of the Goddess," she whispered back. "The priestesses keep it up, and no one really dares steal anything from them because they're afraid of the Goddess."

"Well, we shan't steal anything but some time," Eros murmured. "I love you. I want . . ."

"What?"

"You."

Psyche sighed and leaned against his shoulder as they walked. He enveloped them both in his cloak, and they ran through the empty street laughing. Eros kept an eye about them. There was no telling whom you were likely to meet in the streets now, but the merchants of Tiryns, Psyche's father had told him, had gotten a civilian watch together, and they would generally come if you screamed loudly enough. Eros kept the cloak from hampering his reach for the sword belted at his side.

No one troubled them as they came to the garden of the Goddess and pulled open the gate.

"Shhhh!" Eros put his finger to his lips.

"Shhhh!" Psyche said back to him, stifling a giggle. She wondered for a moment what would happen if the priestesses of the Goddess caught them, and then Eros tugged her into the dark shadow of an ancient laurel tree and she forgot about the priestesses.

"Eros? Why haven't I met your family?" Sometime later, Psyche traced the line of his lips with a fingertip, brooding on this.

Because my mother would have a fit. It was probably not tactful to say that. "They're odd," he said. "I'll take you to see them in a while, but it's a long way away, and I have to make arrangements."

"How far away? Not over the sea? You come here so often!"

"No, not over the sea. But just a long way."

"Did you mean it when you said you loved me?" Psyche was propped on her elbows in the grass now, her face puckered into a worried frown in the moonlight.

"I did." And oddly, he had. It hadn't happened before, but he was certain it was true. It just wasn't the right time to bring her home to Mother. He would think of something eventually, he was sure. But there was no need to worry about it yet. Plenty of time when they were a bit older. For now, they had the Goddess's garden and each other, and who needed more than that?

Psyche twisted the rings on her fingers. "They are beautiful. Where did you buy them? Did you bring them from your city?"

"Aha! Cleversides, you're trying to trap me." Eros kissed the top of her head. "I'll tell you someday. I'll take you there. But it can't be just yet. You'll have to trust me. Do you trust me?" He tipped her head up by the chin.

"Of course," she murmured. She played with the rings.

"I'll bring you something finer even, next time."

"Are we going to get married?"

"Er, yes. When it's time. We have lots of time," he said cheerfully, hoping that she felt the same.

Psyche thought about that. "Well, can we come to the garden again?"

"Always." He nuzzled her ear, relieved, and she giggled. "But come along now before your father sends your dragon sisters for you."

When they came back to the house behind the shop, the sisters were waiting at the door. Chloris snatched Psyche inside, and Eros bowed low at her. "We took a walk in the moonlight. It's very lovely tonight. Have Psyche show you," he suggested.

Chloris glared at him and closed the door, not quite a slam. Eros fetched his horse and found Follow waiting for him, tongue lolling out and his legs wet to the belly with mud. Eros looked at him suspiciously. Follow grinned. Eros laughed. Someone would have pups they weren't expecting, but they would be good ones.

When he got home, Hephaestus was lying in wait for him, apparently dozing by the hearth. Eros tried to sneak past him, but it turned out he wasn't asleep after all.

"You're a fool to think you can put one over on your mother," Hephaestus said.

Eros stopped. Follow looked guiltily at Hephaestus and slunk behind a hanging so that it appeared to have four gray feet.

"Put what over?" Eros asked.

Hephaestus sighed. He sat up in his chair, straightening the blanket he had draped over his knees. "I am not so old as you think just yet, nor so unobservant. Neither is your mother. She knows you are seeing a girl, and you had better tell her about it before she takes finding out into her own hands. You won't like that."

Eros looked aggrieved. "I tried to tell her. Psyche is a respectable girl; she comes from a decent family. Mother has no reason to be angry, but she was anyway."

"No doubt."

"Mother thinks I'm her personal property," Eros said sulkily.

"She does. I might add in her defense that you are rather young."

"I'm older than Mother when she married."

"Ah. Married. That may be the operative word here. And in any case, you aren't older than I was."

Eros paced about the hall waving his arms, but not actually saying anything. He looked as if he had thought of several things to say and thought better of all of them.

"Is there any wine left in that skin?" Hephaestus asked him finally.

Eros tipped it. "A bit."

Hephaestus held his cup out. "Sit down."

Eros poured Hephaestus the rest of the wine and sat.

"Now then. What have you told this respectable girl and her respectable parents?"

Eros bit his lip. "Nothing, really. She thinks . . . she thinks I live a long way away. Well, I had to tell her something!" he said when Hephaestus raised an eyebrow. "Or she'll wonder why I don't bring my family to meet hers!"

"If she'd met your family, she wouldn't wonder," Hephaestus said. "But that's exactly the problem now, isn't it?"

"I've told her it's complicated."

Hephaestus gave a short hoot of laughter. Eros thought it was a laugh. "Love is complicated," Hephaestus said. "I assume you do love her? If you don't, your behavior is outrageous."

"No, I do. I was surprised," Eros said. "But I do."

Hephaestus studied him. He had his mother's coloring, and he was beautiful in a way that neither Ares nor Hephaestus had ever been, but Hephaestus could see his own face in him. Or Ares's.

"I can't think about anything but her," Eros said. "And dodging Mother. It's awful."

I do believe you are mine, Hephaestus thought. *Ares never thought about anything but what he could fight next*. Even his love for Aphrodite had been the love of a possessor for the possession. Hephaestus wondered if Aphrodite had considered this possibility. He sighed lightly, dismissing that, and returned to the matter at hand. "Are you telling me that you are courting this girl . . ." He narrowed his eyes suddenly. "And has it gone beyond respectable courtship?"

"Well . . ."

"Well?"

"In a way. I suppose." Eros looked at his feet.

"In what way? How many ways are there?"

Eros grinned at him. "Lots."

"Don't dodge," Hephaestus snapped. "I'm trying to save your skin."

"Yes, then. I suppose." Hephaestus raised the eyebrow at him again. "Yes."

"So, you are courting this girl, you have made love to her already, you bring her presents, you raise her family's hopes, and you won't tell her where you live?"

"Mmm. Yes."

"You'll be lucky if her father doesn't kill you before your mother has a chance."

"I'll think of something."

Hephaestus drained the cup and handed it to Eros. "You had better pray to the Goddess that you do."

"Mmm." Eros looked glum. The wine and euphoria were wearing off. Follow had come out from behind the hanging and was lying with his nose on his muddy paws, watching Eros worriedly.

"Do you want to marry this girl?" Hephaestus demanded.

"Yes."

"But not just yet, because you aren't as old as you think you are, are you?"

"Mmm. No."

"You're going to burn yourself. Don't say I didn't tell you. Better to face down your mother now and have done with it. You have to marry sometime. I'll back you up."

Eros's face reflected the horror this thought inspired in him. "No!"

"Then go to bed, you young idiot." Hephaestus heaved himself out of his chair and put his blanket over his arm. He limped toward the chamber he shared with Aphrodite, shaking his head. In the hall behind him, he heard Eros still pacing, muttering to himself. Aphrodite was curled in the bed, wrapped around a pillow, her gold hair braided for the night. Hephaestus stripped off his tunic and pulled his nightclothes over his head. He lay down with a thud, grumpily uncaring whether he wakened Aphrodite or not. The two of them gave him a headache.

XV

❧

Everyone's Business

Eros turned the key in the bolt of the tiny house. It stood compressed between a vegetable stall on one side and a laundry on the other. The smell of hot wet clothes and soap bubbled toward them from the laundry, and the vegetable stall, where a black-and-white cat lay asleep in a basket of turnips, gave off a faint aroma of onions.

"It's little," he said cheerfully to Psyche and her family outside the door. "But you'll be cozy here. I've had everything I could think of sent in." He opened the door onto a tiny chamber painted deep green, with a border of golden birds around the walls, and Psyche drew in her breath with pleasure. In the center a small hearth was flanked by two bronze braziers filled with glowing coals. The furnishings were small, to fit the room, but elegant: chairs with birds carved into the backs, a couch with sumptuous red pillows, tables inlaid with ivory and shells. A hanging embroidered with more birds screened another doorway. Eros held it back to show

Psyche a yellow bedchamber with a bed furnished
as elaborately as the couch, a carved ebony chest for
clothes, and a dressing table fitted with a silver mirror, ivory pots for rouge, and a blue glass scent bottle
shaped like an ape.

Psyche flitted about the rooms examining things
while her sisters stood suspiciously in the doorway.
"Oh, look! Chloris, look!" She ran to the door with
the scent bottle and one of the ivory pots in her hand.
"Alecto! Look! Isn't he dear? And look at this one;
there are lions carved around it."

"Very nice," Alecto said repressively.

Chloris sighed. "Father has no more sense than
you do."

Leonidas was consulting solemnly with Eros. "This
is my youngest daughter, mind. I'll see her treated
properly."

"Of course." Eros smiled at Psyche. "She is my
treasure; I would never mistreat her."

"And there will be a wedding as soon as your
family can travel here?" Leonidas prodded him.

"Of course. I consider us wed already."

"And I suppose you'll consider yourself wed when
the baby comes along?" Chloris asked. "You'll remember that you considered yourself wed then?"

"Chloris!" Psyche turned on her. "Stop that! You
are being horrible!"

Alecto folded her arms. "We are being practical.
Men have convenient memories."

"Father!" Psyche turned to Leonidas.

"That's enough now," Leonidas said to them. "I
have young Eros's word, and that's good enough for
me. He's been very good to us so far."

"They're right to look after their sister," Eros said
gallantly. "I have a present for each of you, too, to

show you my good faith." He took two small packages out of his tunic, and handed them to the sisters.

Chloris and Alecto took the little wooden boxes gingerly, but they lifted the lids. Inside were two matching pairs of earrings, amber teardrops set in silver.

"Oh, they're beautiful!" Psyche said. "Much nicer than anything else you have. *Now* will you be nice?"

Alecto put hers in her ears. "Hmm."

Eros took their hands, one in each of his. "Now, my dear sisters, let us be friends. You used to think me not so bad."

"That was when we used to think you were going to marry Psyche," Chloris said, but she put her earrings on, too.

"And so I shall, but these arrangements are complicated and will take time. Until then, this house will show you my good intentions." He smiled at each of them, charmingly, cajolingly, and they felt less sure of their objections. He *was* charming. And he had given them all *lovely* gifts.

Out of his presence, the sisters felt uneasy again. They scratched their heads and tried to think why they had been so easily won over. They complained of this to Psyche, who smiled at them pityingly and said it was a shame they were so untrusting. They'd have a hard time catching husbands of their own if they kept that up.

Psyche loved living in the little house, because it was all hers. She could get out of bed at noon if she felt like it, and it didn't matter that she didn't have a servant because it was so easy to keep clean. In the mornings she yawned and stretched and patted the place in the bed where Eros had lain—he always left before morning—and then she washed with water from the well that was only a few steps from her house, and put on a clean gown. Eros bought her clothes—dresses with flounces and ruffles, and stiff starched skirts as lovely as anything her father's best customers wore—and if they got soiled, she could have them washed for her by the laundry next door instead of taking them to the river herself. At the grocer's she could play with the cat and fill her basket with fresh beans and apples and figs and pomegranates, and at the fishmonger's down the street she could buy oysters and eels and even a turtle, and put it all on Eros's bill, which he paid every ten-day.

Then she would take her purchases home and fix a meal for Eros in the tiny kitchen that also opened off the central chamber. It was smaller than her bedchamber, but it had its own hearth and a stone sink to wash the dishes in. She could make eel pie in the brick oven and turtle soup over the fire in her new bronze-and-copper soup pot. It was like living in her dollhouse. As a child she had spent hours with the tiny set of rooms she had furnished for her clay dolls, taking satisfaction from the placement of a miniature rug or a minuscule wine jar.

When Eros came in the evening, she would bring him water to wash his hands with, and then a pitcher of watered wine, flicking a few drops on the floor for the gods, as befitted the mistress of the house. She would serve him the meal she had made, dishes of fruit and olives in pretty pottery bowls, and the main course on a piece of flat barley bread she had baked herself.

Eros came nearly every night, late in the evening, and stayed until just before dawn. Sometimes he didn't come, and she fretted, waiting for him, but he was always there the next night, with a kiss and a smile. Usually his dog, Follow, came with him, and curled up beside the hearth in the spot he had chosen for himself, or amused himself barking at the grocer's cat until Eros dragged him inside.

Eros didn't mention the marriage or his family, and when Psyche did, he looked so worried that she felt sorry for him. His family was "difficult," he said. Psyche understood. And it was so much fun in the little house that it would almost be a shame to spoil it. She invited her sisters to dine on an evening when Eros had said he wouldn't be there, to show off the house and ease their minds.

"I've even learned to bake bread," she said proudly to Alecto. "You'll see." Both sisters had always pronounced Psyche's bread somewhat less tasty than a wool blanket, but she had practiced carefully, and the old grocer's wife next door had shown her a few tricks. She had shown Psyche some tricks they didn't know about as well, married ladies' knowledge (Psyche hadn't mentioned not being actually married) having to do with not making babies until you wanted them. Those were not respectable things for her sisters to know, Psyche thought smugly, since they were still single, even if they were older than she was.

"Here. Sit down and I'll bring you some wine—Eros has brought me a very fine vintage from Argos—and you can see about the bread. Eros praises it." Psyche escorted her sisters to chairs by the hearth and bustled about pouring them each a cup of wine, the opal rings sparkling on her fingers. There were hot coals in the bronze braziers against the fall chill.

"Eros says it's a shame this is nearly the last of

this pressing; we won't see as good again for a few years."

Chloris rolled her eyes. "And what does Eros say about bringing his family to Tiryns for the wedding?"

"That part is very complicated." Psyche bustled into the kitchen and came back with a tray on which she had arranged the barley bread and slices of roast duck with mint leaves and rosemary.

Alecto sniffed cautiously. "It does smell good."

"Eros lets me buy anything I want at the market."

"Psyche, doesn't this bother you?" Alecto looked about the room suspiciously, as if she expected something to pop out at her from behind the walls. "All this mystery? Why should he have to make it all such a mystery? Has he even told you where he lives?"

"Well, no. But I won't hound him. He's very kind and I'm very happy and I don't care where he lives."

"Honestly!" Chloris bit into an olive, snapping her teeth closed around it. "He could be anyone!"

"Father approves of him."

"Father approves of him because he has money. But how do we know where he *got* this money?"

Psyche looked puzzled. "Well, where would he get it? His family has it, or they own shipyards or . . . or something."

"You don't know, do you? How do you know they aren't bandits?"

"Oh, that's ridiculous!" Psyche stood up indignantly. "He is a well-bred man from a good family and not a bandit."

"He could be a rich bandit," Alecto suggested. "Awful things are happening everywhere these days. What if he's a murderer?"

"Why would he be?"

"Why won't he tell you who he is?"

"He says it's a matter of my having faith in him," Psyche said. "If I have faith in him then everything else will come out right."

"Oh, you ignorant child! Have you ever heard of a bridegroom not telling a bride who he *is*?"

"I know who he is," Psyche said.

"No, you don't," Chloris said. "You know his name, *if* that is even his real one, and you know he gets money from somewhere, and you know he's ashamed for his family to meet you."

"Or the other way round," Alecto said darkly.

"What happens if he gets tired of you?" Chloris asked. "What then? You'll wake up some morning with your throat slit."

"If my throat was slit I wouldn't wake up!" Psyche snapped. She didn't like the way the conversation was going. They were always hounding her about Eros, trying to make her mistrust him. "And don't talk to me like that about him."

"You *are* an ignorant child," Chloris announced. "You don't know anything about men. It's because Mother died young, I expect, and you haven't had her to teach you."

"And you know everything about men, do you? No one has ever brought either of you so much as a bunch of flowers!" Psyche let her temper get the better of her.

Alecto sniffed. "We are merely trying to save you from yourself—and probably from that monster— and all you can do is make unkind remarks." She tore a piece of duck off and popped it into her mouth, sucking her fingers reproachfully.

"I'm sorry," Psyche said, contrite. "That was mean of me. But you mustn't be rude about Eros."

"Rude! We aren't worried about hurting his feelings!" Chloris said. "We are worrying about saving your skin from whatever he's plotting."

"Where does he go at night? Tell us that. When he leaves here?" Alecto asked.

"I . . . I don't know. And I won't ask him," Psyche said.

"Well, he can't be going home, if his family lives a long way off," Chloris said. "You did say that, didn't you? That is what he told us all?"

"Well, yes."

"Then where does he go?"

"To his lair, no doubt," Alecto said.

"What lair?" Psyche demanded.

"Where he lives with his bandit crew. They only leave it to prey on travelers, I expect."

"Oh, you are ridiculous!"

"You won't think so when you wake up some night and he's standing over you with a knife."

"You'd better find out where he goes at night," Chloris said.

Psyche glared at them in exasperation. "I trust my husband, and that's that."

"He's not your husband," Alecto said.

"Let her be," Chloris said with a sigh. "She'll find out. I expect. We've tried to do our duty."

Duty didn't stop them from eating everything they were served and finishing the wine, Psyche noted. She treated them with chilly courtesy until they left, and then paced the little house in a fury. But with Eros not there, her sisters' words rang in her ears. Why *wouldn't* he tell her where he went at night, or where he was from? She did have faith in him, but shouldn't he have some in her? If she asked him again she would just get the same sweet talk, and in his presence she would rapidly forget all about it. She could threaten to move back in with her father, of course, but what if he let her do it? What if it was so important a secret that he simply couldn't tell her? And what if it was not a dreadful secret but a good one? This thought took hold of her as she paced, warring with the awful ones at the back of her head. Supposing he was a king's son? In these uncertain times he might have to be very careful. She could ruin everything by announcing their marriage. He might be the heir to Mycenae. There were factions everywhere fighting for that throne. What if he was supposed to marry some royal bride, and he had to prevent that until he could take the throne?

But if he was a king's son, he should trust her to keep out of sight and be discreet until the right time. Alecto's words came back to her. What if he *was* fleeing some horrible crime? If he was a murderer, maybe he thought she would leave him if she knew. Or betray him. Or . . . there was always the question of whom he had murdered, and why. But most likely he was a king's son. But what if they never let her marry him?

By the time Eros arrived the next evening, Psyche had worked herself into a terror of either answer being true.

"What on earth is the matter?" he said when she dropped the wine and spilled the broth.

"I don't know! I'm just clumsy tonight." She mopped up the broth while he picked up the pieces of the shattered jug.

"Then you shall sit down and let me serve you!" He made a show of tying on her apron and mincing as if he were a serving girl, swaying his hips until she laughed.

Her fears calmed as they ate, and by the time she
was clearing away the sodden bits of barley bread
and the dishes of olives and sweets, her heart had
stopped pounding. He came up behind her and
kissed the back of her neck and she melted. So they
went to bed.

But afterward, as she lay propped on one elbow
watching him sleep, her mind flooded with all her
daylight worries again. He was so beautiful; how
could he be the bandit of Alecto's bloody descrip-
tion? But who was he?

Psyche put her head on the pillow, careful not to
wake him. He would leave in a few hours, near dawn
but still in the darkness. If she followed him, she
could see where he went without his knowing. And
then she would find out, and it would be all right
because her mind would be at rest. And he would
never know she knew, and she wouldn't tell a soul—
unless it was something awful, of course, but she
was sure it wouldn't be, and even if it was she would
protect him because he couldn't have meant to do
it—so everything would be all right.

She rested, half dozing, but not letting herself fall
into full sleep. Usually she didn't wake when he left,
and she didn't want to risk not hearing him go, because her courage might fail her by tomorrow. At
last she heard him stir and stretch. She kept her eyes
closed and felt him kiss her on the cheek. That made
her want to cry for not trusting him, but now that
she had begun to worry the thoughts wouldn't leave
her. She had to know.

She heard his soft footsteps cross the outer chamber and the click of the closing door. Psyche leaped
out of bed and snatched up her mantle and sandals.
She slid through the door, trying to tie them as she

went, and nearly fell on her nose in a dung pile outside the stable where he left his horse. She flattened
herself against the wall as the horse clopped out of
the yard with Follow at its heels.

How am I going to keep up with a horse? That thought
hadn't occurred to her until now. It was disappearing
down the dark street already, and she began to run,
trying to keep in the shadows. Psyche was a strong
girl who could carry two full buckets of water from
the well, or a whole cowhide, but the horse had outdistanced her by the time they came to the city gates.
She stopped, panting, and saw the faint flicker of its
movement in the moonlight on the road leading
south. *Well, I know what direction he goes in,* she
thought. There was nothing that way past the harbor
but the sea, and the road that curved across the valley through the farms south of Tiryns. Psyche went
home and thought.

Eros never gave her money; he just bought her
things. In the morning she took a silver hairpin she
thought he wouldn't miss to the silversmith and sold
it for enough to pay the stable keeper for the hire of
a horse. On horseback she could keep up with Eros's
horse, and outrun anything lurking on the roads. The
next night she gave Eros a head start, knowing where
he was heading, and then got the horse from behind
the laundry where she had tethered it. Psyche had
ridden her father's cart horses since she could toddle,
and she swung up onto this one's back without much
trouble and turned its head toward the gates. A
sleepy sentry, posted by the citizens' watch commit-
tee, waved her through with little interest. Once clear
of the steep ramp that rose up from the harbor, she
kicked the horse into a canter until she saw Eros on
the road ahead. She slowed then, wrapping her man-

tle about her face, and stayed far enough back to just keep him in sight. He wasn't headed for the harbor. He took the road south.

Eros seemed to be in no hurry. His horse ambled along the road while Follow zigzagged back and forth, sticking his nose in the brush that grew beside the wagon tracks, occasionally sending a rabbit rocketing across their path. The moon washed the landscape with the same silvery shine it had given it a month ago, when Psyche had gone to the Goddess's garden with Eros. Then it had seemed magical, an enchanted light that could only bless anyone it fell on. Now it had an eldritch cast, and the landscape looked the way leaves did when they turned their undersides up in the wind of a coming storm. A chill fall breeze whipped her mantle about her and spooked the horse so that he danced sideways in the wagon tracks as leaves blew past his nose. Psyche tried to stay well back from Eros's horse, but the night had begun to scare her. She didn't know what else might be riding on that wind. The ghosts of the dead of Troas, brought back by returning sailors, maybe. An owl went by her on silent wings and thudded her heart into her throat. After a moment she heard the shriek of whatever it had caught.

She followed Eros a long way down the road and was both relieved and frightened when he turned his horse up a narrow track that led past a barley field belonging to some farmer. Could this be where he stayed at night? And could she follow him in there without being seen? She drew rein to think about it and nearly turned tail to run when a pair of farm dogs came racing down the track, barking furiously. And then it was too late and the dogs were dancing about her horse, barking, while Follow, who plainly knew who she was, watched them. Eros spun his horse around, and then she heard a shout of fury, and a woman in white erupted out of the barley field, a shrieking apparition among the bundled sheaves that scared Psyche out of her wits. The woman turned her face to the moonlight, and at first Psyche thought it must be the Goddess herself, beautiful and terrible in her anger. Then she recognized her: It was the lady who had bought the red sandals in Father's shop. Psyche tried to back her horse away from the barking dogs, but they circled him, nipping at its heels every time it tried to move. Finally it stood stock-still, quivering and rolling its eyes.

The woman in white grabbed Eros's horse by the reins, still shouting at him. "What do you think you are doing, coming home at this hour? And who is that? That's her, isn't it? That girl from Tiryns!"

Eros swung his head around. "Psyche?"

Psyche stared back at him, too terrified to move.

"That's the one you've been spending all your money on, isn't it?" the woman screamed. "Begging your father for an advance on your allowance! And your lyre is gone, and your good bow is gone, and you sold them, didn't you? And I have to wait in a barley field just to catch you at it! Shivering in the cold all night! You ought to be ashamed!"

Eros jerked his horse's reins out of her hand. "Mother, be quiet!" he shouted back at her. "Will you stop lying in wait for me?" He spun back toward Psyche again. "And you! You followed me! How dare you?"

"I want . . . I was afraid . . . My sisters . . ." Psyche fumbled for some explanation, watching his terrifying mother all the while.

Eros reined his horse toward her, wading through

the barking dogs. She could see his face twisted with
anger in the graying light. He looked from one to
the other of them in a fury. "You followed me! I told
you I would take care of you, and I have, haven't I?
But you didn't trust me!"

"I just wanted to know where you live!" Psyche
burst into tears.

"And I told you to be patient! Now look what
you've done." The woman in white came after him,
pulling at his reins again, and he slapped her hand
away.

The woman advanced on Psyche. "You! Girl! Girl
from Tiryns! Go home!"

"Stay out of this, Mother!" Eros shouted. "Shut
up!" he bellowed at the farm dogs, who were still
barking.

"Eros . . ." Psyche reached out her hand toward
him.

Besieged, he looked from his mother to Psyche to
the dogs, which were still barking hysterically. He
backed his horse away. "Go home. Go away. You
didn't trust me." His expression was grim.

"Eros, please . . ."

"I don't want to see you anymore," he said fiercely
as his mother and the dogs surged around him.

"Slut from Tiryns! Go home!" Aphrodite spat the
words at her and flung a handful of stones from
the road.

Psyche sobbed and yanked her horse around past
the dogs. She put her heels to its flanks and they
heard the thud of its hooves on the high road.

"Get in the house!" Aphrodite shrieked at Eros.

Eros leaned down until his face was close to hers.
"You! How dare you lie in wait for me like that?
You stay out of my life!"

"Then conduct your life in an honorable fashion! Selling your things to pay for that little—"

"That's enough! I don't want to see you, either, until you can learn to stay out of my business! Maybe not then!" He kicked his horse hard and it thundered up the track to the farm, with Follow loping behind.

The farm dogs were still barking at the empty high road.

"Be quiet. You are idiots." Aphrodite cuffed them and stalked off, following Eros.

XVI

☙

Next Morning

In the morning all Aphrodite's bones ached, and she had a cold.

"You are too old to be sitting out in a damp barley field all night," was Hephaestus's comment.

"Thank you. That was just what I needed to make me feel decrepit." She spread olive oil and honey moodily on a piece of bread. She didn't look decrepit. He thought life would be easier when she did.

"Well, what possessed you?" he asked her. "I heard the commotion clear up here. Mother will be down shortly to find out all about it, I expect."

"I'll be sure to explain it all carefully," Aphrodite snarled. "I woke up in the night and went to see if he was home, and he wasn't, so I went out to the stable and his horse was gone. I just thought I'd walk down the road to meet him. And he didn't come home till nearly dawn!"

"While you sat in the barley field waiting for him."

She suspected that Hephaestus was trying not to laugh.

"He's been lying to me," Aphrodite said furiously.

"And you've been spying on him."

"I'm his mother."

"Ah, of course. I always welcomed having Mother know my intimate business."

"You listened to her when she told you to marry me," Aphrodite pointed out.

Hephaestus was silent. Finally, he said, "There wasn't anyone else I wanted to marry."

"Mmm." Aphrodite poked at a plate of boiled eggs and goat cheese and put some of that on her bread as well. She ate it while Hephaestus watched her as he might watch a volcano that had begun to smoke. She ate grimly, as if it were her duty, and when she had swallowed the last bite, she announced, "He hired her a house. He admitted it last night."

"Enterprising of him," Hephaestus said.

"Disgraceful of him. He sold his lyre." She took up her cup and splashed more wine into it. Breakfast wine was always well watered, but the addition of the wine kept one from disease. Aphrodite paced the hall, circling the hearth like a lioness moving in on a hapless rabbit. "I don't want you giving him any more money. His allowance is stopped as of right now. And I want you to put him to work. Take him to the forge and let him learn to do something besides chase girls."

"He already knows how to," Hephaestus observed. "He seems to prefer chasing girls."

"Are you taking his part?"

"No, not exactly. I am merely trying to get you to see past your anger."

Aphrodite snorted. "And what would you do, oh Most Wise?"

"Let him marry this girl if he wants to."

"Never!"

Hephaestus poured his own cup full and took an egg. He bit into it ruefully and watched Aphrodite pace, still ranting. Everyone in the family agreed that, of them all, he was the one with the best sense and wisest counsel, whose advice should be listened to; and they all did. And then they never took it. He hadn't told her yet that he had gotten a message from Ares, sent by a soldier in Menelaus's army. Ares was making his way back. The soldier said: "I was to tell you he'll be home for the olive harvest." It would be an interesting year.

"Father!"

Hephaestus jumped and laid down the hammer with which he had been sheathing a wagon wheel in bronze. "You are like an explosion," he said mildly.

"I will explode if Mother doesn't stay out of my business!" Eros blurted. "Do you know what happened last night?"

"I do. She has mentioned it several times."

"She treated me like a child!"

"You behaved like one," Hephaestus pointed out. "I understand you've been selling things."

"Well, that doesn't matter now," Eros said angrily, diverted. "I don't want to see *her* again, either, if she can't trust me. Why does no one trust me? Anyway, those things belonged to me."

"I could count the reasons and run out of fingers," Hephaestus said. "Beginning with deceiving that girl."

"I didn't. I asked her to trust me. I needed time to get around Mother."

"And now they're both angry at you?"

"I'm angry at *them*. I won't marry; I'll go join the army."

"You wouldn't like it," Hephaestus said. "You have to get up in the morning."

Eros glared at him.

Hephaestus laid the cooling wheel rim aside. If he tried to work on it and talk to Eros he would smash his thumb. "It seems to me," he said, "that you had it arranged very neatly to have what you wanted without paying any price for it. You had it all worked out, with a nice little house in town, and your lover and your mother kept at a comfortable distance from each other."

"What's wrong with wanting that?" Eros demanded.

"Nothing," Hephaestus said. "I have often wanted it myself. It's the accomplishing of it that presents the problem. The girl deserves respect, and not to be treated like a concubine—she'll get pregnant eventually, you know. And your mother also deserves your respect. You've given it to neither, going behind both their backs."

"I couldn't tell Mother!"

"I advised you to, if you recall."

Eros propped himself against the forge wall, arms crossed, his beautiful face petulant.

"Don't pout."

"I'm not pouting!"

"Shall I fetch a mirror?"

"Never mind!" Eros stomped out. Follow was nosing in the dung heap for rats. When he didn't come, Eros shouted at him. Follow regarded him solemnly and then lay down beside the forge. Eros cursed him and stalked off. Follow stuck his nose mournfully into Hephaestus's hand.

*   *   *

Psyche flung herself, sobbing, through her father's door. Alecto was just raising the wooden partition that screened the shop front at night. Chloris stopped with a bucket of mop water in her hand and stared at her.

"This is your fault," Psyche shrieked at them. "Why did I listen to you? Now he's gone!" She burst into loud, racking sobs, and sat down on her father's work stool with her face in her hands.

"Stop that!" Chloris said. She put the bucket down and shook her. "Everyone will hear you."

"I don't care!"

"Well, we care," Alecto said primly. "Chloris is being courted by a very nice young man from the fishmonger's shop, now that *you're* gone."

"Now that I'm gone?" Psyche raised her head. "I never looked at that boy from the fishmonger's!"

"When you were here nobody looked at us!" Alecto snapped.

"Then you should have left me alone," Psyche sobbed.

"Did you find out who he is? I told you he was a bandit."

"He isn't a bandit," Psyche said, hiccupping. "He's just a boy from a farm south of here, and his mother hates me, and now he hates me, too, for following him, and he said to go home, and now I won't have my nice little house anymore, and I hate you all!" She stood up, glaring at them, scrubbing at her eyes.

Leonidas came through the door from the house in his leather apron, frowning at the commotion. "Psyche?"

"I told you he wouldn't marry her, Father," Chloris said. "Now he's abandoned her, and who's going to pay the bills she's run up for turtles and wine from Argos?"

"What did you do?" Leonidas demanded.

"I didn't do anything," Psyche wailed. Her face was red and slick with tears. "Chloris and Alecto kept telling me I ought to find out where he lives, and they frightened me."

"What did you *do*, you foolish girl?"

"I followed him, and he got angry."

"And now he won't pay your bills?"

"I don't know! He didn't say. What does that matter? He told me he doesn't want to see me anymore!" Psyche sobbed.

"This is a respectable house," Leonidas said. "We can't have this. What will everyone say?"

"*You* wanted me to go and live with him!" Psyche said. "You said he had money and he was a good catch!"

"Then you should have behaved properly."

"Chloris and Alecto said . . ." Psyche looked at her sisters for help, but they crossed their arms and glared at her. Every man who came into the shop had always wanted Psyche and never looked at her sisters, even though Psyche had never wanted any of them. Since she had moved out, Chloris and Alecto had suitors. Chloris's young man was expected to discuss a bride price with Leonidas any day now, and Alecto had recently begun walking out with a grain merchant's apprentice.

"I love him," Psyche sobbed. "And now he doesn't love me."

"I love you, sweetie; come live with me!" a voice called, and there was a burst of laughter outside. A young man in a butcher's apron stood smirking at her from the street.

Leonidas glared through the shop window. Three housewives with baskets on their arms peered back curiously, and two small children pulling a wheeled dog had stopped behind them to stare. Leonidas slammed the wooden window shut.

"I won't have this," Leonidas said. "If you're going to stay here—"

"Father!" Chloris and Alecto said together.

"—you're going to stay in the back, inside the house. You can keep the place clean while your sisters take care of the shop. I won't have it said any daughter of mine disgraced the family."

Psyche looked up at him miserably. "You were happy enough for me to live with him when you thought he had money." She sniffled.

"What? He hasn't even got money?"

"He lives on a farm south of here. His mother shouted at him because he sold things to pay for my house and all the presents he brought us," Psyche said dolefully.

"I shall go and see these parents," Leonidas decided. "And demand payment for his ruining you. They should at least pay us that."

"No!"

"Someone has to pay for this," Leonidas growled. "Someone owes me."

The sisters nodded. Psyche stood up. She felt like lead inside. Someone outside banged on the shop window, and she slipped into the house in back while her father went to open it. When no one followed her, she went out the house door into the street and took the horse by the bridle. She took him back to his stable and then turned her key in the lock of the little house by the laundry. It looked stark and empty, and the bed was still rumpled from the night before. She lay down in it, pressing her face into the depression in the mattress where Eros had lain, and cried herself to sleep.

Psyche woke in the late afternoon, with the room full of long shadows and her head stuffed up so that she could hardly breathe. She got up, scrubbed her face in the basin on her dressing table, blew her nose, and pulled off the gown she had ridden the horse in. It was ruined, a sad wad of torn ruffles and stained skirts. She balled it up and threw it in the corner. She bathed in the water from the basin and put on another dress, her best one. She might as well keep up a dignified face. Then she put on all of her jewelry, and went to pay her bills with it.

XVII

❧

What You Let in the House

The soldier in the battered armor paused where the track turned off the Tiryns road and wound away through barley fields and trees. The farmland looked shabby to him, down-at-the-heels and too weedy in the fall light, as if whoever owned it had grown tired. The barley's pale stalks had been cut and baled into sheaves, and looked as if they were waiting for something, standing like a silent army in the morning mist. He hefted the sack on his back and grinned fiercely at them, a ragged grin with fewer teeth than he had possessed when he left. Everything in Argolis looked like the farm, ratty and falling to bits, and there had been thieves on the road who had had the bad judgment to waylay him. There were two fewer of those now.

He set off up the track toward home. A furious barking erupted, and a pair of dogs raced toward him. One, gray-muzzled and even more toothless than he, stopped suddenly, head cocked as if puzled. Then she leaped on him, paws on his shoulders, nearly knocked him down. The other dog kept barking until the older one dropped back, spun around, and snapped her teeth at his nose. The younger dog sat down abruptly in the road.

"Chaser?" Ares bent to scratch the old dog's ears. "You're an old girl now, aren't you?" She whined. "Ha! She still knows me. We'll see who else does."

He followed the wheel-rutted track past the fields and through the laurel thicket, where a second track branched off toward the Goddess's spring. He could hear the chickens clucking in the yard up ahead and he snort of a pig rooting somewhere in the trees. A goat bleated in the distance out of sight, and a woman's voice called to it. He shifted the heavy sack on his shoulder again, using his spear for a walking staff. His gait was uneven, and dried blood caked the greave on his left calf and the padding under it. The tile roofs of the farm, perched on a hillock, showed just above the trees that ringed it, and he hobbled faster.

He was nearly to the house before anyone saw him. A woman throwing grain to the chickens paused, hand outstretched. She peered at him through the mist. Then she flung the bowl away from her and raced down the track, holding her skirts in both hands.

"Ares!"

He dropped his sack and his spear and stood waiting for her.

Aphrodite's heart thudded in her chest as she ran. She felt the pins coming out of her hair, and it tangled about her face as she flung herself at him as the dog had. Ares's arms crushed her to his chest, and she squirmed against the cold angles of his breast-plate. He laughed and gripped her by the shoulders, holding her a little away from him.

"Now there's a woman worth coming home to!"

She stared at his face: His beard was grizzled gray and his cheek scarred with what looked like the mark of a spear point. His hair hung dankly under a dented helmet with half its horsehair crest torn away. The shield that he unslung from his back was bat-tered and scarred as well, the bright blue eye blind with dirt and scratches. His own gray eyes were sunken under ragged brows, and when he laughed she could see the dark places where two teeth had been. His right ear was as ragged as a tomcat's. She stared and her eyes filled with tears.

"By the Bull, you are beautiful," he said, and pulled her against him again, kissing her hard. His breath was foul.

She staggered as he let her go and wrapped one arm around her waist instead. He handed her his spear to carry and picked up his shield and the sack.

"We've been waiting for you," she told him, wob-bling as she tried to walk with his weight against her hip. She could see the blood on his calf now, and saw he was limping. "You're hurt!"

"A Trojan arrow. I caught it when we took the city. Nothing a little salve and some nursing won't cure." He took another step, leaning on her heavily. "It festers."

"I'll call Hebe. She's the best at that."

"Everyone else still alive and kicking? The old ones as poisonous as ever?"

"They died. After you left."

"Now there's good news." Ares grinned at her.

After the king killed his daughter for a wind. She didn't

say that. Ares hadn't done that. There wouldn't have been anything he could have done to stop it, surely.

"And my dear brother? I don't suppose you're a widow?"

"Hephaestus is well."

"A shame."

"He's a good man, Ares. He's been good to me. *You* weren't here!" she said, suddenly angry because she didn't feel lighter, more joyful.

"I couldn't have borne to miss a war like that," Ares said seriously. He stopped in the road, his bundle over his shoulder, the mist clinging to his beard. "Ten years we fought them, Aphrodite. Ten years. We fought every ally they had, every kingdom surrounding them, fought them one by one and brought them all over to our side, all into *our* army. Then we went for Troas's throat."

His eyes gleamed, little sparks of fire in the sea-gray irises. He was remembering, she thought. Remembering the blood and the noise and the thrill of it. He had always liked blood. *I will get used to you like this,* Aphrodite thought. *I still love you. You haven't changed too much for me to love you.*

She nodded at him, and they picked their way up the road. The chickens left their spilled grain to greet her and peck about her feet.

"Do you still have that pet hen?" he asked her.

"She died long ago. But they all come to me still."

Ares looked around the farmyard. "Well, I've seen worse on my way home, but not much."

"What do you expect with most of the men gone to your army?" Aphrodite demanded. "Half the men in Argolis, at least. And now the king and queen are dead and the royal family is fighting itself, with the army taking sides, and no one has time or money for keeping up the roads or the water channels, or even the temples to the Goddess. Zeus is old now and so are the Uncles, and you know Dionysus and Hermes were never any use. And sometimes we can't even sell what we do raise. The markets here are complete chaos, and the shipping is unreliable—the waters are full of pirates." She looked at him with exasperation. "Heracles does most of the work by himself. He'll be glad to have you here."

Ares snorted. "And my dear brother?"

"Your brother has plenty to do, mending every broken thing from soup ladles to wagon wheels."

"Ah. Well, now that I'm home, we'll see. I suppose I'll have to use my plunder to put the place to rights."

"Plunder?"

"Wondrous things," Ares said, winking. "A gold necklace off a princess of Troas. The captain got the princess, but I got the necklace. Maybe I'll give it to you. Come along. I want a hot bath and some wine. I've been thinking of it since we docked."

As they passed the forge, Hephaestus saw them and came out, wiping sooty hands on his leather apron.

"Ho, brother!" Ares said. "Your wife is going to give me a bath."

Hephaestus gave them a long look and turned back into the forge. They heard his hammer clang on the anvil.

"You didn't have to say that!" Aphrodite hissed. "That was cruel."

"Ah, he should be used to it. He knows you're mine."

"You needn't rub his face in it. And you've been gone ten years!"

"How does that matter?"

Aphrodite had told herself the story of their love over and over in those ten years, and the other men hadn't made much difference to it. She had told herself how she waited for him, and how he came home a hero in the gleaming armor he had ridden away in and swept her into his arms. Now it wasn't like that.

In his mother's house, Ares stripped off the battered armor and piled it in a corner of the hall with his spear and the sack he had carried. The sack settled on the floor with a clang. The tunic beneath his breastplate was ragged and stank. Hera threw her arms around him as Aphrodite had done, while Zeus regarded him with caution.

"I am glad to see you unharmed," he said.

Then they both stood back, as if he were a stranger to whom they didn't know quite what to offer.

Ares pulled off his greaves and winced as the left one came away. "Nearly unharmed," he said, and that gave them all something to do.

Hera sent for Hebe, who looked at his leg and pursed her mouth and ordered Semele off to find a long list of herbs and ointments. Hebe took him off to the bath, and Ares, suddenly malleable, let her order him into a chair, and gritted his teeth while she probed the wound in his calf.

"Hold my hand," he said to Aphrodite, who was hesitating at the door, so she gave it to him. His fingers clamped down on hers as Hebe squeezed foul-smelling pus out of the wound.

"Anngh!" The veins in Ares's neck stood out.

There were maggots in the pus. Aphrodite gagged.

Hebe gave him a cup of unwatered wine spiked with tears of poppy to drink, and opened the wound further, probing while he shook until his teeth rattled. When she poured vinegar into it, Aphrodite thought he would break her fingers. At last Hebe sat back and said, "That'll do. Get in the bath and soak it."

Ares stood, still shaking, and pulled off his filthy tunic. Semele had come with the things Hebe had asked for, and Maia and Hermes brought jugs of water. They all fussed over Ares, helping him wipe himself down with oil and then scrape himself clean. Aphrodite thought he was enjoying that, being the hero. It wasn't fair to blame him for that, she told herself.

Hebe took the basket from Semele and made up a poultice of flowers of copper mixed with hypericum, honey, and olive oil, while they filled the bath and helped Ares into it. His body was lean, the ribs showed, and he had more scars than Aphrodite had seen at first: a long white gash that must be years old along his ribs, and a twisted scar, newer and an angry red, that ran from his shoulder to his left elbow.

Ares sank into the bath, head nodding from the poppy, and Semele washed his hair and beard and rinsed it with lavender water. Aphrodite retreated to the doorway again as they bustled about him.

"Glad to have the old man home?" Hermes asked her with a wink, smacking her backside.

Aphrodite whipped around and swung a fist at him, and he dodged, sending a water jug clattering across the stone floor.

"Get out before you break something," Maia snapped at him, and Hermes departed, hooting with laughter.

"Aphrodite, come and help me," Hera said abruptly, and Aphrodite followed her.

"You stay away from him now that he's home,"

Hera said. She carried a bundle of linens and spoke to Aphrodite over her shoulder as they crossed the hall to Ares's old chamber. "That war hasn't done him any good. He frightens me."

"You're his mother!" Aphrodite said.

"I am. And I know what I'm talking about." Hera bent to put the linens on the empty bed, pushed her graying hair back from her face. "I bore him and I raised him, and I know him best."

Aphrodite fidgeted with the washbasin and ewer on the table, and stumbled over the empty chamber pot that had somehow wandered into the center of the unused room.

Hera made a "Tchah!" noise and said, "Come help me with this bed. My back is troubling me."

Aphrodite obeyed.

"What's in that sack of his?" Hera asked.

"I don't know. He talked about his plunder. He said he had the necklace of a Trojan princess."

"Hmm! From what I hear, it's lucky he didn't bring back the princess. Men are barbarians." Hera straightened the covers on the bed with a jerk of her hand.

"He said the captain got the princess," Aphrodite said. "As if she were a piece of plunder."

"That's what I mean," Hera said. "That was a bad war. And I don't like to think what happened to the princess. I've heard tales."

"You mean about King Agamemnon?"

"And others. War is dreadful, and dreadfulness is catching. It eats away the soul."

Aphrodite listened curiously. She had never heard Hera discuss philosophy. Her attention was usually on the cleanliness of the house and the amount of cheese coming out of the dairy.

A splashing from the bath chamber told them Ares was out of the tub. "No," he said, coming into the hall wrapped in a towel and plainly still under the influence of the poppy juice. "I want my sack. Bring me my sack." He started across the tiles for it.

"I'll get it," Zeus said, rising from his chair. "Put him in bed, for the Bull's sake. He looks half dead."

"Not so dead as I was," Ares said. "Get me my sack." He stood stubbornly in the hall, dripping water on the floor.

"Get into your bed; someone will slip in that," Hera said.

"Get me my sack!"

Zeus brought it, panting a bit, and set it on the floor beside Ares's bed. Ares lay down, propped himself on one arm, and said, "Now, see what treasures I bring home!" He reached into the sack and took out a cloth-wrapped bundle, stained and filthy. As he unwrapped it, Aphrodite's eyes widened. It was a gold necklace, finer than anything she had ever seen, finer even than the one Hephaestus had made her as a wedding gift. Loop after loop of gold beads cascaded from Ares's fingers, with a pendant in the shape of a lion's head hanging from the longest. The lion had carnelian eyes. Interspersed between the gold beads were pearls and beads of coral and amber.

"Shall I give it to you?" he asked Aphrodite. "It was a Trojan princess's, but she won't want it anymore." He laughed.

"She's dead, isn't she?" Aphrodite whispered.

"They're all dead," Ares said. "All dead. Look what else." He looked up at Zeus. "Fix up this goat shed." He waved his arm about him at the room. "Look here." Ares drew out a gold vase nearly as long as his forearm, with a relief of a bull hunt around its middle. The top and bottom curved gracefully inward and then out again, and the narrowest points were girdled with bands of twisted silver and silver leaves. "Ha! Better than my brother can make!"

"Where did this come from?" Hera asked him.

"Troas, Mother dearest."

"You know what I mean."

"From a temple of their goddess. They all went to hide in the temple, old Priam and his lot; much good it did them. We pulled them out and pulled their temple down afterward."

Hera compressed her lips. "A temple of the Goddess?"

"Their goddess, not ours. Here"—he tossed the vase to Zeus, who staggered catching it—"pay for some repairs on this place before the roof falls in."

"All goddesses are the same Goddess," Hera said.

"Bah. And the old bull in the pasture out there is the Bull who rides her," Ares said.

"He may be," Hera retorted, and Aphrodite felt the hair stand up on her neck. "That is part of the mystery."

"Silly," Ares said dismissively. "If the Goddess was fighting on our side, how could she be the goddess of Troas, too?"

"It is a mystery," Hera said again. "A women's mystery."

"Then the Goddess won't mind if Father sells that vase," Ares retorted. "Since men aren't in on the mystery."

"We can use it," Zeus said to Hera. "I'll give you some of the money to put a roof over her spring."

"Sell the necklace!" Aphrodite said abruptly. "Sell the necklace and give me the vase to give the Goddess." Maybe she could undo a little of what she had done.

Zeus raised his brows. No one had ever known Aphrodite to turn down a present.

Ares looked startled, too, but Aphrodite was adamant. "I'll take it to the Goddess and put it in the spring, and maybe she'll give us a good olive pressing this year." He would just be angry if she said that the more she looked at the dead princess's gold the less she wanted to touch it. Or that she couldn't bear to wear the necklace in front of Hephaestus and rub his face in his wife's love for someone else. Ares would just laugh, and then he would taunt Hephaestus with it. "Give me the vase, Ares," she wheedled, smiling at him.

"I can't watch you wear the vase," he said.

"No need for you to be watching your brother's wife!" Hera snapped.

"Very well, since you insist . . . Mother," he said, but he was looking at Aphrodite.

They left him alone to sleep, and Aphrodite wandered out into the yard again, trying to think what she ought to do next. She should tell Eros that Ares was home, but Eros wasn't speaking to her. She felt reluctant to face Hephaestus. She picked up the spilled bowl that had held the chicken's feed and found it cracked through the middle. She swore at it and threw the pieces in the midden. The sun was burning off the mist, and the birds that swept over the land every spring and fall on their way to who knew where were circling above the trees. She thought it would be nice to be one of them, and then went and got the gold vase before Ares changed his mind.

Zeus had taken it and set it on a shelf in the great

hall. When she lifted it down, she held it for a moment in her hands, feeling the heavy, cold heart of it.

Hebe came out of Ares's chamber, wiping her hands on a cloth, while Aphrodite was studying it. "You're quite right," Hebe said. "Give it back to the Goddess and maybe it will turn the ill luck Ares has brought home with him."

"What ill luck?" Why was everyone acting as if he were a black crow lighting on the rooftop?

"Nothing good comes off a battlefield," Hebe said. "And don't think he's out of the woods yet, either. That leg is very bad."

Aphrodite looked up from the vase. "I thought you said he would be all right?"

"I said I did what could be done," Hebe said. "A salamander repairs itself more easily than we do. It can grow a new leg, bones and all. All we can do is grow patches over our wounds. If inflammation sets in, or the black rot . . . Well."

"Well, what?" Aphrodite demanded, but she knew—she had seen the vintner last year who had caught his arm in a press. Now the bottom half of it was missing, with a bit of bone sticking out the end, nearly grown over with proud flesh. If you were lucky, the limb died and dropped off. If you weren't, the inflammation and rot went through your whole body and you died.

"Make him let me tend it then," Hebe said. "You can get him to do more things than most of us. If I don't tend it, his chances won't be so good, but it will hurt, and I don't intend to have him strangle me in a rage because I've hurt him."

"I'll sit with him when you do," Aphrodite said.

"Very well. Now go and talk to the Goddess for us." Hebe watched her set out with the vase held carefully in both hands. Aphrodite did talk to the Goddess in some strange way, she thought. All women spoke to her, but Aphrodite spoke with her whole body, as if she were a little piece of her that had somehow got detached. No wonder she was so much trouble, Hebe thought. You didn't want the Goddess in your house, not really. She was too strong a force, like a fire or a whirlwind or a great wave out of the sea. You worshiped her at a comfortable distance and hoped she blessed you and left you alone.

Dark stains still marred the stones around the lip of the Goddess's pool, but there was green moss growing over them now, and the water was clear and cool, its surface mysterious, faintly rippled with the little breeze that whispered through the laurel leaves. Aphrodite knelt and dipped some up in cupped hands, an offering to pour down the round, inscrutable face of the omphalos stone. She cupped a hand into the water again and drank, peering into the depths. Her own face looked back at her, wavy in the wake of her fingers. She set the vase on the lip of the pool and looked for a long moment at the hunters chasing the wild bull eternally around its girth. Then she took it in both hands and plunged it into the dark water so that it filled to the lip. She let go and it sank slowly, drifting into the depths like a gold ship sailing into some unknown night. She watched until it was out of sight and then whispered to the Goddess, "I have brought it back. We are sorry he took it. Mother says it was yours."

A single bubble rose from the bottom of the pool like a breath, a sigh. *Mine*, a voice whispered in Aphrodite's ear.

"I am to ask for your blessing, Lady, on the olive harvest," Aphrodite whispered back, frightened at the intimacy of the voice.

Mine, the water said again. It paused. *It. You. Everything*.

Aphrodite sat very still.

The girl, the voice said now.

"What girl?" Aphrodite asked, startled.

Something gold stirred at the bottom of the pool, as if the vase moved, swam in the darkness. *Let her in*.

"Let her in? Where? Do you mean that girl my son is infatuated with?" Aphrodite's voice rose in indignation, forgetting fear.

The voice was silent. A frog plopped off the lip of the pool and scissored away from her into the black water.

"She's gone, anyway," Aphrodite said. "He doesn't want to see her again."

A winged insect, delicate as a cobweb, lit on the water, skating on the surface tension. The frog erupted openmouthed from the pool and swallowed it.

The voice was still. Aphrodite drew her knees up to her chin and wrapped her arms around them, leaning against the omphalos stone. An ant crossed her feet, white feet with long toes, and she let it walk clear over her instep and down her big toe without swatting it. There were bunions on the right foot, ugly red knobs that she hadn't had when she was young. No one stayed young but the Goddess.

She sat by the pool until the sun was low in the sky and its orange light filtered through the leaves and shot off the surface of the water. Then she got up slowly, stiff from having sat on the ground for so

long. She peered into the pool and thought she
caught a glimpse of the vase again, but it might have
been a fish or even her bronze horse and chariot. She
walked slowly back up the track to the house and
found Hephaestus just leaving the forge.

"Has my brother settled in?" he inquired.

They didn't speak of each other by name now, she
noted, the way Helen had said "my husband." "He
has a festering wound in his calf," Aphrodite said.
"Hebe treated it and put him to sleep with tears of
poppy. He'll be awake by now, though, I expect."

"You'll be wanting to see him," Hephaestus said,
looking straight ahead.

"I have work to do," Aphrodite said. "At home. I
thought maybe you would want to." They walked in
silence to the house. "But maybe not." She lifted the
latch. "He brought home a gold vase that he took
from a temple of the Trojans' goddess," she said
abruptly. "Mother said we couldn't keep it. I made
him give it to me and I put it in the pool by the
spring."

"And what did you ask her for?" Hephaestus
said quietly.

"A good olive harvest."

He was silent, considering her.

"What did you think I asked her for?" she demanded. She knew, and knew he wouldn't say it.

"Happiness?" His voice was almost a whisper.

Aphrodite ignored him. She crossed the hall
briskly into the kitchen where Cook was baking whit-
ing in garlic sauce. Aphrodite sniffed. "Too much
garlic," she said, and went through into the garden
while Cook glared at her.

In the garden she sat down on the chair Helen had
sat in and put her head in her hands. Her lover had

come home with a wound that might kill him and an aura of darkness she couldn't dispel. Her husband thought she had been praying for his death. Her son wasn't speaking to her. In this light, love looked unwieldy and discouraging. She sat there until Cook called grumpily out the door that dinner was ready. She came in and picked at her food, a dish of beans and eels stewed in fig sauce, while Eros bolted his and refused to look at her. Hephaestus, his expression enigmatic, called Teacher out of the kitchen, where he had been dining with Cook, and brought out the draughts board and pieces. He set them out and motioned Teacher to a seat opposite him.

"And where is my devoted brother?" Ares inquired when Aphrodite went up to Hera's house to see him. "Not going to visit the wounded hero?"

"He's playing draughts with Teacher," Aphrodite said, and left it at that. She remembered Ares fighting the village boys who had taunted Hephaestus, and then bedeviling Hephaestus himself once they were at home. She had asked Ares why he did that and still defended his brother from outsiders, and Ares had looked at her as if she were stupid and said, "Because he's *ours*."

"Hebe says I'm to sit with you and make you behave when she comes to dress that leg," Aphrodite said. "She says she won't do it otherwise for fear you'll hurt her."

"I will," Ares said.

"Do you want to die of the rot? Hebe says you will if she doesn't tend it."

"Hebe says. Bah! Tell me what Aphrodite says." His hand shot out and caught hers and he pressed it to his lips. They were dry and rough, but the old familiar lightning shot up her back. "I thought about you all the way home in that cursed boat," he said. "It pitched and I lost everything I ate, but I still thought about you."

"Just on the way home? Not before?"

"With the war going on? No time, love. No time."

"I suppose not. I thought about *you* the whole time." She stroked his cheek and then his ragged ear with her other hand. "I used to sit and think of what I would tell you when you got home. How the vines made such a good vintage one year, and about the year there were so many owls. And about Eros. He's the best shot of anyone with a bow now. I used to watch him and be so sad that you couldn't see him grow."

"He grew anyway, didn't he?" Ares seemed more interested in wriggling his hand along her skirt, seeing if he could get under it.

Aphrodite batted his fingers away. "I wanted him to know you."

"What for? Are you going to send him into the army? He wasn't the type when he was small; I doubt he's changed."

"Ares, he may be your son," Aphrodite said, aggravated.

"He may not, too. And I'm sure my brother has done a fine job of raising him and teaching him to make jewelry." Ares's lip curled.

Aphrodite looked hurt.

Ares took her hand again and squeezed it. "I know you're fond of him. I'll try to be fatherly if you want."

"I don't want you to be fatherly," she said. "That would upset him and Hephaestus both. I just want you to be . . . well, to take an interest."

"I take an interest in you." Ares grinned. "Come a little closer here."

Aphrodite stiffened. "Not here!"

"Why not?"

"I can't," she said fretfully. It had been different ten years ago, when she was young and wild, and thought nothing of making love to him in the barn or the woods. But now he was in bed in his mother's house. "Hebe will be here any minute to dress your leg. And anyway," she added, suddenly aggrieved, "you've been gone ten years! You went off and left me for *ten years!* And you want me to just hop into bed with you and get caught by Hebe?"

"Why not? Give old Proper Behavior something to liven up her evening."

Aphrodite giggled in spite of herself.

Ares's hand clamped more tightly on hers. "And I suppose you're going to tell me you've been faithful all this time?"

"Have you?" she demanded.

"That's different. A man at war needs a release. And Trojan girls were easy." He laughed. "Once you tied them up."

Aphrodite pulled her hand away.

"No, come back, love. I'm sorry." Ares looked contrite. "I won't even ask what you did while I was gone."

He didn't look as though he meant it, she thought. He'd get around to it.

"Just tell me you haven't fallen in love with my brother while I've been away."

"He's a good man," she said again.

"Good men are dull," Ares said.

Aphrodite couldn't think of an answer to that. Hephaestus wasn't dull. He knew more things about the world than anyone else in the family, even Ares, who had been to Troas and back. Hephaestus noticed things, like the dance of the stars through the seasons, and showed them to her, pointing out the Sacred Twins and the Horns of the Bull on a clear, cold night. He watched. Ares was like the Bull itself, charging blindly down his path. But Hephaestus had never given her the dreadful yearning in the heart that Ares did.

Hebe came in to dress Ares's leg again, and Aphrodite sat and held his hand until she had finished. Afterward Ares was pale and flopped back against his pillow, grunting with pain. He glared at Hebe.

"When I was at war, the captain pulled out a triple-barbed arrow from his own leg and treated it with oil and wine," he said.

"And has this captain still got the leg?" Hebe asked him.

"I don't know," Ares admitted. "It was festering."

"So is yours. Lie down and give your body a chance to heal it. If it will." She swept out with her basket of herbs and salve and the bowl of bloody water, and Ares closed his eyes.

Aphrodite left him sleeping restlessly. Hephaestus was still up when she got home. Teacher had gone to bed, and there was no sign of Eros. Hephaestus was fitting points to a sheaf of hunting arrows, tying them down with sinew.

"Where is he?" Aphrodite demanded.

"Gone to bed, I expect," Hephaestus said.

"Are you sure?"

"Do you want me to sleep with him to be certain?"

"What was it I saw in men?" she muttered, and stalked down the hall to their bedchamber. Behind her, she heard Hephaestus laughing.

XVIII

❧

Talking to the Snake

In the morning Hephaestus rose before Aphrodite did, whistling as he dressed and making no mention of Eros or Ares. Aphrodite followed him to feed the chickens and tend the goats whose milk gave the household its cheese. The sun was barely up, and the sky was already a clear, startling blue, like the ocean on a bright day. There was no whisper of wind, and the air was warm, golden on her shoulders. She took a deep breath, savoring its taste. This was the last trace of summer before winter's chill. Aphrodite had always loved that season, the last warmth made the more lovely because you knew for certain that winter was coming. The hens clucked around her feet, pecking interestedly at her toes. She counted heads—Heracles had said he had seen a fox in the woods—and scattered their feed on the ground. They rustled after it, muttering and clucking, while the rooster paced back and forth in front of them, displaying his tail feathers. Every so often he dived at the feed and chased a hen from a particularly large bite.

The does were waiting for her in the goat shed, their gold eyes and strange black-barred pupils gleaming in the shadows. Aphrodite sat down in the straw, leaning her cheek against Seashell's back. Seashell butted her gently with her horns and switched her tail while the others bleated and stuck their noses in Aphrodite's lap. Sometimes she had apples.

When she had filled the buckets with warm milk she took them into the kitchen and gave the snake his bowlful. "Have you seen Eros this morning?" she asked Cook, just casually.

"Took a loaf of bread and the last of a rind of cheese," Cook said, kneading dough, "without asking, mind, and said he was going up the vineyards. Don't know why, with harvest over. Just for a place to get into trouble, I expect. That dog went with him." Cook cracked an egg disapprovingly.

"Oh." Aphrodite went out into the kitchen garden, skirting a bucket of eels at the door, and stared aimlessly at the cabbages and the last of the beans drying in their pods. The farm dogs began to bark, and she shaded her eyes, looking down the road into the trees. Someone was coming along, a small someone in a skirt. She squinted her eyes. Peddlers weren't usually women. This one had a bundle over one shoulder.

The dogs danced around the woman, and she stopped near the forge, probably frightened of them. Aphrodite saw Hephaestus come out, and she was about to go down and see who it was when she recognized the intruder. It was that girl. A brief memory of herself in her nightdress, calling names and throwing rocks in the darkness, flooded embarrassingly back.

Hephaestus was talking to the girl. Very well. Let

him chase her off. She couldn't stay here. And he would see exactly how brazen she was and why Eros should be kept from her at all costs. Or . . . Aphrodite folded her arms and stared at him. He saw her and lifted a hand. Aphrodite shook her head to indicate the absolute necessity of driving that girl off at once. Hephaestus bent his head to the girl's blond one. She was explaining something to him, moving her hands pleadingly.

Aphrodite went back through the kitchen door. Now it seemed to her a good thing that Eros had gone off so early. Hephaestus would send the girl away, and Aphrodite wouldn't have to talk to her, and Eros wouldn't even see her.

Cook had disappeared on some errand, and the kitchen was empty, so Aphrodite sat down on the floor to consult the snake. The snake belonged to the Goddess, but he had never actually said anything out loud. Aphrodite felt more at ease with him than with the voice that came out of the pool into her head.

"She's not the right girl for him," she informed the snake. "And yes, I do know he has to marry sometime, but he's not nearly old enough. Mother says a man should be thirty before he takes a wife. Of course, Hephaestus wasn't thirty, but she wanted to get rid of me, and he was the only one who would take me. Or the only one she thought could stand me, or something. Maybe she was right. If I'd been married to Ares and he went off and left me for ten years, I might have done what Clytemnestra did. What do you think?"

The snake looked at her enigmatically with golden eyes and then laid his flat head on her thigh. Slowly the rest of him flowed after until his whole length was piled in her lap. She was the only one of the household that the snakes seemed to actually be fond of. With snakes it was hard to tell, but they never socialized with anyone else. Even the young snake in Hera's kitchen, who had replaced the venerable serpent of Aphrodite's childhood, came out to see her when she was there.

Aphrodite shifted until she sat cross-legged, with the snake in the hammock of her skirts. His cool gray-green coils were smooth to the touch. "I made a fool of myself the other night," she confided to him. "Throwing rocks and shouting. I was so angry, and cold and tired with sitting in that barley field waiting for him. I must have looked like a harpy. It's a wonder she has the nerve to come back here. But she needn't think I'm going to take her part."

Take her part. The words hung in the air like an echo, a faint shimmering of sound about her head.

"Oh, no. No. She isn't going to stay."

Stay.

"No. I misunderstood what the Goddess said at the pool. I'm positive. Don't try to make me think I didn't."

Didn't.

Annoyed, Aphrodite glared at the snake. "Don't play silly tricks. Hephaestus must drive her off," she added to see what he did with that.

Silence. No echo shimmered about those words.

"She can't stay," she whispered.

Stay.

The snake lifted his head and looked at her out of round gold eyes. He slithered off her lap and back into his basket.

Cook came bustling back into the kitchen with a fresh cheese from the cold cellar and peered at her. "What are you doing on the floor?"

"Talking to the snake," Aphrodite said.

"Not a good idea," Cook said. "Never ask the gods questions; you're as like as not to get answers. Just feed them and give them their proper due and don't talk to them."

Aphrodite stood up, wincing as her knees creaked. None of her was as young as it had been. She used to be as limber as the snake. "Too late for that advice," she said crossly. "And I didn't ask for it anyway."

"What did he say to you, then?" Cook put her fists on her broad hips and looked suspiciously at Aphrodite.

"He didn't say anything." Aphrodite had no intention of discussing that girl, or her son's shortcomings, with Cook. "And I don't want eel again for dinner," she added, looking at the bucket.

"I was going to make a pie," Cook said.

"Well, don't put eels in it."

"What am I going to do with them then?"

"Wear them for a necklace," Aphrodite said irritably. "I'm sick of eels." She went back out into the garden to see if Hephaestus had gotten rid of that girl yet.

"They're very nourishing," she heard Cook shouting after her, but she didn't answer because she met Hephaestus and the girl face-to-face, coming through the gate from the yard.

"My dear," Hephaestus said before she could open her mouth, "this child is called Psyche, and I'm afraid our son has not treated her very well."

Aphrodite favored Hephaestus with a look of infuriated reproach, intended to indicate her total dismay at his flagrant lack of regard for her feelings, as well as her wounded trust in him and her sorrowful real-

ization that he lacked all fatherly feeling into the
bargain.

Hephaestus ignored all of it. "Eros has put her in
a very bad position indeed," he informed Aphrodite.

"No one can put a girl in any position she doesn't
want to be in!"

"Not all girls are as resourceful as you were, my
dear."

"What is that supposed to mean?" Aphrodite inquired, while the girl eyed her with an unbecoming
curiosity.

"Psyche finds it difficult to go home just now,"
Hephaestus said, "and the quarters that Eros arranged for her are no longer available, due to lack
of funds to pay the rent."

"Please, my lady." Psyche looked straight at
Aphrodite. She was as lovely as Aphrodite remembered her, even with her face powdered with road
dust and her gown torn at the hem. She set her bundle, tied up in what appeared to be bed linens, down
at her feet. "He's angry with me because I didn't
trust him, but I do love him. Give me a chance and
you'll see what a good daughter I can be."

"I am not in the market for a daughter," Aphrodite snapped.

"I could be a lady's maid," Psyche suggested.

"Not mine!"

"Perhaps Hebe," Hephaestus suggested. "Or she
could help nurse my brother. He was injured in the
war," he said to Psyche.

"Have you lost your mind?" Aphrodite looked
from one to the other of them. They had conspired,
she could tell—they had reached some agreement before coming to her. She felt extremely angry and betrayed. Hephaestus had never so much as looked at

another woman. Well, so far as she knew. But this girl was beautiful enough to stop any man in his tracks. She used to be able to do that herself, so she knew. Now all anyone said, she thought petulantly, was what a beauty she must have been. Nurse Ares? "If you have enticed our son into some ill-advised relationship," she said now, "that is your own doing, I'm sure. Certainly Eros has not asked me to welcome you. So I shan't, until he does." There.

"Eros is angry at the moment," Hephaestus said. "But I rather think he will come around."

"He won't."

"Then what harm in letting the poor child stay on a bit? Until she can make other arrangements?"

Aphrodite glared at him. What had gotten into Hephaestus? She pointed a finger at Psyche. "You stay here." She grabbed Hephaestus by the arm. "Or go away," she added hopefully. "But leave us alone."

She dragged him out of earshot, through the garden gate as quickly as he could hobble, and as far as the ancient oak tree that shaded the forge. "What do you think you are doing?" she hissed.

"Undoing what Eros has done." Hephaestus looked angry now. "She can't go home; her father thinks she's disgraced the family, and he wants to lock her up where no one will see her. She can't stay in the house Eros took for her because he isn't paying the rent anymore. And for all I know she may be pregnant. She can't swear she's not."

"This is too much!" Aphrodite said furiously, spitting the words out between her teeth. "Ares comes home and talks of raping Trojan girls, so that I feel sorry for *them*! Eros takes up with that shoemaker's child! And you—trying to bring her into my house!"

Hot tears flowed down her face suddenly, and she turned away from him.

She felt his hand on her shoulder. Then his cheek against her hair. "No one will ever be more beautiful than you in my eyes. Or in my brother's, either, I'm afraid. But Eros needs to go his own way; you know that. He loved this child, or he wouldn't have gone to such trouble and lied to us so thoroughly. Give them time to work it out. If they don't, I'll find her a place somewhere. If they do . . . well, you want him to be happy, don't you?"

"Happier than we've been?" She sniffled.

"Well, yes. That would be nice."

Aphrodite tried to think. Really think, not just fling angry words at him. The Goddess had as good as told her to take the girl in. The snake had told her. She had thought she wouldn't have to listen because the girl was long gone. Now the girl was here, not gone at all, and Aphrodite felt uneasily that she had better listen.

"Where would she live?"

"In our house?"

"Ha!"

"We do have an extra room."

"The little room?" The little room next to Cook's chamber was a storeroom that had gradually accumulated eighteen years' worth of odds and ends. It was smaller even than Cook's and had no window. Aphrodite was reasonably sure Psyche would hate it. "I suppose she could clean it out," she said grudgingly. She looked back toward the garden. The girl was still standing there in the beans, like a statue, where they had left her. "What will you tell Eros?"

"That it is our house, not his. Eros has made this mess. He will have to live with what we do about it."

"I assumed you thought *I* had made it," Aphrodite said. "Because I forbade him to see the girl."

"Eros decided what to do about that. There were more intelligent paths he could have taken."

"Very well. But she will take orders from me. And she will *not* be a member of the family. Is that clear?" The Goddess hadn't said anything about coddling the girl, and Aphrodite intended to take the Goddess very literally.

"Agreed."

Aphrodite set off toward the garden again without waiting for him. The girl looked at her hopefully as she came through the gate. "Have you ever milked a goat?" Aphrodite inquired.

"No, lady."

"Well, you'll be expected to make yourself useful, so we'll start with that. After you have cleaned out your chamber." Aphrodite looked at the bundle at the girl's feet. "What's in that?"

"My clothes."

"Completely inappropriate, I'm sure. You won't need fancy gowns here." The one she wore was of good fabric despite the tear, Aphrodite noted, with the tucks and flounces that took time and expertise to stitch. Over Aphrodite's own work clothes, a rough woolen skirt and a plain bodice, she wore an apron much stained with use. The girl needn't think she was going to dress like a concubine in *her* household.

"I sold the nice ones," Psyche said. "To pay the bills."

The bills Eros had run up. Aphrodite's lips compressed. "Come along then."

She led Psyche through the kitchen—no need to take the girl in the way that guests came—and to the little chamber next door. "You can sleep here. Cook has the one on the other side. You'll take your meals with her. My son's teacher most often eats with Cook as well, unless we ask him to dine with us." Her tone made it plain that that invitation would not be issued to Psyche.

"Yes, my lady." Psyche peered into the little room. Its dim recesses were piled with broken bed frames, dented oil lamps, rolled and moth-eaten carpets, and what looked like a loom that someone had taken a hammer to. Crates and baskets were stacked in wobbling piles, coated with dust, and when Aphrodite stepped through the doorway, something vaguely mouselike scurried into a hole in a trunk.

Aphrodite looked at Psyche's bundle. "When you've got it straightened out, I expect you can make up the bed with that sheet."

"My lady? What shall I do with all this?" Psyche waved a hand at the contents of the room. "There's no room for me."

Astute of you. "Well, I imagine you can use some of it. You'll need a bed. The things you don't want you can put in the barn." Aphrodite disappeared down the little hallway that connected the kitchen and servants' quarters with the main house and left Psyche staring at the jumble in the room.

She was still in the doorway, trying to think what thing to take out first without the rest falling on her head, when she heard footsteps and whirled around. Eros stood staring at her.

His face blazed with surprise. "What are you doing here?"

"I am to stay here," she whispered. "Your father says it."

"I told you to stay away from me!"

"Where else am I going to go?" Psyche snapped,

losing the humble demeanor she had been at pains to cultivate during the walk from Tiryns.

"Does my mother know about this?"

"She told me to clean out this room and make up a bed in it," Psyche said.

Eros backed away. "She's up to something. I'm not having any part of it."

Psyche pulled a disintegrating basket off the top of a stack and coughed as the air filled with dust. "I'm to put these things in the barn."

Eros glared at her. "You needn't think I'll help you now. This is your fault." He was uncomfortably aware that family sentiment might rather put it at his door.

"You needn't think I want you to," Psyche shot back, and felt a surprising satisfaction when she heard his footsteps going away. She hadn't lied when she told his mother she loved him, but it was interesting how angry you could be at someone and still love him. She opened the basket and dropped it when a cricket sprang out into her face.

"Shoo! Or I'll squash you!" She stomped threateningly at the cricket and it leaped away into the shadows. Psyche picked up the basket again and a wooden box that had been stacked below it. The box held nothing but three old sandals with holes in the soles.

Psyche set out for the kitchen with a burden in each hand. Cook's broad form was visible, muttering over the eels, and she stopped to ask, "Where is the barn, please?"

Cook looked her over curiously. "Ah. You'll be the new servant girl, I suppose. Madam told me about you. Barn's yonder, but don't go through the garden door; you'll trample the beans. Go that way." She

pointed at a second doorway that opened into a
dusty yard where a few of Aphrodite's chickens
clucked morosely and a pig nosed at the dung pile.
"You want the goat barn; it's the first one. Stay away
from the horse barn. They're jumpy creatures, and
that Poseidon doesn't like strangers messing with
them."

Psyche went through the door, skirting the dung
and the pig, and saw the goat barn, a weathered
structure of stone and plaster and thatched roof, with
a crumbling shed attached to one side. She entered
gingerly, peering into the dusty shadows while barn
swallows swooped over her head. In the light from
the doorway she made out the stall that housed the
plow ox. He stared back at her with huge dark eyes,
his horns a wide curve to either side of his face, like
an upturned moon. Beyond him were milking stalls
for the goats and a doe asleep in the warm straw,
her knees buckled under her and her beard waggling
as she snored. Psyche had seen the other goats in the
field beyond the barn, grazing with a herd of sleek,
dangerous-looking horses.

She didn't see anyplace that looked like somewhere she should leave her burdens, so she went
outside again and inspected the shed. Its cobwebby
interior was already littered with a broken wheelbar-
row, two cracked wine jars, and a stool with two
legs. She left the things she had been carrying among
them and went back for more.

Aphrodite saw her going back and forth, carrying
wobbling stacks of baskets, or tugging the heavy
frame of the broken loom. The loom had been her
marriage gift from Hera, and she had broken it apart
with a hammer from Hephaestus's forge one day a
month after the marriage, after Ares had gone back

to the army. Hephaestus hadn't said anything, just set about making her another one. He had waited a ten-day and then set it up in the hall where the old one had been. Aphrodite had sat down to it and woven a blanket for their bed on it, and neither of them had ever said a word about it. Ares wouldn't have done that, she thought suddenly, watching Psyche dragging it along. Ares would have beaten her with one of the pieces.

Aphrodite watched the girl all day as she went about her own chores. Psyche was still at it, red-faced but determined, when the family gathered in late afternoon on the rocky slope where the olive trees grew, for the annual fall argument over the harvest. The fruit hung heavily in the branches now and had begun to turn the purpley black of a moonless summer night, like dark mysterious eggs among the gray-green leaves. The family gnawed samples from each tree and argued over whether to let them ripen further or pick now.

"They're ready," Zeus said. "Another ten-day and they'll be too ripe before we can finish. The oil will be acid."

Aunt Demeter licked her fingers. "Two more days," she pronounced.

"Three," Heracles said.

Hebe closed her eyes and chewed. "Two," she said. "And what is that girl doing here?"

"That's Eros's little mistake," Heracles answered. He smiled at Hebe in the satisfied way of parents whose own children aren't yet old enough to cause major trouble.

"Where is Eros?" Hera demanded. She seemed to have acquired the whole story already.

"Skulking," Hephaestus said.

Aunt Demeter spat out the olive pit. "Two more days," she said again. "That girl can help. And Eros. He can come out and take his medicine; we'll need him. Hermes and Dionysus are getting too old to climb trees."

Hermes and Dionysus looked offended.

"And you stay away from that girl," Hera told them.

They gave everyone to understand that they had no such thought in their heads, wouldn't dream of it, poaching on young Eros's turf, never.

Aphrodite saw the girl coming out of the shed, brushing cobwebs off her dress. Her hair hung limply about her face, and she scrubbed at her eyes with her fist. Aphrodite took a certain satisfaction in the notion of keeping the girl as unattractive as possible, and marched off to see to that. Behind her in the olive grove the family took up the discussion again amid the lengthening shadows of the trees, but she knew it would be Hebe and Aunt Demeter who would have the final say. She caught Psyche sitting on a hay bale outside the shed.

"Have you cleaned out the room?" Aphrodite asked, hands on hips, disapproving.

"I have the things out of it, yes. It needs mopping."

"You can do that tonight. Right now, you can come with me and I'll show you how to milk the goats."

Psyche looked dubious, but Aphrodite appeared not to notice. "Come along," she said briskly, and led her into the barn, where the does in milk had begun to gather. They crowded expectantly around her knees, bleating and pushing Psyche and one another with their horns and their hard heads. Aphrodite took a tin bucket off its hook on the barn wall.

"Sit," she said, pointing at the floor. Psyche crouched in the straw.

"Not like that." Aphrodite sat down with a sigh to show Psyche how exasperated she was. "Like this." She tucked her knees under her. "Come, goat." Seashell butted her way to the front of the herd and swung her bony rump against Aphrodite's shoulder. Aphrodite gripped the teats, warm and goat-smelling, and squeezed. Milk squirted into the pail. "Like that." She stood up and motioned Psyche toward the goat.

Psyche sat down gingerly. The goat rolled an eye at her and switched its tail. Psyche wrinkled her nose.

"That won't be the worst thing you'll smell here," Aphrodite said with satisfaction. "You can come in the kitchen and ask Cook for some dinner when you've milked all of them."

She disappeared up the path to the house. Psyche eyed the goat. Its strange horizontal pupils looked inscrutably back at her. It snorted and kicked the pail over.

"I don't like you either," Psyche muttered, righting the pail. The goat nibbled the sleeve of her dress. She tugged on its teat the way she had seen Aphrodite do, but nothing came out. The goat looked affronted. And it was getting dark.

She tried again. And again. The goat chewed her hair. She batted at its head and started to cry until the sound of something scraping on the dirt floor made her lift her head. It was Eros's father, leaning on his cane, dragging his lame feet.

"It's not as easy as it looks," he said.

"It didn't look easy." Psyche sniffled. "And it's not. And the goat eats my hair."

"All right." Hephaestus lowered himself carefully to the floor. His lame feet stuck out at odd angles. Psyche tried not to stare at them. "Stand still, you dreadful old bitch." He shook Seashell gently by the horn and she waggled her tail. Hephaestus took the teats in his hands and squeezed. "Like this. Watch my fingers. There's a rhythm to it, to get the milk flowing."

Psyche scrubbed her face with the back of her hand and watched him curiously. The white streams of milk jetted into the pail. "My mother used to set me to milk the goats when I was little," he said. "I wasn't much use for anything else. You don't lose the knack. My brothers laughed at me, of course."

"I've always lived in the city," Psyche said. "We never had a goat. Or a cow. I can make a shoe, though," she added. "Father only had girls, so he taught us."

"So you make things, do you?" Hephaestus smiled at her past Seashell's flank. "So do I. Now you try this. Sit here and I'll put my hands on yours and you'll get the hang of it."

She sat in front of him, and he tipped her head with his hand until it rested against Seashell's flank. The goat was warm and even smellier than before, and her hide tickled Psyche's ear. Hephaestus leaned against Psyche's shoulders and put his arms around her sides, hands on hers. He squeezed her hands, clamping her fingers on the teats, until the milk shot out into the pail.

"I did it!"

"Very good. Just keep going. Squeeze. And squeeze." His hand opened and closed hers in repetitive rhythm. "They like to be milked—it's uncomfortable for them to have a full udder—so once you get going, they stop bothering you."

He was nice, she thought. Maybe Eros would grow up to be like him. If his awful mother didn't drive her away first.

"Now try it on your own." He scooted back in the straw. She kept her fingers on Seashell's teats, trying to remember the rhythm of his hands. The milk dribbled out a bit, and then a respectable stream fell into the pail. "I did it!" she said again, pleased.

"You're a quick study."

"I was afraid I'd never be able to do it," she confided, liking him. "And your wife says I'm not to have dinner until I've milked them all."

Hephaestus scooted along the barn floor to the wall and pulled himself upright. He took down another pail and chirped at one of the waiting does. "What my wife does not know will do her no harm," he said as he sat down again.

They milked in silence for a while, listening to the zing and splash of milk in the pails. Hephaestus milked three goats to Psyche's one, but her speed gradually increased.

"You'll do all right with them in the morning," he said.

"Is she going to make me milk the goats every day?" Psyche asked him. It seemed a ghastly prospect. But perhaps it got easier.

"I expect so," he said. "If you're going to live here, it's a skill you'll need to learn. And you'll soften her up if you get on with the goats. Aphrodite regards every living creature as her personal property. They all come to her. I've seen wild rabbits come to her in the woods."

"She'll never like me," Psyche said dolefully.

"Do you know, I rather think she will. She isn't a cruel woman by nature; she's just ruled by her heart. She clings to this child because she lost one once."

"Eros told me he was the only one," Psyche said, intrigued.

"He's the only one of our marriage," Hephaestus said. "Before that she fell in love with a young man from Troas, who loved her back in his way, I suppose, but he sailed away for home afterward, and when my parents found out Aphrodite was pregnant, they let her have the baby and then they took it away and shipped it off to the young man's family in Troas."

"Your parents?" Psyche frowned, trying to puzzle it out.

"My wife is a foundling. My parents raised her, and she led them such a dance they decided to marry her to me to tie her down." He shooed the last goat away and dragged himself to his feet. "I've never been certain that was the best idea. At any rate, the child was raised in Troas and is very likely dead now in this terrible war. Give her some time, and let her know you won't try to take this one away from her."

What would it be like to have a baby and have someone take it away from you? Psyche wondered. Enough to make you angry forever, maybe. She knew women like that, women whose babies had been exposed, who went about their lives now in silent, merciless hatred of their husbands; hatred the husbands never noticed but that left a faint blue light shining about the wives, as if they emanated some fierce poison. She thought it might be even worse to know the baby was still alive, growing up somewhere without you, and you couldn't have it; although she also knew women who kept themselves sane with just that thin hope. It was the one thing about marriage that frightened her. She looked at Hephaestus's twisted feet.

"We do not, in this family, expose babies, if that is what you are wondering," Hephaestus said.

Psyche nodded.

XIX

❧

Washing a Pig

Hephaestus didn't volunteer any information when he came inside to dinner, smelling of goat, but Aphrodite looked at him suspiciously. Eros, on the other hand, looked as if some sorcerer had molded him out of clay and then animated him just enough to eat his dinner. He stared at the plate of bread before him, piled with a helping of partridge pie and turnips, poured his wine cup too full and slopped it, ate and drank hurriedly, and departed onto the portico with a mumbled excuse too incoherent to be understood.

Aphrodite rose to follow him.

"I doubt that's a good idea," Hephaestus said. "You'll just set his back up."

Aphrodite turned around. "I have no intention of following him. I was just going to see that that girl is settled," she said with elaborate dignity, and started the other way down the hall.

Before she could set out on that mission either, one

of Hebe's babies jangled the bell at the door and said that Mother was going to dress Uncle Ares's leg again, and would Aunt Aphrodite come please, and help her.

"Oh, very well." Aphrodite turned around again and took her cloak off a hook by the door. She scooped the child off the doorstep and put her on her hip, snuggling her into the cloak. "What are you doing out without your mantle? It's getting cold," she scolded.

"Not cold," said the child, with automatic denial of adult attempts to manage her, but she snuggled her face into Aphrodite's armpit. Aphrodite set the child down in Hera's house, where her siblings were playing on the floor with a bag of marbles, and found Hebe in Ares's bedchamber, laying out fresh bandages beside a basin.

A brazier of glowing coals stood in the corner by the bed, making the room close and hot. Aphrodite wrinkled her nose. A faint, sweet, unpleasant smell hung in the air, just noticeable through the smoke. Ares lay propped on pillows, his injured leg covered with a sheet that reached to his waist. The sheet was stained with smears of blood and something clear that had left it stiff in patches.

"It feels fine," Ares said, clutching the sheet. "No need for you to dig at it again."

"It smells," Hebe said. "A wound that's healing properly doesn't smell."

"How would you know? Have you been traveling with some army or other while I've been gone?"

"I've tended dogs who've torn each other open, and goats who got caught in fences. And Hermes when Uncle Poseidon's horse threw him and came down on his hand. There's very little difference between any of them and you." Hebe snatched the sheet away.

Aphrodite sat down on the clothes chest that was the only furniture in the room besides the bed, the brazier, a stool, and the table that held the basin. Ares's chamber had always been spare, undecorated except for his quiver and arrows and his hunting spears. Now his armor was piled in the corner of the room, a jumble of dented bronze and sweat-soaked leather. He had a greave in his hands, and she could see that he had been polishing it with a rag.

"Leave me alone," he said.

"Stop it!" Aphrodite said. He looked at her, startled. "You're behaving like a child. I have real children to annoy me; don't you start."

Ares laughed suddenly. The smile twisted his worn face, but it didn't look friendly. "Now that's what a man comes home from war for! A beautiful woman with a sweet tongue."

"Let Hebe treat your leg if you want to keep it," Aphrodite said bluntly.

"I might end up like my brother. Now there would be irony for you."

Aphrodite moved to the stool beside the bed and took his hand. He gripped it while Hebe took the dressing off his leg. "I could give him tears of poppy," Hebe said, "but he won't take it."

"Evil stuff. It puts my head in a fog," Ares said. "What if I needed to fight?"

"Who would you need to fight on this farm?" Hebe asked scornfully.

"Ahhh! Curse you, you bitch!" His hand tightened on Aphrodite's. "I'll fight you!"

"You're better off without the poppy," Hebe conceded. "It dulls the mind, as you say, and the effect lingers. Some people crave it if they take it too long." She looked critically at the pus still coming from the wound. "But it cuts the pain in the short term."

"Tears of poppy is for people who don't want to see things," Ares grunted.

"I wouldn't want to see what you have seen," Aphrodite said thoughtfully.

"I've seen sights. I could tell you. . . ." Ares's eyes wandered away from her, looking through the far wall. "When they came out from behind their walls and we rushed them, then I saw things. It was glorious, Aphrodite! The ground was red with blood."

"Whose blood?" she asked, aghast.

"Ours, theirs. Does it matter? Blood is blood. The smell of it—it's unmistakable. There's nothing else like it. When the spear goes in, and you know his life is on the end of it, and you drive it just a bit deeper. You can watch the flame go out, I swear."

"That's dreadful."

"That's glorious. You don't know. You're a woman. You've never fought a war. That's when you know you're alive."

Aphrodite caught Hebe's eye as she worked on his leg. Hebe's face was blank, impassive. He might have been the dog she had spoken of, torn open by its fellow. She wrapped a clean dressing around it and threw the stained bandages in the basin. She swept the sheet off the bed as well. "I'll send someone with a clean one."

"Solicitous, isn't she?" Ares said. "Dear sister."

"You ought to be glad she's seeing to that leg," Aphrodite said. She tried to feel the old tenderness toward him, but all she could see was blood. When he was well he wouldn't brood so on the war, she thought. "I must go. I have our new maidservant to get settled in. Mother has told you, I'm sure." Everyone else on the farm had been snickering about it.

Ares appeared to know all. He grinned. "Young Eros got it caught in a snare, did he?"

"You could put it that way," Aphrodite said, irritated. A man would put it that way.

"Stay awhile." He put his arm around her waist. "I'll tell you about Troas. You never saw such a city, bigger than Mycenae, and built of marble. Their temples had gold altars, and mosaics on the floors, pictures of lions and apes made of little stones pieced together. The biggest temple was in a grove of trees so old no one knew when they were planted. People brought offerings and piled them behind the altar—gold and silver plates, collars of beaten gold. Silver ewers. I had a pair of wristbands a hand span wide made of gold, but I lost them on the ship home."

"Tell me about the people." Her son—Aeneas, she was practicing the name—had lived there. She tried to put a face to him, maybe one like her own, and see him in that marble city.

He ignored her. People didn't interest him. "The streets were paved with flat stones, cut square, and smoothed so that chariot wheels didn't catch in them. The whole road that spiraled up the hill to the palace was like that, not just the last bit. The Trojans had the shipping that came through the Hellespont to pay them for each ship that passed. The whole city sat on stacks of gold, but it didn't do them any good in the end."

"What were the houses like?"

"Painted colors, like a paintbox. Blue and green and red ocher. They were wealthy people. One woman had chairs made out of ebony, inlaid with ivory, and jars for wine carved out of carnelian. Two of my men were fighting over the chairs, and I had to knock their heads together. How would you get something like that home?"

"So you left them?" Aphrodite imagined the woman, maybe too old to be attractive to soldiers, clinging to her chairs, spared something.

"We burned them."

"Why?

"We burned the whole city. They held out against us. They should have let us in when we told them to."

"I have to go." Her hands felt clammy, even here in this overheated room.

Ares lay back against the pillow and looked sulky. "You never spend time with me."

"I do. I will. Just as soon as you are up and about. We need you here; it's good to have you back."

"You needn't think I'm staying!" He sat halfway up. "Stay here and herd goats, with hay in my hair?"

"Well, where would you go?"

"Laconia! Menelaus will be readying an army to take Mycenae; it's ripe for picking. They say young Orestes is a gibbering madman." He picked up the greave he had been polishing. "Just as soon as this leg heals. There's a place in King Menelaus's army for an officer from the war."

"You aren't young," Aphrodite said quietly.

"All the more reason to go while I can."

"I thought this time you might stay with me." She stood up.

He grinned and slapped her backside. "I'll be back to see that you behave yourself," he said.

Aphrodite gritted her teeth. Men had seemed such a wondrous thing to her when she was young. Now she wanted to drive them from the house at the end of a broom. What had happened? "There is very little time for anything else these days!" she snapped, and stalked off.

When Aphrodite looked in Psyche's doorway, she found the girl sound asleep on her rickety bed and snoring. Eros would find that unattractive if he decided to come sneaking around, but she didn't think he would have the nerve, not under her nose. She undressed with an irritable satisfaction and climbed into bed beside Hephaestus. He put an arm around her, apparently in his sleep, and she sighed and let him, because he had told her about finding a nest of young rabbits in the woods at dinner, and not about blood.

In the morning she introduced Psyche to the pigpen.

Psyche looked at the pigs with horror, her lip trembling. "I already milked the goats," she said hopefully.

"Excellent. Now then. I want this pen shoveled out until I can see the dirt."

"It's all dirt!" Psyche said.

"The ground. Pigs aren't very particular, but we have to live next door to them, and these could use an airing."

Psyche stared at the pigs, who all stared back at her, a gigantic sow and four bristly youngsters destined, she knew, for sacrifice at the winter solstice and at the Festival of the Goddess in the spring. They snorted at her and snuffled hopefully in the heap of dung and oddments, whose origins she didn't want to know, that littered their pen. They weren't confined to the pen, but left to wander and eat acorns in the woods, but they came to its enclosure to be fed household garbage and, apparently, to roll in the dung.

"Wash the pigs, too, while you're at it," Aphrodite said briskly. "Then you may ask Cook for breakfast."

Psyche nodded faintly.

"Wash the pigs?" Cook said when Psyche asked her for a bucket. "No one washes pigs."

"Madam says I am to," Psyche said grimly. "And I mayn't eat until I have, so give me the bucket."

"Better wash yourself when you're done with the pigs," Cook advised. "If you're coming in my kitchen."

"Washing pigs? No one washes pigs."

Psyche spun around at the voice and the sow trundled away in a lather of soapsuds. Eros had hoisted himself on the fence to watch her. "Did my mother tell you to do that?"

"Your mother wants them washed." Psyche advanced on him with the bucket and he backed away. "This is your fault!" She flung the contents of the bucket at him in an arc of pig-scented water. "Now I have to catch her again!"

Eros flapped the hem of his wet tunic, curling his lip in revulsion. "It's all over me!"

"You're a pig anyway!"

"I am not! I gave you a nice house, and presents, and anything you wanted!"

"And didn't tell me who you were!"

"And you didn't trust me!"

"And why should I have?"

They glowered at each other while the sow came cautiously back to see if maybe there was food in the bucket now. The soapy water had been an unpleasant surprise.

"I don't know," Eros said. He looked at her uncertainly. She was barefoot, her legs black to the knees. Wet, dirty hair hung in her face, and her gown was smeared with black, greasy mud. "Um. I didn't expect this to happen. Maybe I can talk to Mother." He looked as if he didn't relish the idea.

"You can help me catch that horrible pig," Psyche said.

Eros began to ease toward the sow, who watched them warily. Her piglets waited in the road, snuffling at a few grains the hens had left. Eros began to skirt around to the sow's left. "Get more water. When we catch her she won't wait while you fill that bucket."

Psyche nodded. She ran to the well and drew up another bucketful. Her bare feet squelched unpleasantly in the muck as she walked, and she could feel horrible water trickling down the back of her neck from her hair. She began to creep to the sow's right.

Eros saw a snail on the kitchen wall. He detached it and held out his hand enticingly. "Come, pig."

The sow regarded it with interest.

"When we get her," Eros said, "I'll hold her and you rinse her."

Psyche nodded again. They crept closer. Eros held out his hand, and the sow snuffled at the snail. She snapped it off his hand and chewed it with a revolting crunch. Eros caught her around the neck and held on. Psyche upended the bucket on the sow's back, scraping away dirty soap with her fingers. The sow snorted in alarm and began to back up, dragging Eros with her.

"Hurry!"

Psyche emptied the last of the water on the sow's

head, dabbing ineffectually at the dirty streams running off her ears.

"That will do!" Eros let the sow go and she shot onto the road, snorting and kicking. She and the piglets disappeared into the trees. Psyche sat down hard in the muck of the pigpen, her legs out in front of her, her hair a vile-smelling tangle in her face.

Eros got a fresh bucket of water from the well. He poured it over his head, drew up another bucket, and handed it to Psyche. "Here. I'll talk to Mother," he added. "When I get my nerve up."

Psyche didn't know whether he had spoken to Aphrodite or not, but the next day no further mention was made of pigs. She milked the goats, was fed in the kitchen, and went out the following morning with everyone else to bring in the olive harvest and press its oil. This was another activity unfamiliar to Psyche, although olives were the crop that fueled the cities of Argolis. Their oil lit the lamps and cooked the food and soothed the skin in the bath, but it had always arrived at her father's shop in jars.

The family set out at daybreak, hurried along by Hera, Aunt Demeter, and Hebe, the men carrying flails and sailcloth tarps, the women with their gowns tied above their knees to keep them from the brambles in the rocky orchard. Eros's grandmother's serving women balanced stacks of baskets on their heads, and Hermes followed, driving the wagon behind the plow ox.

"Can you climb a tree?" Eros's rather frightening Great-Uncle Hades demanded.

"I did when I was a girl," Psyche said. "Father used to tell me not to. He said it wasn't ladylike."

"Not a lady then, here, are you? So take this." He

handed Psyche a flail. "Up you go. The idea is to beat all the olives out of the branches onto the tarps down here. Then we tip them into the baskets. Use a light hand, mind; you don't want to injure the branches or bruise the fruit."

Psyche saw Eros scrambling into the gnarled branches of another tree, climbing lightly as a cat among the gray-green leaves. "All right, then." *If I can wash a pig, I can climb a tree,* she thought. She tucked her skirts higher into her girdle and caught the lowest branch in her hands, swinging herself onto its rough surface. Above her the olives hung glistening purpley black among the leaves, glowing with an edge of fire as the early sunlight caught them. Around her, Eros's uncles began to climb the trees too, with directions from his grandfather, Zeus, and the great-uncles. Even Eros's father, with his lame feet, was at work spreading the tarps below to catch the olives, and Psyche saw him shade his eyes with his hands and smile up at her, leaning on his cane. She waved down at him and balanced herself on her branch, wielding the flail as she saw Eros doing.

"She looks like a tree nymph, doesn't she?" Hephaestus said to Aphrodite as she tugged the corner of the tarp into place below.

"Hmmph!"

"The child washed a pig when you told her to. Give her some credit."

"Eros helped her. He needn't think I didn't notice."

"Well, that's a good sign, isn't it?"

"Worry about getting Dionysus up in that tree without cracking his head open," Aphrodite said, watching him hanging precariously from a low branch. "And if he's brought a wineskin with him, take it away from him. *That* would be a good sign."

"He can give me the wine," Hephaestus said. "I don't have to climb a tree."

"At daybreak?"

"Well, maybe not." Hephaestus shaded his eyes, peering into the tree again. A little shower of olives descended on him. "That's right! Good girl!" he called into the branches.

More olives thudded onto the tarp, and Aphrodite busied herself with tipping the edges up so that they didn't run off into the weeds. One of Hebe's babies came to the other side to help Hephaestus.

In the tree, Psyche was beginning to get the hang of the flail, raking its long whippy end through the branches, knocking the olives to the ground. Their fall made a sound like hail drumming on the tarps below the trees. She hadn't been up in a tree since she was ten, when Alecto had told on her and their father had smacked her for it and said she was to be a lady now. Maybe if she stayed here she would be allowed to climb trees.

The shower of olives slowed and stopped. Psyche's face peered down through the leaves. "I think that's all. Shall I climb another tree now?"

Hephaestus nodded, and Aphrodite said, "Come down carefully and don't step in them!"

Psyche slid down the trunk and stepped gingerly among the fruit that had fallen next to it, escaping the tarps. Hebe's child was picking them up one by one and putting them in a basket.

"Were you *trying* to get Eros to help her wash that pig?" Hephaestus inquired quietly as Psyche set her bare foot against the trunk of the next tree in the row.

"Certainly not!" Aphrodite said.

"Because I thought it particularly wise of you, you know, bringing them together that way. It worked on him far better than a lecture from either of us, I imagine. I always think washing a pig makes a bond between a couple."

Aphrodite looked at him thoughtfully, trying to decide if he was being devious. She began to say that that was exactly what she had *not* had in mind, but she bit the words off before she spoke them. No one, least of all Hephaestus, had ever complimented her on her wisdom before, for any reason.

She thought it over during the rest of the morning, as the olives were tipped into their baskets and loaded in Hermes's cart. The harvest would take days, since the oil had to be pressed as soon as the olives were shaken off the trees, or the fruit would ferment. Today's pressing would be the finest, at the peak of proper ripeness, and they wouldn't take more fruit than they could press by nightfall.

At noon Hades declared that quantity attained, and the pickers climbed down from the trees and followed the cart back to the granary, where the olive press stood in a flat courtyard beside the threshing floor. The press was a huge circular trough of stone, into which the olives were dumped and pressed by a stone wheel turned by the plow ox. When the fruit had been crushed, a lever squeezed the oil out to run into a tub, leaving the pulp and pits behind. The household servants brought bread and cheese and flagons of wine to the press, and they ate them in the shelter of the threshing floor roof while Hermes unhitched the ox and fastened his collar to the shaft that drove the press. The day had turned gray. A stiff little wind whipped through thin clothing.

"Let's get moving," Uncle Hades said, looking at the sky. "Let's go!"

The men laid down their meal and began pouring olives into the press. Hermes took the ox's head and started him on his endless circular journey, while the women poked at the mass of olives with sticks, knocking them loose from the sides of the press and rolling them under the wheel. The heady tang of crushed olives rose from the press as greenish-yellow oil began to trickle from the spout at its base. They stirred the mass of broken olives back under the wheel again and again until finally the ox halted at a shout from Hades. Eros, Heracles, and Hermes put their weight on the lever together, and more oil flowed out. When the olive pulp was raked from the press, another load of fruit went in, and the ox started his circle again. The pigs, hoping for the olive mash, snuffled their way out of the woods at the scent.

By evening, Psyche's arms and back ached, and her shoulders felt as if they were on fire. She and Eros had passed and repassed each other in the dance of the pressing, but he never spoke to her, nor she to him. She thought, though, that he knew just where she was in the same way that she marked his position in the space of her peripheral vision. As the sun was setting, he walked back to the house with his father, leaving Psyche and Aphrodite to trail wearily behind them.

Cook had laid out buckets of warm water and clean towels in the bathing room, along with flasks of oil, and strigils for scraping the skin clean. Psyche hung back as Aphrodite headed for the bath, pulling her mantle from her shoulders as she went. She turned and beckoned to Psyche. "Come along. I'm

too tired to be prissy, and you aren't entitled to."
She threw her gown in the corner and doused her
filthy arms and legs with water.

Psyche shucked her own clothes off, feeling Eros's
mother's eyes on her.

"It's hard work, living on a farm," Aphrodite said.

"I like it," Psyche said stubbornly.

Aphrodite snorted. She poured sweet oil from a
glass flask into her palm and rubbed it along her
arms and legs and down her ribs. "I've lived here
all my life, except for a month when I went to the
court at Mycenae with Father, and nearly every day
of it I would have traded to live in the city. Nearly."

"Which ones wouldn't you have traded?" Psyche
asked cautiously, since Aphrodite seemed willing to
talk to her.

"The day my son was born," Aphrodite said. "Both
of them," she added quietly. She began scraping oil
from her skin with the strigil, not looking at Psyche.

"Your husband told me about your first son," Psyche said softly.

"Did he now?"

"Yes. That must have been awful."

"It was," Aphrodite said shortly. And what had
possessed Hephaestus to tell this child about it?

"I don't know how you stood that," Psyche said.
"I don't think I could."

"You stand what you have to stand." She saw Psyche scrubbing at her arms with her fingers. "Here."
She handed her the flask of oil. "This is mine. Hephaestus has it made up for me in Tiryns. It smells
of roses."

Psyche took it gingerly. "Thank you."

"What day wouldn't *you* trade?" Aphrodite
demanded.

"Any day I saw Eros," Psyche said promptly. She rubbed oil into her flanks. "Well. Maybe not the night I followed him here."

"Ah. Yes. There was a madwoman in the road, as I recall."

"I was terrified of her." Psyche handed back the oil flask. "She threw stones at me."

"You came back anyway."

Psyche began to scrape her skin with an ivory strigil. She was lovely, Aphrodite thought, and she was completely unself-conscious. *I used to be that way.* Now Aphrodite was acutely aware of every wrinkle, every fold of skin no longer tight and smooth, of the sag in her belly and the corns on her feet.

"I don't give up easily," Psyche said.

"Hephaestus may not be his father," Aphrodite said abruptly.

"What?"

"It may be his brother Ares. He was the one I loved."

Psyche stopped, breath drawn in.

"Are you appalled?"

"No. But that's so *sad*."

"Not scandalous?"

"Love isn't scandalous," Psyche said.

Aphrodite put the strigil down and dipped fresh water from a full bucket with a ladle, pouring it over herself again. "Child, I have been a scandal my entire life. And it was mostly due to love. All due to love, now that I come to think of it. This horrible war was due to love."

"That's not what Eros said. He told me his father says the war was due to our side wanting to send our ships through the Hellespont without paying. The queen of Laconia was just the excuse, he said."

"I told you he may not *be* his father," Aphrodite snapped. "Ask Ares what the war was about and he'll tell you it was about blood. You haven't met Ares yet. You won't like him. I don't like him myself just now."

"Do you still love him?"

Aphrodite nearly told her to mind her manners and her business, but the words that came out instead were, "Yes, but you don't always like what you love; it's awful."

"I didn't like Eros the night I followed him. Or he me," Psyche said thoughtfully.

Aphrodite sat down on the three-legged stool beside the drain and washed her feet. "When we press the grapes they're always stained scarlet," she said, rubbing fresh oil between her toes. "I always thought it was beautiful, but this year I just thought of blood. I don't know why. Ares hadn't come home yet, but all that grape juice just looked like blood, rising up around my ankles."

"It's all the things that have happened at court," Psyche said. "When we heard about the king, and then about Queen Clytemnestra, I had bad dreams for months. I used to wake, and Eros— Well."

"Love isn't a talisman against death. I used to think it was," Aphrodite said.

"I do love him," Psyche said. "It wasn't just the presents and the little house."

"No. Eros is charming. He was always able to talk me around, convince me that whatever he wanted was a splendid idea."

"Except for me."

"Are you a good idea?"

"I am. I'm a good idea for Eros. He loves me, even

if he's mad at me just now. I'm mad at him, if it comes to that, so we're even."

"Well, you have nerve. I'll give you that much."

There was another stool, so Psyche sat down on it, trying to comb her long hair with her fingers. "Why didn't they let you marry the one you wanted?" she asked.

"Mother thought he couldn't control me. That he'd hurt me if I wasn't faithful."

"You wouldn't have been faithful?"

"Probably not." Aphrodite handed Psyche a bone comb, carved with doves, something else Hephaestus had made for her. "Definitely not."

"Oh. I would be faithful to Eros, if that's any help."

"It will be a help to Eros, I'm sure. I'm not certain I want a daughter-in-law who will be scornful of me, though."

"I wouldn't be scornful," Psyche said. "I think you're . . . I don't know what you are exactly; you're like a piece of the Goddess, sort of . . . You . . . well, it's no wonder men all want you. They don't follow me about like that, you know. Oh, they all want to look at me, but none of them ever wanted to do more than that, except Eros. It's as if I wasn't quite human to them. I don't know."

"Maybe you're a different piece of the Goddess," Aphrodite said. "The piece that behaves herself. And how do you know men all want me?"

"Eros said. He's quite proud of you. He says men follow you everywhere you go, and his teacher is in love with you."

Aphrodite chuckled. "Poor Teacher. Maybe he'll fall in love with you now."

"I don't think so," Psyche said. "I told you, men don't. Anyway, I only want Eros."

Aphrodite stood up. "We'll see. I wouldn't dream of forcing Eros to do anything, so we'll see." She wrapped a towel about herself grandly, a queen's gesture, and sailed out, leaving Psyche to pick up the dirty clothes.

XX

Love and Goats

The olive harvest went on for a ten-day, until everyone's hands were as raw as their tempers.

"Father and Grandfather used to hire a crew every winter to get the olives in," Eros said grumpily. "But now Grandmother says you never know who you'll get, and better to do it ourselves."

"Your mother told me she almost wishes the king of Laconia *would* come, and get the bandits off the roads," Psyche said.

"My mother told you?"

"She says Cook had her purse stolen just going into Tiryns for flour."

"Why are you talking to my mother?"

"She says I was foolish to come all this way alone; it's not safe for a female to be alone on the roads anymore, not even poor Cook."

"*Why* are you talking to my mother?"

"She talks to me."

"Well, I don't like it," Eros said. "Were you talking about me?"

"No. We were talking about love, and goats, and the best way to cure Cook's boils."

Eros looked appalled, but whether by their subject matter or the fact that she was talking to his mother, she couldn't tell. He stalked off, waving his arms.

At the Solstice they killed two of the pigs and roasted the bones on a bonfire on the hill above the farm, for the Goddess and the Bull. The family and its servants gathered around the fire to feast and to welcome the sun back to his northerly course again. Even Eros's old Great-Aunt Hestia, who hardly ever left her little house, came out and made the prayers to the Goddess, holding up quivering white arms to the sky and the thin horns of the moon. The flames leaped up from the bonfire, red and yellow, throwing dancing shadows on the ground. The younger ones linked hands and began to dance around the fire, slowly and then faster and faster, pulling the sun with them out of the darkness. Eros grabbed Psyche by one hand as he passed, and she followed him, startled, into the dance. Hebe's little girl grasped her other hand, a slightly sticky grip tinged with honey and nut meats.

Aphrodite found herself swaying to the beat of Dionysus's pipes and Teacher's lyre. Her foot patted the ground, itching to dance for the Goddess. Ares had hobbled out to sit in a chair, and she caught him watching her from one side and Hephaestus from the other, canes propped against their chairs, dark, saturnine brows drawn together, heads cocked at the same angle, each an unlikely mirror image of the other. Hephaestus smiled at her suddenly and nodded his head toward the dance. She ran, skipping across the rocky earth, and caught Hebe's daughter by the hand. The flames threw their dancing shadows on the hillside so that they might have been a race of giants.

She watched Eros's girl skipping after him, her head thrown back, laughing, gold hair streaming out behind her like a comet's tail. As they circled the fire she saw Ares and Hephaestus still watching them, only Ares was looking at the girl now. Aphrodite stumbled. She righted herself, saw his eyes slide over her and back to the girl. Psyche had said men wanted only to look at her, but Ares would be different. Psyche was Eros's, and Ares would want what Eros had, because Eros was his son; or because Eros wasn't. It wouldn't matter.

The dancers stopped, gasping for breath, drained the wineskins, and circled the fire again. Two of the stable boys joined in with another lyre and shepherd's pipes, Hera's old cook beat a copper spoon on a pan, and the dance circled faster, spinning the sun up over the eastern hillside.

When its first fire lit the ridge, they dropped, exhausted, and then staggered through the cold, dew-wet grass to the farm below. Hermes and Dionysus carried old Aunt Hestia on their crossed arms like a chair. They passed the graveyard, and Aphrodite wondered if Cronos and Rhea had heard the dancing. She saw Zeus stop at their tomb and pause, as if he spoke to them.

Hephaestus lagged behind the rest, with Eros and Psyche walking with him, but Ares, his leg much healed, caught up to her. He slid an arm around her waist.

"I'll be leaving soon."

She waited for that to set the old longing clamoring in her chest like a bell, but it didn't come.

"Come out to the barn with me and we'll bring in the Solstice the old way."

She looked over her shoulder. Hephaestus, Eros, and Psyche were behind them.

"What are you worried about? Eros's little piece?"

"No, I—"

"She'll never tell. And it's not as if old Hephaestus isn't expecting it."

It was the first time he had named his brother since he'd been home, and he had done it to shame him. Her stomach heaved. *Why do I love you?* Aphrodite shook her head. "I can't do that," she said before she changed her mind. She could feel his fingers on her waist like hot coals.

Ares's eyes glinted, but he shrugged. "I suppose I shall have to find something else to amuse me then." He looked over his shoulder at the three behind them.

Aphrodite spun away from him. She turned to face him. "If you touch that girl, I'll cut it off," she said.

He glared at her, the rising sun outlining him with a red glow. She glared back, fists balled at her sides. The silver horns of the moon were still in the sky, hanging above her head. She spread her arms out and seemed to grow taller, and he thought for the moment that she grasped two snakes, one in each hand, sinuous bodies coiled about her arms. It was only the sun on her gold armbands. He shook his head and the vision dissipated.

In the morning Ares left for Laconia.

"You aren't well enough," Hebe said. "That leg will fester again."

"I'm well enough to ride a horse."

"You haven't got a horse."

"I gave him a horse," Poseidon said. "Let him go. It's worth a horse to set him on the road. Three mares have foaled dead foals since he came home."

"That isn't his fault," Hebe said. She looked at Aphrodite, who could be counted on to defend Ares.

But Aphrodite thought that it might be, some way. She shook her head.

Ares grasped the saddle and swung himself into it. If it hurt his injured leg, he gave no sign of it. He wore his breastplate, the one that Hephaestus had made, its dents pounded out and polished, the wolf's head gleaming in the cold sun. The horse danced sideways under his weight. A leather bag was tied to the back of the saddle.

"Good-bye, Brother. Keep the fire burning; it'll keep the ghosts at bay. Good-bye, Father. Remember me when the roof fails to fall in on you this winter." He looked at Aphrodite. "Good-bye, Sister dear. Remember me in your dreams." He turned the horse's head toward the road and kicked it hard, scattering the chickens in his path.

"Marry that girl," Aphrodite said.

"What?" Eros eyed her nervously. Mother had been odd ever since Uncle Ares came back—Eros had heard all the rumors, too—and no telling what his leaving would do.

"You heard me. You're young, but you got yourself into this. So I expect you have enough stamina to survive."

"You told me not to see her," Eros said sulkily.

"Don't pout."

"I am *not* pouting—"

"Come and help me get the eggs." Aphrodite took his arm. The chickens that had flown squawking into the trees settled slowly to the ground, ruffling their feathers and clucking to themselves, a running chicken commentary on the recent disturbance. They looked suspiciously at Eros as Aphrodite led him into the henhouse.

Eros peered about the roost. Three hens were asleep in the dim, feathery light, heads tucked into their wings.

"Here." Aphrodite handed him a basket. "This is always a good place to talk, or think. Hens are calming." She felt along the nests on the top of the roost, white fingers moving lightly in the straw. "Look over there."

Eros patted an empty nest cautiously. "I used to do this when I was little. I remember you lifting me up. A hen pecked me in the nose once. I still have the scar.

"It makes you look dashing," Aphrodite said.

"It makes me look cross-eyed."

"Psyche doesn't seem to care."

"Mother—"

Aphrodite slid her hand under a sleeping hen and put an egg in her basket. "Good girl." She looked at Eros over the hen's back. "I mean it. You told me you were serious about this girl."

"And you said I wasn't to have anything to do with her."

"So you only said that because you knew I'd forbid you?"

"No! Well, not really. I just thought—"

"That you could have a concubine?"

"No! Well—"

"Concubines are as much trouble as wives. Marry the girl."

"You're a fine one to give marriage advice." Eros

stuck his hand under a hen, and she clucked at him grumpily and flapped her wings. "Ow!" He put an egg in his basket and sucked at his thumb.

"You're getting quicker," Aphrodite said. "It wasn't your nose this time. I *am* a fine one to give advice. I have been married a long time."

"And how happy have you been?"

Aphrodite sat down on an upturned bucket, the egg basket at her feet. "I honestly don't know. I was miserable at first, and then you were born and it didn't seem so bad. I thought I was making the best of things, in my way." She smiled. "Lately, I've begun to think I was happier than I thought."

"With Father?"

"Yes. It's odd. He's the one who mends things as well as makes them, you know. When your grandfather dies, he'll be the one we all look to. He's the . . . sort of hub that the whole wheel turns on. When you're fifteen it's hard to appreciate that."

"Doesn't sound romantic," Eros said doubtfully.

"It's not. It's solid. It's dependable. And kind. That's love, not romance."

"Don't you miss romance?"

She smiled again and stood up, brushing feathers off her dress. The hens muttered sleepily, resettling themselves. "Maybe I'll just romance your father and scare him to death."

They took the eggs up to the house and gave them to Cook. Eros was still eyeing his mother uneasily. She pushed him out the other door, toward the goat barn. "Go help her carry the pails."

When he had gone off, she looked at Cook and said, "That's that, then. They'll get married and things will settle down around here." She cracked an egg into a bowl and set it down for the snake. She got down on her hands and knees as he slid out of his basket, not caring whether Cook heard her or not. "I listened to you," she told it as his tongue flicked out around the egg. "Now do something for me."

Hephaestus was at the forge, straightening the bent tines of a pitchfork. The day was gray and raw, and the warmth of the forge fire drew her in. He turned at her footsteps. When he saw who it was he raised one eyebrow. Aphrodite rarely visited the forge.

"I told Eros to marry that child," she said.

A smile twitched the corner of his lip.

"If you want, I'll admit to being a beast."

"Certainly not. Eros behaved like a lout, independent of any beastliness on your part."

"Well, I wasn't going to admit it to Eros. I was going to admit it to you."

"You needn't. I don't find you beastly."

She held her hands to the warmth of the fire. "Ares won't be back," she said.

He turned his attention to the pitchfork. "I don't think so, either. I'm sorry."

"Well, you shouldn't be. *He* was beastly to you."

"He always was."

"He was worse."

"He was just more so. The war . . . concentrated him, I think. Cooked him down until anything superfluous boiled away."

"Ugh. You make him sound like a carcass."

Hephaestus was silent.

Her eyes filled with tears. "He is," she said. "I know."

Hephaestus put the pitchfork down. He rested his hands on her shoulders. "I *am* sorry."

Aphrodite sniffled. "No, I am. I haven't been a good wife at all."

"Well, you didn't *want* to be a wife, so I suppose that's understandable."

"I do now." She sniffled again. "I want what Eros and Psyche have."

He stood perfectly still. "You can't have that."

"It's too late?"

"It's too late."

She let out a long breath. "Then I want what *we* have," she said finally.

His hands tightened on her shoulders. He laid his head against hers. "I think we can manage that."

The Festival of the Goddess welcomed in the spring and the long, warm, slow slide toward summer. In Tiryns the bull ring was cleaned of winter debris, and the bull leapers danced for the Goddess, their short white tunics bright against bronze skin. They balanced on their toes, waiting for the bull, and Aphrodite's heart balanced on her breastbone as it always did, watching them. They were young, with the muscular slenderness of their kind, dedicated to the Goddess at five or seven. At fifteen they would be too old to dance with bulls, and then the priestesses of the Goddess would give them a purse of gold coins and their freedom to marry—those who lived. Sometimes the bull took one. Life was always that way, Aphrodite thought—prayer was dangerous and might be answered. Hephaestus had prayed to the Goddess to send Ares home alive from the war.

On her right, Psyche and Eros sat disgracefully holding hands; their heads garlanded with twin wreaths of anemones. They had been married a ten-day and had moved into a little house Eros had helped build. Aphrodite had give Psyche her golden girdle as a wedding gift. Psyche wore it now, sitting golden and lovely in its aura. There would be grand-children, Aphrodite thought with satisfaction, and then, *I was right not to have them live with us.* Her own marriage was relatively new in its current incarna-tion, and she didn't know what she thought of that, but whatever it was, it didn't need a pair of newly married children under her roof.

She saw Psyche's father and sisters in the crowd on the other side of the ring and nodded regally at them, all forgiven on both sides since the wedding. The girls nodded back.

"Poor things," Aphrodite said to Hephaestus on her left. "Surely they can do better than a fishmong-er's boy and an apprentice grain merchant, always sailing off to who knows where. I'll look around for them."

"An excellent use of your talents," Hephaestus murmured, and she snickered because she couldn't help it.

Hephaestus wasn't sure where their marriage was taking them, either, but *he* had gone to *her* last night, and she had opened her arms to him. He would take that and be grateful.

The priestesses of the Goddess were passing below them now, their arms held high, the sacred serpents twined about them. Their stiff flounced skirts swayed as they walked. Wide girdles laced with gold were buckled beneath bare breasts with painted nipples. They paused at the north end of the ring, just barely acknowledging the couple who sat in the high seats. The king of Laconia had honored Tiryns with his presence and was said to be heading for Mycenae to reclaim his brother's throne. The acknowledgment of the priestesses gave him their blessing. Order was needed, and Menelaus could restore it.

When the priestesses had made their circle, they went through the little door at the south end of the ring, and the dark gate at the north end rattled up. A spotted bull came through it, his dark eyes wild at the sudden light. His wide horns curved out like the horns of the moon. The bull dancers ran around the edge of the ring, tumbling on their hands, righting themselves, flowing like a ripple of heads and legs. There were three of them, two boys and a girl, naked now, nothing to snag by ill chance on the horns as they flew past.

The first boy bounced on his toes and faced the bull. He began to run. Two paces from the horns, he leaped and caught them in his hands, vaulting him over. He flipped in midair, somersaulting onto the bull's broad back. The bull was lumbering faster now, swinging its head dangerously from side to side. The boy balanced there for a heartbeat as the bull galloped, then flipped backward into a hand-stand, and backward again to the ground.

The girl came after him. The bull tossed its head as she caught its horns, flinging her higher, breaking the smooth arc of her leap, and the crowd drew in its breath. She righted herself, danced on the bull's back, flipped backward into the boy's waiting hands. The third boy followed.

Aphrodite held her breath. She loved to watch the bull leapers flipping in the bright sun like birds, the pleasure always tinged with terror. She imagined what it must be like to feel the smooth horns against your hands and then to stand poised on that fearful back, with the bunched muscles under your feet.

They tumbled head over heels about the ring again while the crowd cheered them and threw flowers, and the bull stood panting, his horns lowered, as they spun about him.

"It's a fearful dance," Hephaestus said, watching her.

"Life is a fearful dance," Aphrodite said.

"But there's always the moment when you're on its back," Hephaestus said. "That transcendent instant of . . . of joy." He watched her solemnly.

Aphrodite nodded. In the ring she saw the girl leap to the bull's back again and hang there, painted against the bright sky. Behind her she saw Helen on the dais, sitting beside her husband.

Aphrodite slipped her hand into Hephaestus's. *Joy sometimes*, she thought. Joy sometimes would do.

Read on for a preview of
Athena's tale

All's Fair in
Love and War

Coming from Signet Eclipse in January 2006

She is tall, frozen in painted marble, forbidding as the stone from which she was carved. Her gaze is stern, as befits the tutelary goddess of a city as great as Athens. The citizens come and go on the Acropolis beneath her marble gaze, bringing offerings to her temple. Poets and philosophers argue the meaning of life while sitting on her steps. Despite her patronage, it is men who run her city; the lawmakers, the soldiers, the gentleman farmers. Respectable women stay at home, minding the servants and the children, venturing outside their houses only for festivals. Only occasionally the hetairae, the elegant, well-educated concubines, come to see her, painted faces a mark of their freedom from domestic tyranny.

This is the classical age, the Golden Age of Greece and of Athens, the proudest of its city states, its economy fueled by the source that feeds and lights the whole Aegean—the olive.

Once it was not like this. Once there was a village of stone and mud huts. Once there were only flocks of goats; tallow to burn in smoky lamps; a bloodstained stone altar to the older gods. The olive is old, but not as old as Athens. Once there was a real woman inside the marble shell.

Metis lay gasping with the new baby, bloody and squalling, clutched to her breast.

The midwife clucked her tongue sadly. "Pity it's a girl," she said to Kosmetas. "She may not carry another one. It was a hard labor and she's done herself damage."

"Get out!" Metis shrieked at her.

"I was just saying I was sorry," the midwife said. "They're often like that," she added to Kosmetas. "After a long labor. Especially the first ones. They get a little mad in the head."

"I am not mad in the head."

Kosmetas looked as if he wasn't sure. He had not been allowed in until after the baby had come, and from the sound of it, his wife had been trying to kill the midwife. Now she lay on the bed, her hair a wet, dark tangle about her face, and glared at the midwife in the smoky light of the tallow lamps.

"That baby needs to be washed," the midwife said briskly, and held out her hands for it.

Metis looked at her suspiciously.

"Let her have it," Kosmetas said. "There's a good girl."

Metis's eyes narrowed and she glared at him, too, but she held out the baby. The midwife took her and dipped her in a pot of warm water on the stone floor. The cut end of the umbilical cord stuck out like a twig from her navel. The baby stopped crying when she felt the warm water. "There now," the midwife cooed at her. She lifted her out, washed her face with a wet cloth, and wrapped her up in blankets. She laid the baby in the wooden cradle beside the bed.

"Go away again," the midwife said to Kosmetas, "while I bathe my lady. Then you can come back in."

Kosmetas looked relieved and disappeared into the hallway outside.

Metis lay back resignedly and let the midwife bathe her and change the bandages that absorbed the seeping blood between her legs. The afterbirth, a translucent mass that had once sheltered the baby, lay in another pot beside the cradle. Metis looked at it pointedly. It had magical properties and the midwife had been instructed to burn it in the proper fashion, according to the customs of Metis's people. The midwife had snorted in annoyance, but Metis had instructed her maids to follow her and make sure she did it. If the afterbirth wasn't given to the Goddess, she would have no reason to look after the child as she grew.

"I'm sure I'm sorry if I insulted my lady," the midwife, said, gathering her kit of rags and knives and picking up the pot with the afterbirth. "I only meant it's a shame for the king not to have a son to come after him and all. If you don't have a boy, I suppose it will be that brother of his."

"Certainly not!" Metis said.

The midwife handed her the baby and Metis closed her eyes, snuggling the child against her breast. A daughter was fine. Old ways were the best ways.

Metis named the baby Athena, which was a name from her own language, mostly given up in her public speech now that she had married the king, but spoken with her maids, and in the times when she wanted to be easy in her speech and not hunt for words. Kosmetas argued that it was a name he couldn't get his tongue around, but he let her have her way since the child was a girl.

"I hear she's not likely to have another," his brother Poseidon said cheerfully, slapping Kosmetas on the back.

"You never know with women," Kosmetas said. "Don't measure your head for my crown just yet."

Poseidon laughed, a cheerful bellow. "Early days yet indeed." He stretched his long legs out in front of him and grinned at his older brother.

Kosmetas chuckled. Poseidon was nearly twenty years his junior, barely fifteen this winter, but already a better horseman than anyone else in Attica. He would make a good king if it came to it. But Kosmetas wasn't old yet. He might make another baby, on Metis or someone else, the way his father had done. He couldn't divorce Metis, of course, he thought ruefully. He had married her in the first place to cement his rule over the Pelasgians, the people who had held the land before the Achaeans, Kosmetas's father's people, had come. She had been an unsatisfactory wife, never quite refusing him or going against his wishes, but always managing somehow to do the things she wanted to. She was thick as thieves with the priestesses of the Pelasgians' goddess as well. One of them had told her what to name the child. It was necessary to show regard for the Pelasgians' goddess, who was represented by a crude stone that they anointed with tallow and fed on festival days, but Kosmetas's ancestors had worshiped the Goddess in her Achaean form and she had done well by them.

Metis knew what he was thinking. She generally found her husband transparent enough to interpret without asking, a talent that she knew irritated him enough that he might change his mind on an issue just to prove her wrong. She also knew that she was regarded with suspicion by the Areopagus, the council of nobles named for the rock where they met with the king to decide matters of state. The Areopagus had decided on her marriage, for instance, but they had expected her to be a subservient wife and they had gotten a surprise. The Achaeans didn't pay attention. It was necessary to pay attention. Metis paid attention to everything, as the priestesses had taught her.

As her daughter grew up, Metis saw that Athena learned to pay attention, too. She was given a nurse to follow her and the run of the palace, a lime-washed stone building two stories high that sat beside the temple of the Achaean goddess at the top of the Acropolis. The city spread down the slopes below, a collection of tile-roofed stone houses and temples giving way to mud and thatch huts on the lower slopes. Beyond were wheat fields and goat pastures on the landward side, and the blue harbor on the seaward side. Athena's room in the palace had fish painted on its plastered walls, but the houses of most of the citizens were rough stone.

When she was old enough, her mother taught her to count, and to do small sums in her head, which her father couldn't do. She taught her the names of the birds that flocked along the shoreline or nested in the meadows or flew overhead in their twice yearly migrations to distant lands. She spoke to her in the Pelasgian tongue so that the child grew up with two languages in her head. She taught her to weave fine cloth and tapestries with pictures in them, from the wool of the goats who also gave Attica milk and leather and meat for sacrifices. What her mother didn't teach her, Athena paid attention to herself at the smith's forge or the carpenter's bench or the smelly confines of the fishmonger's stall. When she was five she burned her fingers on a swordblade in the forge when the smith turned his back.

"Child, you oughtn't to be in there," her nurse said. "What was Smith thinking of?"

"Amoni goes in there," Athena said. Amoni was the smith's son, a year older than Athena.

"And he is a boy," Nurse said, "if I recall correctly."

"That does not make any difference," Athena said, sucking her burned fingers. "Ask Mother."

Nurse sighed. She didn't need to ask Mother: She knew what the queen would say. She was raising the girl like a boy, and no good would come of it, but Metis wouldn't listen.

When Athena was six, she was allowed to explore the city, safe in the knowledge that everyone knew who she was. Beside the palace was the temple of the Achaean goddess where Kosmetas and the Areopagus went each spring and fall to kill two goats and a boar and burn the bones on the altar. Behind the altar was a statue of the Goddess, a fierce figure with great birdwings, and snakes in her hands, brightly painted. The temple was stone, with four stone pillars holding up the tile roof. The temple of the Pelasgian goddess, where Athena's mother went to worship, was older, and smaller, but Athena thought it held more magic. The statue of the Goddess there was just a stone, dark with old blood and smears of tallow from the sacrifices, but when Athena looked at it she was sure she could see a face. The goddess in her father's temple was just a carved lady, but somebody was *in* the stone.

The Greek goddesses have seduced
readers—and lovers—for centuries.

Now Signet Eclipse introduces a new series—
tales of love and seduction filled with
passions of mythic proportions.

✳✳✳✳

Now Available:
Love Underground: Persephone's Tale

Coming January 2006:
All's Fair in Love and War: Athena's Tale

✳✳✳✳

SIGNET ECLIPSE

Available wherever books are sold at penguin.com